AFTER THE
BLOODWOOD
STAFF

LAURA E GOODIN

ODYSSEY
BOOKS

Published by Odyssey Books in 2016

www.odysseybooks.com.au

A Cataloguing-in-Publication entry is available from the National Library of Australia

ISBN: 978-1-922200-72-3 (pbk)
ISBN: 978-1-922200-73-0 (ebook)

Cover design by Rachel Roberts

This work is dedicated to Mr. George Kaiser, my high-school English teacher, who taught me more about writing than any other single person before or since; and to the memory of my grandfather, Jesse S. Sohn: engineer, inventor, unsung hero, and lifelong adventure-fiction enthusiast, who taught me that adventure waits around every corner.

Chapter 1

In Which Hoyle Meets an Adventurer

The bookstore was a barn of a place. Hoyle thought it might have been an actual barn at one point, judging from the smell that underlay the scents of musty paper, old leather, and expensive coffee. He'd driven an hour from the DC suburbs to get here; a post on his favorite adventure-fiction forum had recommended it as a good source for overlooked authors. And he needed a change of scene. The pile of what looked like sawdust pellets that he'd found in a corner of the garage last week had filled him with a vague but relentless dread that somewhere in his house lurked a brood of termites. He'd been trying to get the nerve up to phone somebody for days. The dread had swooped again as soon as he had woken up. But it was Sunday. *Can't do anything about it today*, he had thought almost jauntily. The bookstore would be the ideal distraction.

He could feel his mood lifting as he wandered along the first aisle, turning from dull worry to the bright eagerness of the hunt. He knew the look of the books he wanted; he almost didn't have to read the spines anymore.

Oh, that one looked about right. He reached, and his hand was knocked aside by a painful swat.

"I saw it first," snapped the woman who'd hit him. Her was hair slightly grey, like his. She was significantly shorter, but stocky enough to put a bit of sting in the swat.

"What the hell?" he cried. But she was already striding toward the cash register.

Hoyle felt a wave of loss and frustration. He rushed to the

register. "Hey," he called to the woman as she finished paying and carefully placed the book in her tote bag. "Hey, wait." She gave him an annoyed look over her shoulder. "Please," he said. He caught up to her. "Please. Just let me see what it was. I didn't even get a chance …"

She hesitated, then drew the book out. *After the Bloodwood Staff*, by C.G. Ingraham. The cover was a faded mustard color, the title printed in an enticing Art Nouveau font. Without thinking, he ran one finger gently across the cover, feeling the rough cloth, and the slightly smoother lines of the title. The woman did not pull the book away.

"Ingraham," murmured Hoyle. "Never heard of this one."

"Fabulous stuff," she said. "He was a bit of a maverick. Not many of them wrote about Australia. It was all Africa this and South America that and the South Sea Islands the other. I've been looking for this one forever." She cleared her throat. "I'm sorry I was so rude."

"That's okay," he said. On an impulse, he added, "Coffee?"

They stared at each other for a moment.

"Thanks," she said.

Hoyle and the woman placed their orders at the cafe counter and looked for a table.

"There," Hoyle said. "You go grab it."

Once he had the coffees, he twisted and shuffled through the chairs, holding the coffees at head height to keep his elbows safe from jostling. He had an uncomfortable feeling that raising his arms like this made him look paunchy. When he got to the table, he set the coffees down and sat.

"I'm Hoyle," he said.

"What's your first name?"

"That is my first name."

"Your parents *named* you Hoyle?"

"Well, what's your name?"

"Sybil."

They sipped, not quite companionably. She kept glancing at him, then away, as if she were *expecting* something from him.

"So, um, you read a lot of adventure?" he ventured at last. Oh, God, what a stupid thing to say.

"Since I was little," she said. "My grandfather got me started on one of Mundy's novels."

"*King, of the Khyber Rifles?*"

She sat back, astonished. "How did you guess?"

Hoyle shrugged, feeling bashful. "It's my favorite of his, that's all. Thought maybe your grandfather might have felt the same."

"What's your favorite Conan Doyle?"

"I confess it's the Brigadier Gerard stories."

"Oh, don't be embarrassed. Just because they're obscure, doesn't mean they're not good."

On the strength of this, he said, "Tell me about Ingraham."

Sybil leant forward, suddenly eager. "It's such a sad story. He spent years of his life as a sort of groupie of Conan Doyle—followed him around from one speaking engagement to another, never getting up the courage to introduce himself or even write Conan Doyle a letter. He did write Haggard once, in 1899—at least, Haggard's reply was found in Ingraham's papers, although Haggard seems to have thrown out Ingraham's letter. Typical."

"What did Haggard say?"

Sybil closed her eyes. "'My dear sir, your suggestion is entirely untenable—indeed, bordering on the insane—and I trust you will seek out competent assistance. Please do not contact me or anyone associated with me again.'" She opened her eyes and took a sip of coffee. "That was all. What in the world could Ingraham have suggested? I've been reading his books for clues. He was prolific, too—nearly thirty-five by the time he died. He starved himself to death. He'd become convinced that an evil parasite lived in his liver and the only way to kill it before it propagated was to starve it—and, by necessity, himself."

"Wow," said Hoyle, feeling queasy.

"Oh, yes, you can look up the case study."

"Was he English?"

"No, American, believe it or not."

"I take it you're doing a PhD on him or something?"

She blinked. "Oh, no. No."

"But you know so much about him."

"It's a mystery, that's all," she said, suddenly irritable. "I want to know what his suggestion was."

"Ah," he said.

"That's why I needed this book. It's one of the last three I didn't have. I'd checked out online sellers, everything. When I saw you reaching for it … sorry."

"That's okay."

"Will it help make up for it if I let you in on a secret?"

"Really, it's okay—"

She lowered her voice. "There is evidence that Ingraham travelled to Australia in the 1890s." She sat back with an air of having given him something for which he should be very grateful.

"Wow," he said again, somewhat more weakly.

She frowned. "Of course, wow. You … don't get the connection?"

"Nope." He started drinking his coffee as quickly as he could.

"His letter to Haggard was written in 1899."

"Okay."

"Ugh! I'm glad I did nab *Bloodwood*, it would have been wasted on you. He'd found something in Australia and he wanted to mount a second expedition."

Something in her voice made Hoyle say, "Whatever it was can't possibly be there now. It's been, what, over a hundred years?"

"Do you think I should go and find out? Or that I shouldn't?"

"Well, it's none of my business, is it?"

"Because if you're thinking that I'm just a middle-aged woman who should stay home with her cats and her book club for a couple of decades until it's time to go into a hospice and die, then you can just think again."

"No! No, of course not, no, sorry." The silence descended again. She finished her coffee and stood up.

Hoyle stood as well. "It's been a pleasure talking with you."

"Oh, no it hasn't. Don't patronize me. Oh, and thanks for the coffee." He watched her go, then went back to the shelves. There was an unpleasant, dogged feel to his browsing now, but it was not entirely fruitless: he found a couple of Talbot Mundys he'd been looking for, and, over in the kids' section, a copy of *Richard Halliburton's Complete Book of Marvels*. He bought it, even though he had three copies already; there were nephews and nieces, and Christmas was less than two months away. The oldest of them was almost too old now for the book, and, to be frank, too interested in black nail polish, but maybe there was still time to instill a love of adventure.

Not that Hoyle himself had ever been on an adventure. In fact, he'd devoted a fair bit of effort over the years to arranging a calm life. A job that suited him, if it didn't inspire him. A few friends, whom he saw at comfortable intervals. His sisters' kids, when he wanted someone to give something to. The thought of trudging through a jungle somewhere, picking leeches off his privates and drinking blood from a cut on the neck of his packhorse to stay alive …

Sybil, though—she seemed raring to go. Maybe she would go to Australia, find Ingraham's secret—or something else entirely. A thousand possibilities, straight out of a thousand musty books with frayed and mottled covers.

He drove home past the endless rows of bland, northern Virginia strip malls and office buildings, fast-food places and office-supply stores. What kind of adventures could he have here? Finding the best price on red peppers at the supermarket? Crossing the street to avoid a group of sullen teenagers?

He pulled into his driveway, got out of his car, and went inside. Sunday afternoons were for reading. But today he couldn't settle in. Tea, then doing the breakfast dishes, then checking email, then more tea, then filing a few bills, then a walk to the convenience store for some milk, then more tea. After each task, he tried again to engross himself in one of the books he'd just bought. Each time, he was overwhelmed by the need to walk, to straighten, to *do*. He kept finding reasons to think of Australia.

* * *

Hoyle stretched at his desk, his arms flung wide. His back was killing him and his eyes burned. It was hard to stay focused at the best of times; harder at the moment because of the rumors that the downsizing was happening at last, and that claims managers like him would be the first to go. They'd all seen the signs: a sudden increase in pointless staff meetings, a proliferation of closed doors and lowered voices, the endless stream of staff-development workshops. Hoyle now had an extensive collection of acronyms and animal archetypes that described his "workplace personality" and "risk-embracing aptitude." Usually he was something like an elephant. He thought Sybil might be a llama: moody and combative, but good at mountains.

Hoyle had been telling himself for weeks not to panic; the bosses had probably made their decisions months ago about who would get the chop. He'd survived the downsizing eight years ago; no doubt he'd get through this one as well. Only … the rumors were troubling. Especially since his staff was down to four people. You didn't need a manager for just four people, did you? How much management did a bunch of claims clerks need, anyway? Claims come in, claims get paid, job done.

Just before lunch, he heard footsteps stop at his cubicle.

"Hi, Hoyle," said Michael. The boss. Karen, the other boss, stood at his elbow. They both had pained smiles. "Come on," said Michael. "Take a break. We'll buy you a coffee."

Hoyle went cold.

His mind split into two levels: on one, he returned their smiles, got up, and walked calmly with them to the cafe downstairs. On another, shame and terror thundered through him in turns—oh, God, how could he be the one let go? What had he done wrong? What would he do now? What now? *What now?*

He paid little attention to the preamble about tough times. He paid a lot more attention once Michael started talking about the severance package. It was meager. Very meager.

"Hang on, Michael," he interrupted. "Let me make sure I understand. I've been here for ten years, and all I get is six months' salary?"

Karen said, "I swear, Hoyle, it's all we've got. Michael and I are taking pay cuts to even afford that. If you were the only one we had to cut, maybe we could have done better, but we're letting sixty people go. Sixty! That's thirty years' worth of a full-time salary, all in one hit."

"Besides," said Michael, "if you don't take the package voluntarily, it drops to two months' salary."

"Who thought that up?"

Michael dropped his eyes.

"Unh." He felt like iron gates were slamming shut all around him, one after the other. He had to choose one, quickly, before all his choices were gone. "All right, then, I'll take the voluntary package. I assume I leave today." With that, the terror and shame disappeared, replaced by … nothing. He felt nothing.

"Well," stammered Karen, "we were planning on a handover …"

"Today," Hoyle said. "If I'm dispensable, then there's no need for a handover. If what I do is important enough for a handover, then I'm not dispensable."

Michael and Karen glanced at each other. Karen gave the smallest of shrugs.

"All right," said Michael. "I'll stop by Personnel and have them get your exit paperwork ready. I'm really sorry."

Hoyle gave his own shrug, took his coffee, and went back to his desk to pack up.

It was just a few minutes' work. No family photos, no trinkets from his last vacation, no papers; his desk was always pristine. Maybe that was why he'd gotten the chop: nobody could tell he was doing anything. Then a half hour in Personnel to sort everything out, and he was done. Ten years, just like that. Should he cry? He tried, during the drive home, but nothing happened.

He stood in the driveway for a moment and listened—the neighborhood was so quiet in the afternoon. He couldn't remember the last time he'd been home on a weekday.

He went inside and put the kettle on. While it heated, he wandered from room to room, looking aimlessly at his bookshelves. Thousands of books—not all of them adventure, either. Geography, science fiction, history, classics, mysteries, even a couple of romance novels he'd read just to see what all the fuss was about. He could remember where he'd bought nearly every one. He didn't go through them very often; the current reading queue was stacked by his bed.

Most of the shelves were double-stacked. He pulled a few books off the front row to see what was behind. A stream of brown, muddy grit pattered to the floor. For the second time that day, a cold wave washed through him; this one was far, far worse. He turned the books over in his hand. The pages were half-eaten labyrinths, tiny paper tunnels and caves leading into darkness.

He pulled more books off, and more, faster and faster. Nearly every one showed at least some damage.

He gave up after a half-dozen or so shelves. His hands dropped to his sides, and he let the ruined books he'd been clutching drop onto the pile at his feet.

Now he cried.

It was nearly a half-hour later that he blew his nose one last time, mentally gave himself a bracing slap, and thought, *Okay, the house is definitely in danger. No more pretending it can wait.* He had to do something before the termites brought it down around his ears. It took a while longer to bring himself to go to the computer, but he managed to spend the rest of the afternoon trying to find an exterminator who would come out to the house right away. Nothing could save the books, of course. Each time he remembered that, a new wash of sickness filled him. Books that filled his evenings, that kept him from minding so much that he was alone night after night, that gave him something to talk about on those infrequent family visits, even if the nieces and nephews were unsubtle about glancing at their phones.

Finally the appointment was made. He waited at the kitchen table, his hands clenched in front of him. From time to time he found himself rocking, just a little; each time he made himself stop. The doorbell rang.

The exterminator spent a good hour poking and shining lights and tapping on things. Finally she said, "Yeah, good thing you called us. They haven't been here long, but man, they're hungry. They can do a lot of damage in just a month or two. We're talking thousands."

"Of termites?"

"Of dollars. I'm actually free tomorrow morning to make a start. Can you get off work?"

"Sure," said Hoyle dully.

"And I hate to say it, but you're going to have to get rid of any of these books that have termite damage."

"I figured."

"Maybe," the exterminator said carefully, "you want to start sorting through them now. As part of the fee I can get someone to haul them away for you. Jeez, do you really read all of …" Her voice trailed off. "Yeah, um, sorry."

"Yeah."

"I'll see you tomorrow morning at eight, then—is eight okay?"

"Fine. Thanks."

Hoyle was certain he could hear the little bastards gnawing, gnawing, gnawing. The sound rose in his ears until it sounded like cicadas, like chainsaws, like the roaring jeers of a crowd of millions. He couldn't eat, and he knew sleep would not be not an option. Instead, he worked through the night to sort the books. Just enough of the iron numbness that had gotten him through his last day at work had returned to keep him functioning now. By dawn he'd gone through all the shelves. The damaged books formed a massif in the center of the living room; the keepers, a far smaller pile under the dining-room table.

At three minutes past eight, the doorbell rang. He let the exterminator in, and she spent the next several hours drilling holes through his floor and digging holes in his yard, and injecting some very nasty-looking stuff down all of them. When she was done, she helped him move the damaged books out to the front porch.

Once he was alone, he could only stand with his hands dangling, and try not to look at the devastated, empty bookshelves. He hadn't cried since the day before, but the tightness in his stomach was there, relentless. When his hands, then his arms, started to shake violently, he knew he needed to get out. Get away. Somewhere. Even for just a little while.

A flash of yearning memory: the long, dark, endless aisles at the country-barn bookstore. If he couldn't have his own books, at least he could be near someone else's. At least he could start planning how he would rebuild. Lean and mean, that's what his library would be now. This was his big chance for a fresh start. Books that would reflect his wiser, more experienced, more *mature* taste. He'd buy whatever ones he wanted. He had six months' salary showing up in his bank account any minute now.

The drive to the bookstore barn was a bit of a challenge on no sleep: winding roads and sudden turnoffs, and always the danger of a chicken or a cow or something wandering onto the road. But he got there at last. He stepped inside; it was as it had been on the weekend, except that the coffee shop was less crowded.

He picked up where he'd left off on Sunday. He could almost forget why he was there as he gently took books from the shelves and leafed through them, giving each one an affectionate tap with his fingertips as he replaced it.

He reached the end of a row and turned to go around to the other side—and bumped into Sybil, leaning casually against the end of the bookcase. She didn't move, just stared at him with an odd expression. She'd been ... *waiting* for him.

"Hello," he said after a moment.

"Call in sick today?"

"Got laid off, if you really need to know. Excuse me, please." He started to step around her.

"Better yet," she said, and shifted slightly to block him. "I leave for Australia on Thursday," she added conversationally.

"Oh, well, good. I hope you have a nice vacation."

"I've been here all yesterday and today, in case you might show up before I left."

Hoyle took a step back. "Um, why?" He noticed that she'd waited to speak until she'd taken up a position between him and the door.

"How'd you like to come with me?"

"*What?*"

"Sure! It was going to be tricky, but now it's all fine, with you out of work and everything. You could use an adventure." She looked pointedly at his soft, round stomach.

"Insulting me isn't going to make me want to go with you."

"What will? The promise of riches?"

Hoyle thought of his house, now rickety, and the hundreds and hundreds of books piled on the porch. He thought of looking for another job, any job, and of the panic he knew he'd feel as his money trickled away week after week. But—buried treasure? Come on. "No."

"Ah, I almost had you there, though, didn't I?" She was infuriating.

"Why would you want me along?" He added silently, *Fat, unemployed, out of shape ... I can't even keep termites out of my house, how would I stand up to pirates or savages or wild beasts or even just leeches? Even leeches?*

"Would you like me to say that I see hidden greatness in you, and you should come along so that you can blossom into your true and valiant self? I don't see it at all, frankly, but I could say so if that would help."

"No. No, it wouldn't."

"All right, the truth. I want you along because you'd get it. You'd get what I'm doing and why." She looked away. "And there's no one else."

"I'm not good at any of that stuff."

"What stuff?"

"Camping. And stuff. Saving you when you fall over a cliff."

She waved a hand dismissively. "If I needed that kind of help, I wouldn't go. I'm sure you'll learn quickly."

She's already decided for me, Hoyle thought. *Should I feel upset?* He tried to feel upset. Instead, he felt the tiniest glow in his stomach: part "Somebody wants me!", part "Could I really?", and part sheer, glorious mystery. He locked eyes with Sybil, and as he saw a small smile flicker on her face, the glow began to flare, then blaze.

"Sure, okay," he said casually. "Give me the flight details and I'll go home and buy a ticket."

Sybil's smile broadened for an instant into a genuine grin. She took a piece of paper out of her pocket and put it in his hand. "Don't be late," she said. "In fact, be early." And she was gone.

Hoyle stared at where she'd stood, his mouth slightly open. The glow in his stomach felt fantastic. Sybil's smile made him feel fantastic. The paper with the flight details made him feel fantastic. And panicky. Home. He had to get home and get his ticket. And pack! A backpack. He couldn't very well go pulling a suitcase through the—what was it in Australia?—the bush. Did he even own a backpack? And when had he last renewed his passport?

He darted back to his car. Under his windshield was another piece of paper. On it was written, "Thanks."

Chapter 2

In Which Hoyle Meets a Stranger

Hoyle waited nervously near the check-in counters, a new, and overstuffed, backpack at his feet and an equally new carry-on that dragged, book-heavy, at his shoulder. He'd spent the last half-hour scanning the passing crowds for Sybil. There! No, too tall. There! No, Sybil wouldn't be carrying a baby. There—wait, yes! Hoyle started to wave idiotically.

Sybil spotted him and changed course. She, too, had a backpack, but hers was scuffed and dirty. "Good, you're early," she said when she reached him. "But … you know it's five hours to LA, and then another twelve or fourteen to Sydney, right?"

"Um, yeah. Why?"

"You're wearing—never mind. It'll be fine. Let's go check in."

His heart sank. Was this what it was going to be like the whole time? Never being quite good enough? Always somehow making the wrong choices? Too late now. He sighed, heaved his backpack onto his empty shoulder, and struggled through the crowd after Sybil.

They checked in, went through security, and set up camp at the gate. Hoyle got as close to comfortable as he could and pulled out a book.

Sybil said, "Don't forget to wake me at the boarding call," wrapped her neck in a U-shaped pillow, and dozed.

While her eyes were closed, Hoyle risked a good, long look at her. Sleep softened her tough, bristling energy, and she looked almost kind without the scowl. She was dressed in loose clothes that almost hid a roll of fat around her middle. Her carry-on was half the size of Hoyle's; he felt yet another flash of shame.

The people who set off on adventures together—weren't they always friends? Shouldn't Sybil be treating him like a trusted companion? Why had she even offered to take him along? Maybe this wasn't his big chance for adventure after all. Maybe it was just the start of one more sad, sorry mishap in his ordinary life, one more time he would disappoint someone he wanted to impress.

At least he could try, though. Maybe this time would be different. With sudden resolve, he swapped the book he'd first taken out for another: an introduction to camping. With Sybil asleep, he could read it without fear of her dismissive pity. He started the chapter on how to choose a campsite. It seemed straightforward enough: you just had to imagine all the very worst things that could ever possibly happen and pick a spot where they were very slightly less likely than at other spots.

When the boarding call came, he put his book away and said softly, "Sybil?" When she didn't wake, he gave her shoulder a gentle shake. She started awake and raised one arm to shield her face, then lowered it as she recognized Hoyle.

"Sorry," they said at the same time. Together they got in the line and shuffled forward to board the plane. Hoyle's seat was towards the back.

"See you in LA," said Sybil.

Hoyle nodded to his seatmates: a teenage boy and a man who looked like the boy's father.

"You staying in LA or going on?" asked the father pleasantly.

"Going on," said Hoyle.

"We're heading out to meet with a games company," said the father. "Josh has some really good programs he's been working on." The boy smiled shyly. "I just wish he spent as much time on his homework." The boy's smile vanished.

"I'm sure he does fine," said Hoyle, feeling embarrassed for him. "Smart kid like that. If he can program games, he can handle the French Revolution and—and Latin verbs. And stuff." He was rewarded by another smile from the boy.

"Hm, maybe," said the father. "So, where are you going on to? Hawaii? Tokyo?"

"Sydney."

"Cool," said the boy. "One of my Facebook friends lives there."

Once they took off the boy had his nose to the window. That left Hoyle at the mercy of the father's chatty curiosity. He found himself drawn into talking about H Rider Haggard and Sir Arthur Conan Doyle, the termites and his destroyed library, even about losing his job.

Sybil walked up the aisle on her way to the toilet. She noticed Hoyle and the father in conversation, and shot Hoyle a warning look. Then the trip was supposed to be a secret. Well, she'd never *said* so, had she? But he knew that wouldn't excuse him. Adventurers always kept their plans secret. One hour into the flight and he was already a failure as a sidekick. He did as he should have done at first: excused himself and started reading a book.

He sensed Sybil coming back down the aisle. He kept his head down, but watched her through his eyelashes as she went to her seat. Just before she sat down, she glared at him over her shoulder. He wasn't looking forward to the plane-change in LA.

* * *

"What the hell did you think you were doing?" said Sybil.

"Oh, come on. It was a shy kid and his pushy dad. They weren't hounding me about the Blood—um."

She nodded. "Better. New habits, Hoyle. People can overhear, put things together. The microphone is always on. Now. What gate for the Sydney flight?" She started walking.

Well. That hadn't been so bad.

She stopped and put a hand on his arm. "And if you screw up like that again, I'll turn and walk away from you, and I won't look back. If that means stranding you in a seedy bar full of desperate junkies or in a ravine a hundred miles from the nearest road, I mean it, I won't think twice. I like you and everything, and I didn't want to do the journey alone, but …"

She stared up at him until he nodded, then continued on to the gate. Hoyle followed, his face burning.

He kept obsessively to himself on the flight to Sydney. He read, and dozed, and ate, and read, and used the toilet, and watched a couple of movies, and dozed, and read, and ate, and eventually the flight attendants gave everyone a white, steamy towel. A heavy feeling in Hoyle's ears and a sense of being tipped over told him the plane was descending. The pilot announced the local time; he reset his watch.

He was doing his best to feel cool and worldly, but he still jiggled and fidgeted until he was allowed to stand up. And then it was another wait until the walkway was attached, and yet more waiting as everyone tried, and failed, to shuffle forward at once. Once off the plane, he waited for Sybil, and together they went through passport control, baggage claim, and customs, all of which required yet another wait.

Finally they went down a ramp, past the eager faces of other people's relatives, and into the waiting area.

"Now what?" said Hoyle. He checked his watch: Seven-thirty in the morning. Awkward time to do anything.

"There's a hotel in the city center we'll be staying at while we get our bearings. We'll have to share a room, though."

"What?"

"Oh, grow up. You can change in the bathroom. I don't know about you, but I'm not made of money, and halving the cost of the hotel was a little miracle for me. Besides, when I checked the website just before we left, there were no extra rooms anyway." She settled her pack on her shoulders. "By the way, I snore."

Hoyle closed his eyes and took a deep breath. "Okay."

"Train station's this way."

They got out of the train at Central Station, and Sybil led him confidently down and up stairs, through tunnels, and out into the huge, Victorian main terminal.

"How do you know where to go?" he said.

"I don't," she said. "I'm open to suggestion at any time."

"Now you tell me."

"Why? Did you have a suggestion?"

"Um, no."

"Then don't worry about it. Come on, we need to get east of the station. East is this way."

Adventurers always knew where east was. Hoyle never knew. This was going from bad to worse.

The streets of Sydney were cluttered and noisy, and the longer he and Sybil walked, the narrower and shabbier they became. Sybil took a map from her pack, and Hoyle watched passively as she studied it. They started turning corners and going down alleys. Finally Sybil stopped in front of a cramped-looking, four-story building with a sign on the door: "Happy Guest House. Nice Wisdom and Kindness for You. Free Wi-Fi."

"What's that about?" said Hoyle.

Sybil shrugged. "At least it doesn't say 'Bad Service and Bedbugs.'"

The lobby was all dark wood and dusty flowered carpets and odd corners. A staircase going up to a series of landings and hallways took up most of the space. Behind the desk was a woman who looked neither wise nor kind, just tired and a little bit anxious.

"Yes?" she said. "Yes? Yes?"

"Sybil Alvaro. Here's my confirmation number." She pulled a piece of paper from her pocket and handed it over.

The woman squinted at it. She pushed a form and a pen towards Sybil, who wrote for a minute and pushed them back. The woman gave her a key.

Sybil said, "Is there a second key for my friend?" The woman gave her an incredulous look. Sybil said to Hoyle, "I guess we'll have to share."

As Hoyle and Sybil lumbered up the stairs with their packs, a small figure shot past them on the way down.

The woman at the counter shouted, "Ada! Ada! Damn it, Ada! I—ah, shit."

"Nice wisdom and kindness," murmured Hoyle.

"Sh," said Sybil.

The room could just fit the two beds and a small table and chair. The pillows were thin, the bedspreads meager and worn.

Hoyle put his pack on one of the beds. "What's that you were saying about bedbugs?"

"Don't complain, it's cheap."

"How long are we here for?"

"I guess until we figure out where to go next. I'm hoping the State Library might have some information. They've got collections of manuscripts and personal papers, and who knows? There might also be someone in Sydney, an academic or something, to talk to. Breadcrumbs, Hoyle."

"Meanwhile, maybe I'll take a nap. I didn't sleep much on the flights."

"That's not a bad idea. Maybe I'll join you. Um, so to speak."

Hoyle giggled. A second later, so did Sybil. Hoyle realized it was the first time he'd ever heard her laugh.

He thought he might go brush his teeth, which badly needed it, but decided he'd lie down for just a second.

* * *

Sybil woke him. "I'm heading out for dinner."

"What? What time is it?"

"Four in the afternoon, but I'm ravenous. You want to come along?"

"Holy crap!"

"Jet lag is hell." Sybil started for the door.

"I have got to brush my teeth first. You'll thank me."

"Now that you mention it, I believe I will. Go ahead, I'll wait."

Hoyle found his toothbrush and toothpaste and squeezed into the tiny bathroom. He felt like he was brushing the crud out of his brain as well as off his teeth. He rinsed and spat, then splashed some water onto his face. Much better.

Sybil locked the door behind them and they descended the stairs. This time the desk was staffed by a tall man, with skin dark enough that he would have been hard to notice in the gloomy lobby had he not been waving his arms and shouting.

"I'm bloody sick and tired of your bullshit, Ada!"

"*My* bullshit?" It was a young woman's voice, high and angry. "You promised me I could work here until Christmas."

"That was assuming you'd actually do any bloody work."

"What? What haven't I done?"

"I don't have all fucking day to tell you, do I?"

"Oh yeah? What do you reckon Centrelink will say when I tell them—well, when I tell them what I could tell them?"

"You piss off during working hours again and I won't give a shit what you tell anyone."

"Fine!"

"Fine!"

Hoyle could hear her angry, stomping exit even over the carpet. A door slammed somewhere towards the back of the house, and the man behind the counter gave a loud sigh and rubbed his face wearily. Suddenly aware of Hoyle and Sybil, he looked up. "Yes?"

"How late is the front door open?" said Sybil.

"Nine. After that, use your room key."

"Thanks," said Hoyle, trying a friendly smile.

The man stared at him for a long moment. Abashed, Hoyle stepped with Sybil into a hot, humid, grey afternoon. His shirt felt damp in seconds. "That Ada seems like a piece of work," he said as they walked.

"Not our problem. I need to find a money machine."

"I guess back the way we came. I think there were some on that main road. God, it's hot here."

"What did you think? It's November."

They got to the wide, busy street Hoyle remembered from the morning, and Sybil got some cash. It occurred to Hoyle that he couldn't expect Sybil to pay for his dinner—indeed, the thought of it made him feel queasy—so he got some, too. They bought fish and chips from a corner shop, which he found very charming: real fish and chips wrapped in paper, just like in books. Pretty good, too, if more than a bit greasy.

"I want to go make a start at the State Library when we're done here," said Sybil. "It's just a little way up this street—I checked while you were asleep."

"I thought you were going to sleep, too."

"Couldn't. Too much to think about."

"Do you want me to come with you?"

"That's all right, thanks. Here, take the room key. I'll be back sometime before nine, I guess, so try not to fall asleep again until I get there. The way you sleep, you might not wake up no matter how loudly I knock. Do you remember how to get back to the hotel? Take the map, too. We're right here. That street there," she pointed, "is this one here on the map. Got it?"

"I can use a map." He sounded defensive, even to himself, but Sybil was too eager to notice.

Hoyle decided to walk around for a bit. Maybe have a beer. Australians were famous for their beer drinking; it would be interesting to watch them at it. There was a bar up the street—it was confusingly called a hotel, but it definitely looked like a bar. He bought himself a pint, then sat at an empty table and watched some sort of football. At halftime he bought himself another. The conversations around him were warm and jovial. He was really starting to like Australia.

He glanced outside. Uh-oh, it was getting dark. Time to head back. He took out the map to plan a route.

"Need some help, mate?" Hoyle looked up and recognized the figure that had darted past him that morning. The voice wasn't shouting now, but it was definitely the same one they'd heard before. Ada.

"Hey!" said Hoyle.

"Yeah, Happy Guest House—I saw you check in. This is my favorite pub, mainly because it's the first one I get to after I knock off work. You in a rush to get back? Can't think why. The place is a dump, and Mick and Melati are—well, never mind. If you had a choice, you'd be staying somewhere else. Mind if I sit down?"

"No, sure, please."

She was smaller even than Sybil, and thin as a straw. Her hair was spiky, and bleached white-blond, making a bizarre contrast with her deeply tanned skin and wide, dark eyes. Her hands were never still: they gestured, or ran through her hair, or fiddled with one of the piercings in her ears or lips.

"Okay, never mind the map. What you want to do is, see that street there?"

"Uh-huh."

"Go up there three blocks, then turn left, then second right and there you are."

Hoyle blinked.

"Aw, hell, I'll take you back there. If you shout me a beer."

Shout?

Ada spoke carefully. "If you buy me a beer, I'll take you back to the hotel."

"Oh! Oh, sure, yeah. What kind?"

"Whatever you're having."

He got her the beer, which she drank a lot more quickly than he'd expected. She stood up. "You ready?"

"Almost." He drained his own glass. "Okay."

She led him through the darkening labyrinth of streets until they got to the hotel. "Here you go," she said quietly. "Don't tell Melati I'm anywhere near here, or she'll drag me back in to do another shift, yeah? Thanks for the beer." She grinned and was gone.

Mick was at the desk, looking at something on the computer and frowning. He glanced at Hoyle, then back at the computer.

"Good night," said Hoyle, and Mick nodded without looking up again.

Up in the room Hoyle showered, changed into pajamas, and got out his camping book. It would be too easy to sleep if he lay on the bed; he sat gingerly on the rickety chair to read and wait for Sybil.

Despite his precautions, he was dozing when she knocked at the door. He jumped up, hid the book under his pillow, and let her in. She was glowing.

"It's a treasure trove," she gushed. "Letters, monographs, everything! I haven't found anything Ingraham-specific yet, but I'm sure I will—maybe even tomorrow. I have a good feeling about this—we might be on our way to the wilderness before the week is out."

Hoyle thought wistfully of the cheerful pub. Only one week until he was dragged away with nothing to shelter him from the wrath of the wilderness—and of Sybil. His bonhomie vanished, and he lay down to a restless sleep and an early rising.

Chapter 3

In Which a Nice Day Becomes
Much Less So

Hoyle woke to the sound of Sybil's morning ablutions. He put the pillow over his head and clamped it to his ear. His skull felt like it was stuffed with dirty laundry, and his eyes stung. Jet lag, or the two beers last night?

Sybil came out of the bathroom fully dressed. "Time to get up." She pulled the curtains open, and Hoyle groaned like a child.

"You want to come with me to the library today?" she said.

Hoyle sat up painfully. "Frankly, I'm not sure how much help I'd be."

Sybil nodded, as though this was the answer she wanted. "I'll be out all day. You can be back before nine, right?"

"Uh-huh."

"You're Mister Chirpy in the morning, aren't you?"

"Unh-unh." Hoyle lay back down and put the pillow over his head again. He heard the door open and shut, and the stairs creak as Sybil went down to the lobby. He resolutely kept his eyes shut and waited for sleep again.

Even through the pillow, Hoyle heard the crash and the shouting from the alley behind the hotel. A woman was hollering in a harsh voice that made her words sound like someone was banging a garbage can with a stick. It mostly wasn't English, but Hoyle had no trouble picking out the words that mattered: "Ada! You sacked. Get out!"

Ada cursed shrilly and expertly, and there was more crashing. Finally, all was silent.

Sleep was no longer an option. Hoyle threw back the covers and swung his aching legs over the side of the bed. He brushed his teeth, got dressed, and went out for a coffee.

This morning Sydney was bright, with a bit of a breeze. Hoyle stood outside the Happy Guest House and breathed deeply. He realized he had no idea where to go next, and something in him rebelled against going back into the dingy hotel to get the map. He'd be an explorer. No time like the present to start.

He thought to note the street names at the first intersection and felt smug. Maybe he wasn't completely inept after all.

He started walking towards where he remembered the pub and the main road were. After about a block, he heard light footsteps running up behind him. He turned nervously and felt relief wash through him.

"Hey," said Ada. She slowed to a walk, but Hoyle still had to push himself a bit to keep up with her.

"How are you doing?" said Hoyle. "Earlier. It sounded—"

"Oh. You heard all that?"

"Um, well …"

"Yeah, that's Melati. She sacks me every few weeks, but I'm the only one who can stand to work for her so she keeps having to take me back. This time, though, she might really mean it. In other words, I'm in strife."

"Why?"

"Hey, I know! Why don't you hire me as your guide? Like, your tour guide and that? I'd charge you less than those poncy blokes in the suits. And nobody knows Sydney like I do."

"How much is less than the blokes in suits?"

"How about $80 for all day?"

"Actually, that sounds pretty reasonable."

"It does?" Ada recovered quickly. "You have to buy me lunch, too. And a beer at the end of the day. Oh, and a beer with lunch."

"Anything else?" said Hoyle drily.

"Fees and fares for where I take you. Deal?"

"It's starting to sound a lot less reasonable, but okay."

"I'm telling you, mate, even with all that you'd pay a lot more with someone else."

"I *said* okay."

"Hey, what's your name?"

"Hoyle."

"Well, then, Mr. Hoyle—"

"No, it's my first name."

Ada stifled a snort, then said, "Any idea what you want to see first? Old stuff? Big stuff? Famous stuff? Weird stuff?"

"How about some of each?"

"You don't make it easy, do you? Okay, we'll get the famous stuff out of the way. But I gotta warn you, it's boring as bat shit. We could take a cab to start off with, but you won't see nearly as much. Are you good at walking?"

"I guess I'd better *get* good at it."

"Why?"

Hoyle blinked. "Um, I need to lose weight."

Ada glanced at his middle. "You're not wrong."

She led him to the main street he remembered from before and started walking. The street had a gentle incline that Hoyle was humiliated to find left him puffing.

"Don't worry," she said. "There's famous stuff coming up soon. I promise. Oh, okay, here we go. There's Hyde Park, and there's a big fountain and a war thing in there. There's the Australian Museum. Want to go in? It costs a lot of money, but there are dinosaurs and shit."

"No, thanks."

After a couple of minutes' walking, they came up to the cathedral whose spires Hoyle had been admiring.

Ada said, "This here is a great big church."

"I can see that. So far you're not much of a tour guide."

"This stuff isn't my strong point. Here's a place that used to be a jail in the old days. They have a museum. They took us in school. You can buy toy rats—you want a toy rat? Take back to your kids?"

"I don't have any kids."

"Oh." They walked further. "Here's Parliament House, where the Prime Minister lives. Or maybe the Premier. And this is … uh …" She looked around for a sign. "The State Library."

Hoyle tried to spot Sybil, but there were too many windows, and none of them had people where he could see them.

He saw a building that looked like a castle. A few kids came out, carrying musical-instrument cases. He glanced, puzzled, at Ada.

She shrugged and said, "I guess they're like a band or something. It gets *real* boring for a while now. Just hotels and that."

The street started to slope down, to Hoyle's relief.

"We're headed toward Circular Quay," said Ada.

"I've heard of that."

"Good," beamed Ada. "Then I won't need to tell you anything about it."

The waterfront was brilliant with tourists, musicians, jugglers, ferries, and sparkling water. Ahead to the right was the Opera House.

Hoyle said, "Hey, Ada, is that old, big, famous, or weird?"

"Take your pick."

"Ada!" came a shout from somewhere along the crowded footpath. "Ada Drake!"

Ada stiffened. She shot calculating glances along the row of ferry wharves. "Come on, Hoyle, we'll take the ferry over to Manly. It leaves in just a minute, we have to hurry." She dragged him over to a ticket booth. "Two to Manly, return." She motioned urgently for him to pay, then snatched up the tickets and dragged him to the fare gate, shoving a ticket into his hand. Within a minute she'd bustled him through the gate and onto the ferry, the attendants had pulled in the gangway and cast off the ropes, and the ferry had pulled away from the wharf.

Ada led him through the crowd along the rail as the ferry rumbled along and churned up the water. There was a little room towards the front; the seats were all taken, but there was a bit of space to stand and feel the wind and sun and spray. The ferry droned and chugged past the Opera House and out into the broader harbor.

Finally, Hoyle said, "You okay?"

"Sure," said Ada brightly. "Hey, over there, those are the Heads. You're lucky: there's waves today. That makes it a lot more fun— oh, wait. You don't get seasick, do you?"

"Ada," insisted Hoyle gently. "Are you okay?"

Ada dropped her head. The wind ruffled the spikes in her white-blond hair. "Yeah," she said quietly. She looked up at him with a quick grin. "I owe a bloke some money. He says, anyway."

The ferry began to make an odd corkscrew motion as they came abreast of the Heads. Hoyle kept very still, waiting to see if he was going to get seasick, but while he was deciding they passed the Heads, and the ferry steadied. Before long, they'd docked, and he and Ada had shuffled off the ferry along with the crowd. Ada led him along the streets.

"Is that the beach?" he said, pointing to where the street seemed to open out. "Can we go there? I don't get to the beach very often."

Ada shrugged. "You're the boss."

He spent a blissful half hour walking barefoot in the sand, letting the water catch him and splash up to the rolled-up cuffs of his pants. Ada followed along, out of reach of the water. Eventually he rinsed his feet off and put his shoes and socks back on, and they returned to the wharf.

On the ride back, Ada became increasingly jittery.

"What did you do to that guy?" said Hoyle cautiously.

"Nothing."

"Not if you're this scared."

"I'm not scared."

"What happens if someone beats up my tour guide? I'm lost in Sydney—lost!" He clasped his hands in a pleading gesture.

"You big dag," said Ada, and laughed.

"What's a dag?"

"Someone like you."

At Circular Quay, Ada said, "Time for lunch. I'll take you through some old stuff on the way."

The buildings quite suddenly got a lot older and more picturesque. "This is the Rocks," said Ada. "It's really old. Oldest place in Sydney. Or near enough. Here, we'll eat here." She guided him into a restaurant.

They were seated and given menus. Hoyle felt his eyebrows rise in shock as he perused the prices.

"How often do you come here?" he squeaked.

"This is the first time. Always wanted to try it, though."

"Yeah, well, don't go overboard. I'm a tourist, but I'm not *made* of money."

"Don't worry. I'm not out to scam you."

"You're not?"

"Well, not much."

And indeed, Hoyle was comforted to find that she ordered conservatively. He did the same and got a beer for each of them. A deal was a deal. It was good beer, too, and good food. His uneasiness began to fade.

After lunch, he asked Ada to take him toward the Opera House. "Might as well see it up close, since we're here," he said.

"I guess. But none of the bands I like ever play there."

It wasn't long before some sand he'd missed when rinsing his feet started to rub, then scrape, then scour.

"Just a minute, Ada, I'm in hell here," he said, and sat down on a wall near the water to take his shoes off. As he brushed at his stinging feet, she began to glance around.

"We should maybe keep moving," she said.

"It's okay—I'll still pay you if we don't see everything."

"No, that's not it. It's just—" She broke off. "Shit. Here he co—Hoyle, put your shoes back on." Hoyle stared up at her. "*Now*, you dumb fuck!"

Frightened by the change in her voice, he fumbled with his socks and shoes.

"Faster!"

"I'm trying." Finally, he stood up.

"Oh, shit. *Run!*"

She scampered, lithe and quick as a rabbit, among the tourists and toward the steps of the Opera House. Hoyle followed as fast as he could, but he soon lost her. He realized as his lungs started to burn that he should never have run—he looked like any other tourist, and would instantly have vanished into the crowd if only he hadn't started to run. Tourists don't run. He silently cursed Ada. How could he dodge the pursuer? He didn't even know who he was running from.

He risked a look over his shoulder—was anyone else running? He couldn't tell. He looked forward again: the steps of the Opera House loomed before him like a ziggurat. No, oh no. No way. There was a sort of driveway under the steps. Hoyle ducked into the cool, dim space and looked for a door. What thug would venture into an opera house?

Within the dim, carpeted quiet, he felt he could stop running. Indeed, he doubted he'd be permitted to run—there was no shortage of burly security guards in crisply tailored suit jackets. Which meant that neither would any pursuer be running; he could relax. He did his best to slow his breathing. Why should Ada's sordid problems become his? Okay, fine, he'd lost her. She'd never get the $80, even though she'd had a nice lunch out of it. He was well rid of her. She was too wild, too random. Sure, plenty of adventures had plucky urchins in them, but that didn't mean they were *mandatory*.

He could be his own tour guide. He could start right now. He picked up a brochure and decided to have a look around. It all seemed to involve a lot of stairs—everywhere he went, stairs—but as long as he could take them at his own pace, he was fine. He started to enjoy himself. The views were fantastic. And oh, look! There was a bar.

He ordered a glass of red, just for variety's sake, and made himself comfortable at one of the tables. About halfway through the wine, he began to feel … *not* comfortable. He looked around, and jumped: Ada's nose was two inches from his cheek. Wine dribbled over his hand and onto his pants.

"That'd be right—I knew I'd find you in the bloody bar," she said. "Don't you ever do anything else but drink?"

"I'm not buying you one. You ran off and left me. Whoever that was could have killed me."

Ada looked down. "Well, he didn't, did he? So it's all good, isn't it?"

"No!" He took out his wallet. "Here. Take your $80 and leave me alone."

"Awww, no!"

Hoyle frowned. "What do you care? You have your money. Wait, here's another $5 for that beer at the end of the day. Now go, okay?"

"Please?"

"Ada, don't whine, okay? I'm still a bit on edge, and it may make me snap."

There was a long pause. She didn't move.

Hoyle broke first. "Okay, *what*?"

"I … I'm scared. He'll wait until I'm alone. And Johnno … he's a big bloke."

The despair in her voice chilled him. "All right. I'll get a cab to take you home."

"He knows where I live."

"What do you want from me?" Hoyle cried. "Aren't there any police here?"

"The cops don't care about people like me."

"Sure they do."

"Sure," said Ada dully.

Hoyle felt like an idiot. What made him—sheltered, pudgy, middle-class—think he knew anything about Ada's life? He finished his wine. "Come back to the hotel. Then we'll figure out what to do next."

Ada let out an explosive sigh. "Aw, you're a dead-set legend. Thanks. Thanks, yeah? Thanks."

"You're welcome," said Hoyle glumly. Sybil was going to kill him.

* * *

"Damn it, Hoyle!"

"What? She needs a little help, that's all."

Ada shifted from foot to foot. "Maybe it'll be all right now. Maybe I can go to a mate's place."

"No," Hoyle cried. "Remember? You said you saw that guy, that Johnno, hiding when we got out of the cab."

Sybil slapped her forehead. "You mean he saw you with Ada?"

"Um …"

Sybil took a few deep breaths and drummed her fingers on the tiny table in their room. "Hoyle, did you actually see Johnno yourself?"

"Nnno."

"Did you hear anyone making any threats?"

"No."

"Are you sure Johnno isn't just Ada's imaginary friend who lets her get more meals and taxi rides off you?"

Ada squawked. "You see this scar?" She pointed to her temple, where a white line, flanked by a row of dots in each side, ran crookedly to her cheekbone. "That's where Johnno belted me last year."

"I'm sorry," said Sybil brusquely. "But there's nothing we can do, whether or not he's real. You'll have to go now."

Through the window, they heard shouts. Ada said, "Uh-oh," and ran to the side of the window to peer out. She pointed dramatically. "There," she whispered. "There's Johnno. No, Jesus, don't stand right in the window, are you crazy?"

Sybil stood on the other side and looked. Hoyle saw her eyebrows go up, then down in a worried frown. "That's the guy?" she said to Ada.

Ada nodded. "And now he's waiting for Hoyle, too. Mick doesn't scare him. Even Melati doesn't scare him, and she scares everybody. Plus, Johnno knows that Mick knows that if he calls the police, he won't have another quiet day as long as he lives. That's how Johnno works."

Sybil gnawed on a fingernail. "I really don't want to get caught up in dealing with the police, and maybe the consulate—who knows how long all that would take? Looks like we're going to have to head west sooner than I thought."

"Like when?" said Hoyle.

"Well, like now. Pack up, okay?"

"Can I come?" said Ada.

"Absolutely not," said Sybil.

"But have you had enough time to, like, figure out where you're going to go next? I know lots about the country around here. Where are you headed? West, you said? The Blue Mountains? I can be your guide. Katoomba, Blackheath, Warrimoo, I know them all."

Sybil narrowed her eyes. "What about further than that?"

"Mt Victoria, Lithgow, Bathurst, Orange." Ada rattled these off cheerfully. "I told you. I know them all."

Sybil stepped away from the window and turned to Hoyle. "You said she was your tour guide today. How good a guide is she?"

Past her shoulder, Ada was giving Hoyle a panicked, pleading look and shaking her head.

"No, she was okay. Fine, even. We had a good day. She knew lots."

Ada mimed relief; not content with that, she blew him a kiss just as Sybil turned back to the window.

Sybil glanced back and forth between them.

"What?" said Hoyle defensively.

There was a long pause.

"Nothing," said Sybil. "Yet. Now get packing. Ada, how are you going to get your things? You'll need warm clothes, a pack, a water bottle—"

"Um, my mum lives in Punchbowl. Can we stop by there?"

"Is it on the way?" said Sybil, who was already stuffing her possessions into her own pack.

"Yeah, right on the way," said Ada earnestly.

"It had better be," said Sybil. "I'll go get a car and be back as soon as I can. Don't go *anywhere*, do you hear me? Not one foot outside this room. If we're in a hurry to go, and it seems we are, I don't want to waste time looking for you."

"Okay," said Hoyle, eager to placate her.

The door slammed shut.

"Wow," said Ada. "She's heaps aggro."

Hoyle took a guess. "Really irritable? Yeah."

"Gonna be a long trip out west."

"Sure is."

"Still, better than being bashed by Johnno."

"Uh-huh."

"Hey, Hoyle?"

"Yeah?"

"You didn't have to do this. Thanks."

"I sure hope you're a better tour guide out west than you were in Sydney."

"Me too."

Chapter 4

In Which Hoyle Is Made Very
Uncomfortable

"There," Ada said, flinging her arm triumphantly out towards the canyon. "Isn't that pretty?"

It was. The viewing area was just at the top of a cliff, and parrots flew back and forth in the trees below. This shocked Hoyle slightly: it had never really occurred to him that there were such things as parrots that weren't in cages. Their colors showed bright against the dull green of the leaves, and they screeched as they fluttered among the branches. Through the noise, he could just hear the sound of the shirtless, paint-smeared guy up who sat on the sidewalk near the tour buses and played an odd, droning tone on a hollow log.

In the middle distance, three gnarled sandstone pillars rose from a spur that jutted into the canyon. They glowed gold in the late-afternoon sun.

Hoyle read the interpretive sign. "The Three Sisters."

"Yeah," said Ada.

"Turned into stone by a wizard."

"Yeah," said Ada again.

"We should get back to the car," said Sybil abruptly. She was even more irritable than usual: the trip to Ada's mother's place had been a chaos of shouting, disarray, and delay as Ada had stormed through the house grabbing what she figured she needed. Her mother had followed her the whole way, trying to snatch things back out of her hands until Ada had shoved her down onto the couch and yelled, "Shut *up*, Mum! Or I'll pour your fucking grog down the fucking toilet."

That was when Hoyle and Sybil had exchanged a look and gone back out to the car to wait. He spent the time studying the map book; he hadn't wanted to pay for international roaming on his phone—no point, with no-one to call back home—and a quick check yielded no wi-fi in range. He preferred paper anyway. Had Allan Quatermain had Google Maps? Oh—Punchbowl was, in fact, quite a bit out of their way to the mountains. He forbore to mention this to Sybil.

Once in the mountains, Ada had insisted they stop. "It's heaps famous, you'll never forgive yourself. Besides," she'd said, playing her trump card, "I *really* gotta wee."

She'd gotten chirpier the further they'd gotten from Sydney, until even Hoyle was starting to find it tiresome. Still, he guessed it was better than seeing her worried and afraid, or listening to her swear at her mother.

Sybil unlocked the car. The door opened with a grating squeal; she'd bought it from a place that sold cheap castoffs from long lines of backpackers, and it made a lot of interesting noises. She and Hoyle got into the front; Ada had already set up camp in the back seat. "I'm hungry," she said. "Can we get some dinner somewhere?"

"No," said Hoyle. "You just had a candy bar. You can wait."

"Aw," whined Ada. "You're mean."

"Do you want to walk back to Sydney?" said Sybil as she started the car.

Ada retreated into sulky silence and started listening to her iPod so loudly that Hoyle could hear the lyrics from her earphones.

They passed through a few more towns before the road started to drop in front of them. They chased the sun downward until it won, and darkness washed across the gentle hills that were all that was left of the Blue Mountains.

At Lithgow, the first town they came to after the descent, Hoyle realized that he, too, was hungry. He pointed to the McDonald's sign. "What do you think?" he said.

"All right," said Sybil.

Ada looked up when she felt the car slowing. "Sweet, Macca's!"

"What's Macca's?" said Hoyle.

"For God's sake," sighed Sybil. "McDonald's, of course."

"Well, I didn't know," said Hoyle. He felt a sympathetic pat on his shoulder from Ada in the back seat.

The food tasted just different enough from McDonald's at home to make him conscious of how it actually felt in his mouth, how it smelled, the slightly different color of the ketchup. He found it increasingly difficult to swallow, chewing each mouthful longer and longer and washing it down in queasy desperation with some Diet Coke.

Ada had no such problems, eating her burger in a few enthusiastic bites before starting work on the fries. Before long she said, "I'm still hungry. Hey, Hoyle, do you mind if I get some more?"

Hoyle handed her five dollars, and she went back to the counter. As soon as she was out of earshot, Sybil said, "I don't think she's going to be much help in the wilderness, I have to say. And I'm a little uneasy about how you keep letting her sponge off you. In fact, I'm getting sorrier by the minute I let you talk me into taking her along. She acts like an adolescent, and I have suspicions that whenever she says anything definite at all, that's a sure sign she's lying. We're on an adventure, but things in real life don't go the way they do in books. Ada isn't the plucky urchin, and she isn't the noble savage guide. She's a very badly brought up, very selfish, very immature young woman whose only asset is that she knows how to play you, Hoyle, like a violin."

"You don't know she's lying. Maybe we really did rescue her from being beaten. Or raped. You don't know."

"True," said Sybil reflectively. "And that's the only reason I don't drag you back to the car and drive off without her. But I'll be damned if she wrecks my one chance to find the Bloodwood Staff. I—" She broke off as she saw Ada coming back with a bag of food.

"I got it to take away, in case you didn't want to hang around here," Ada said cheerily. "Lithgow Macca's isn't the nicest place in the world, is it?"

"That's okay, thanks," said Sybil. "You can eat it here. Pretty soon after Lithgow we need to turn off onto roads I'd rather not try in the dark, so we'll see if there's a motel here we can stay in. Besides, we have a lot of driving to do, and I'd rather not do it in a car that smells like greasy beef."

Ada shrugged. "Okay."

While she ate, Sybil found out from the McDonald's staff where the nearest decent hotel was, then bustled them into the car and drove them a couple of miles further down the road to where it sat, bland and dimly lit.

Hoyle and Ada sat in the lobby, packs and bags at their feet, while Sybil made the arrangements. Hoyle worried: Ada sharing a room with him was just creepy, and Ada sharing with Sybil was inviting a homicide. To his surprise, Sybil came back and tossed a key to each of them. "We left Sydney early, and this place is way, way cheaper, so I splurged on an extra room. Hoyle, you and I can split the cost of Ada's."

"Wow! Thanks," said Ada. "I never stayed in a hotel room by myself before."

"We leave at eight," said Sybil sternly. "We'll need time to get some food."

"Eight in the *morning*?" squeaked Ada.

Sybil sighed again.

* * *

Hoyle was ridiculously relieved to retreat, alone, into his hotel room. He'd borrowed *After the Bloodwood Staff* from Sybil;

while the few chapters he'd read on the plane hadn't impressed him, he wanted at least to be better informed by the time they got to wherever it was Sybil had chosen to start the real part of their expedition. He could predict the rest of Nestor's journey precisely: Nicholas would die, no doubt, leaving Nestor with a quest for vengeance. Nestor would penetrate the bush and, after unspeakable hardship, find the treasure, which would lead him to his brother's killer. Justice would be served, the treasure would be recovered, the estate back home would be saved, the mother would regain her health, and Nestor would trot back to Oxford to be brilliant and suave, although always with an intriguing air of hidden grief that would cause older men to cultivate his company and younger men to idolize him. And sure enough, it wasn't long before Nicholas met his doom.

Nestor ran to his brother's side. The wound from the staff was grievous: jagged and frenzied, surely the work of a madman. Nestor felt sick at the sight of—no, never mind, he couldn't weaken now. Nicholas needed him.

"Find the staff, Ness. Find it before it ..."

"I will! But not until we get you back to civilization."

Nicholas gave a small, wheezy laugh, then his face contorted with pain. "We both know I'm not going anywhere. The staff has done its evil work on me. But it won't get both of us." He had begun raving. "Will it, Ness? Will it? You'll stop it. Promise me. Promise!"

But before Nestor could say a word, Nicholas's face grew slack, and his eyes—so like their mother's—went cold and glassy.

Nestor knelt beside his brother's body and wept.

* * *

The morning was desperately chilly. As they were loading the car, Sybil said, "I hope your sleeping bag is made for the cold, Ada."

"My what?"

"Your … sleeping bag," said Sybil slowly. "Right. I guess we're stuck here until the stores open. I assume there's a camping store in Lithgow?"

"There'd have to be, this close to the mountains," said Hoyle, anxious to placate her before the storm of her displeasure broke.

"No point in going back to the rooms," said Sybil wearily. "Breakfast, and then," her voice broke with disgust, "*shopping*."

For once, Ada kept quiet. Breakfast passed with hardly a word, and they drove silently up and down the streets of Lithgow, looking for a camping store. The town was entirely functional: dreary houses and Spartan rows of warehouses and workshops, aging cars, the occasional pedestrian with an air of sullen acquiescence. Even the churches were austere. The town was set between two lines of low hills that seemed to block any escape.

"There," said Hoyle. "On the left." The camping store hadn't opened yet, but he could see people inside, readying the store for the day's business. They parked and waited.

The instant someone unlocked the front door, Sybil was out of the car, into the store, and marching toward the rack of sleeping bags. She read labels, tested zippers, squeezed fistfuls of stuffing, and chose a bag already in a stuff sack from the shelves nearby.

"W-which one did you get?" said Ada cautiously.

Sybil pointed to one of the ones hanging up.

After a moment, Ada said, "It's green."

"Yes?" said Sybil in a dangerous voice.

"Is … is there a red one?"

Sybil glared so intently that Ada took a step back. "Sorry. Forget I said anything."

Hoyle tried to change the subject. "While we're here, maybe there are other things we need. You know, that we were—well, that I was—in too much of a hurry to pack in DC?"

"We've already lost more than an hour," said Sybil.

"But it might save us a lot more hours if we just make sure," said Hoyle reasonably. In truth, he was planning to buy everything he could find that even hinted at being useful, just to keep Sybil from looking at him the way she'd just looked at Ada.

"Hm," said Sybil. "I was just going to get some food at the supermarket, but some of this stuff might come in handy. Easier to carry, too." She took a basket and headed over to the aisle with the freeze-dried food.

Hoyle took a basket as well and went up and down the other aisles grabbing things: waterproof matches, a collapsible silicone cup and bowl, a compass, a pair of gloves, an insulated hat, a whistle, an extra pair of socks, a flint-and-steel kit, some biodegradable soap, a signal mirror—

"Enough, enough," said Sybil. "You'll be carrying all that stuff, you know. It adds up. You're already going to have to carry some of the food. And I'll still need to get more at the supermarket, remember."

Hoyle felt a bit deflated. He'd been having fun picturing all the problems he could solve with each gadget, and the thought of his pack being considerably heavier than it already was sobered him. He still managed to surreptitiously tweak a few small and intriguing items into his basket on his way to the checkout.

Sybil insisted on doing the supermarket shopping herself. "The last thing I need is the two of you throwing candy bars and cookies into the basket."

Ada looked at her in wide-eyed innocence.

Hoyle slumped in the car seat and closed his eyes. Not that he was sleepy—the night's sleep in his own room had done wonders (Sybil had not been entirely candid: the noise she emitted as she slept was not so much snore as seismic cataclysm). Rather, he felt like he was trying to shut out the reality of what he'd done: dashed off halfway across the world on a stupid, self-indulgent romp with a stranger, gotten himself lumbered with another stranger out of pity—and they were about to go *camping*, for God's sake. And looking for something that somebody wrote about in some damned adventure novel as if it were real. How much food could they carry? Enough for a week? Two weeks? Then what? He had no idea how to live off the land—not at home, and certainly not here. At least Ada was tough and cunning—that much was indisputable. He was neither.

He sat up and paged idly through the map book to distract himself. He looked up Lithgow—hey, it had a train station! It wasn't too late. He—maybe he and Ada both—could be back in Sydney before dinnertime. He found the intersection where they were parked; the train station was a walkable distance away.

He twisted to look at Ada. Her eyes were closed, and she was bobbing her head to the music. "Hey, Ada," he ventured. Then a little louder, to be heard over her iPod: "Ada!"

"Jesus, what? Quit shouting."

"You sure you want to go on this camping trip?"

Ada shrugged, her eyes still closed. "I got nothing else on. Camping's fun. My cousin says. She's in Scouts, which is dumb, but she likes the camping. I should try it."

Hoyle tried again. "I'm not much good at camping, myself. Maybe we'd just slow Sybil down."

Ada laughed. "Nothing is going slow *her* down. You know," she added, "you should make more of an effort with her. You know?"

"Um, no. Effort to do what?"

"Ugh! You're just like a kid, you know that? She's eyeing you off, mate. You just have to make the offer."

Hoyle was desperately confused.

Ada gaped. "Don't tell me—no, really? You haven't noticed?"

"Ada, noticed *what*?"

"She's got a thing for you, mate." She winked and made a nudging motion. "Mind you, I think you could do better. But she's—"

"You're nuts," said Hoyle with a shocked laugh.

"I'm only saying."

Hoyle would have argued further—how much more ludicrous could anything be?—but saw Sybil coming out of the grocery store.

She fit the groceries in around the packs in the trunk and got in behind the wheel. "Here," she said, handing each of them a candy bar.

"Wow—thanks," said Ada, giving Hoyle a told-you-so look before ripping the wrapper and biting a truly vulgar amount of chocolate from the bar.

"Thanks," said Hoyle.

"That's okay," said Sybil. "They were on sale. Don't leave the wrappers in the car."

* * *

When Sybil shut the car off at the trailhead, the silence dropped over them like a quilt. Hoyle got out. The breeze brought a sharp, resinous scent, and rustled the leaves of the white-trunked trees that spread out as far as he could see.

The morning was warmer already. When Hoyle listened closely he could hear unearthly warbles and wails that he uneasily hoped were Australian birds, and the buzzing of flies (which sounded like American flies, only much, much bigger and more numerous). He helped Sybil get the packs out of the trunk.

All thought of making a run for the train station had vanished in light of Ada's revelation. Could it be true? Sybil *had* gotten him a candy bar. But she'd gotten one for Ada, too. But maybe that was to mask her feelings for him. Maybe Sybil was as shy about these things as he was.

Ada stood still, her head tipped back. "This is the quietest place I've ever been. No cars, no airplanes, nobody yelling or crying or even talking."

"Except you," said Sybil.

"All that quiet makes me nervous. It's scary."

Sybil distributed the food amongst the three packs, taking out a map and a GPS in the process. She fastened the packs, then beckoned Ada over. "Here," she said, and balanced Ada's pack on the trunk with one arm while she guided Ada's arms through the straps with the other. Hoyle grabbed his pack and struggled into it himself before she could do the same for him.

"Have a drink and something to eat before we start," said Sybil. "I've kept a little food and water out of the packs."

As he chewed obediently on a granola bar, Hoyle shifted his weight and experimented with different curvatures of his back to balance the pack. It was already uncomfortable; what would it be like after five miles on the trail? Ten?

"Sybil?"

"Mm-hm?" she said, her mouth full.

"I … may not be able to go very fast."

She swallowed, took a drink of water, and said, "Oh, I know that. I'll have to go slow to make sure we're on the right track anyway. There wasn't much information in the library—that is, I didn't get much chance to find everything there might have been." She cast a meaningful look at Ada. "So I'm needing to piece together some very sketchy clues. I'll be stopping a lot, checking the map, checking my notes. There'll be plenty of chances to catch your breath."

"I hope so," said Ada. "This pack is making my fucking knees buckle."

"Are you going to complain like that the whole time?" said Sybil.

"Yup."

Sybil picked up her own pack. "Hoyle," she said conversationally, "I ought to kick your ass for this."

Chapter 5

In Which the Wilderness Is Faced

"Yes, I said you'd get to rest, but five times in an hour is ridiculous," said Sybil. "Get up."

"No." Ada sprawled against the bank of the dry stream bed, her pack squashing the brush behind her.

"Supposedly, Australian explorers walked all through here, didn't they? I can only assume they didn't complain like this."

"They would've if they'd had you along."

"Get up."

Ada closed her eyes and nestled ostentatiously further into the brush.

"Okay," said Sybil. "Let's go, Hoyle."

"What?" Hoyle had been expecting shouting, shoving, maybe even tears—from Ada at least. But to just … leave her here? Sybil had to be bluffing. She had to.

But she was already several yards up the stream bed.

Hoyle turned back to Ada, who was nonchalantly scratching her leg. She stopped suddenly, and stared, horrified, at her left calf. Then she started to shriek. And shriek.

Hoyle stumbled over to her. "What?"

Sybil ran back down the gully. "What's wrong?"

Over Ada's keening, Hoyle shouted, "I don't know—she won't tell me."

Ada pointed at her leg, still screaming.

Hoyle and Sybil bent in to look. On Ada's bare calf was a thin, pulsing, slug-like thing. In a spasm of disgust, Hoyle tried to brush it away, but it held fast. The feel of his hand rolling over its soft, slimy little body, and the tenacity of its hold on Ada's flesh, made him feel sick. "What is it?" he cried.

"Oh, for God's sake, it's just a leech," snapped Sybil. She peeled it expertly off Ada's leg, and a thick trickle of blood immediately began to seep from the wound. "The longer you sit still, the easier it is for them to find you," she told Ada wickedly. "Well, now that that's sorted out …" She turned back up the gully. In a few moments Hoyle could barely see her through the brush.

"Come on, Ada," he pleaded. "She's really going."

"So?" She had stood up and was anxiously checking her legs and arms for more leeches.

"She has the map. And the compass. And most of the food."

At this, Ada looked even more troubled. But all she said was, "Nah, I'm all right. You go on."

"Ada, this is a hell of a time to try to prove a point. Come on, be reasonable. Nobody will be impressed if you sit here and sulk."

"I'm not sulking."

Hoyle battled the urge to argue. Time was pressing: Sybil was gone, and sitting still meant leeches. The thought of them wriggling towards him in their hundreds as he stood there, a warm-blooded beacon for their hideous hunger—and yet … Ada. Left alone. Clearly no wiser or more competent than he was himself. He could kick himself for falling for her patter back in Sydney. But didn't he owe her something after having dragged her into the wilderness?

No, wait, he told himself. She'd *wanted* to come with them. And if now she wanted to behave like a sullen child, that didn't mean he had to stay here and watch her. He started up the gully.

"Hoyle!" cried Ada. "I didn't mean it. Stay with me."

He made himself ignore her.

She kept calling his name; he could hear her long after she was out of eyeshot. He hated himself more with every step. But how else was Ada ever going to grow up?

Only—she'd been his friend. And he'd left her alone in the wild.

He plunged up the gully, hoping Sybil hadn't turned off it. The thought caused a stab of panic. What if he, too, was now alone in the wild? He took a deep breath. Broken twigs. He should look for broken twigs, bent grass, threads from her clothing, things that would show where Sybil had passed.

He looked at the surrounding brush, trying to figure out if any of the twigs and leaves in the wild tangle were askew, then down to a patch of dirt at his feet. The print of a hiking boot was clear. *Footprints, idiot*, he told himself. *It's not that hard, really.* He moved forward to look for another—there. Sybil was still heading up the gully.

Hoyle glanced up the slope: he could just see sky where the hill crested. It looked like a long way. Maybe he should just go back to Ada. Surely Sybil would come back, once she realized neither of them was following. Or if she thought one of them was in trouble, like she had when Ada screamed. Maybe he should scream. He wasn't actually sure he knew how. There hadn't been much call for screaming in his life, up until now.

He stayed there for several minutes, catching his breath, trying to decide what to do. He frowned: someone was coming towards him from the woods below. From the sound, it was someone either really big or really careless—Hoyle wouldn't have been surprised to see an elephant burst through the brush.

Instead, it was Ada, tiny and desperate, flinging her arms to push the leaves aside, stomping on obstructing bushes, making her way up the gully.

Hoyle waited, feeling guilty. She looked up and spotted him. "You bastard!" she called. "You bastard!" It became her mantra until she reached him; then she fell silent, glaring at him.

"Um," he said. "Hi."

She pushed past him and continued up the hill. All he could do was follow. At least he hadn't had to choose. He just hoped Ada wouldn't mess up Sybil's footprints.

At the top of the hill, Ada stopped. "What the—God damn it!"

A minute later, Hoyle reached her, to find Sybil sitting with her pack as a backrest, reading a book. "All right," Sybil said. "Do we all have that out of our systems?"

"Not because of your fucking nagging, though," said Ada.

"Why, then?" said Sybil.

When Ada didn't answer, she shrugged, and the three of them set off. It wasn't until over an hour of silent walking later that Ada muttered, "Because you were worried when I screamed."

Sybil blinked.

Ada said, "I been screaming about one thing or another my whole life. Might as well have been screaming at a wall, most times. But you came back." Suddenly she turned on Hoyle and hit him, hard, on the arm. "*You*, though—you bastard." Then she hauled off to give him another one. Hoyle let her hit him. He deserved it.

His career as an adventure hero was going even worse than he'd feared.

* * *

Hoyle had never been so exhausted. Sybil had insisted on continuing until the sun had neared the horizon. He hadn't dared object, not after Ada's attempt at rebellion. Ada's chagrin seemed to have become a perpetual sulk, but at least the whining had stopped.

When Sybil finally called a halt, he and Ada collapsed, groaning.

Sybil looked at them, astonished.

"What?" said Hoyle peevishly.

"We need to set up the tent."

"Wait," said Ada, her eyes still closed. "Tent. One tent."

"Yes."

"Which you got before you knew I was coming along?"

"Well, yes."

"So it only fits, what, two people?"

"And their gear," said Sybil.

"So … where does Hoyle sleep?"

Hoyle sat up. "Excuse me?"

"You don't expect me to sleep outside, do you? After you ran off and left me?"

Sybil sighed. "I got a tarp in Lithgow to rig up for the third person. And it's not going to rain tonight. But if nobody wants to sleep under the tarp, we can leave the gear outside and all three of us can sleep in the tent."

"No, that's all right," Hoyle said quickly. "I don't mind."

"Okay," said Ada, her goodwill miraculously restored at the thought of Hoyle's discomfort.

"Who's going to chop up the veggies for dinner?" said Sybil. She'd put a plastic mat on the ground with a couple of carrots and a knife. Hoyle set to work. A piece of carrot shot away from him into the dirt; he started to fling it into the bushes when a cautionary noise from Sybil halted him.

"We don't have enough food to go throwing it around," she said. "Wipe it off."

"Ew!" said Ada. "I'm not eating that."

Hoyle felt the same, but brushed the grit off and resumed cutting. At least he could hearten himself with the thought that in the adventure books, eating gross food was de rigueur. After all, this was no ordinary camping trip.

"Sybil?" he said.

"Mm?"

"What happens if we find the staff? I mean, do we take it home, or what?"

"I'll figure that out when the time comes."

Sybil took the carrots from him and dumped them into a pot that was simmering over a tiny gas flame. "While that's cooking, we set the tent up," she said briskly. Neither of them even bothered asking Ada to help. Hoyle did as he was told, and somehow the poles and the shapeless mass of dull-gray, clinging nylon fabric became a tent. Next, she deftly strung a thin rope between some trees, draped the tarp over it, and pegged the corners down. "There," she said with satisfaction. "Home sweet home for you, Hoyle."

He sat back down and let his eyes unfocus as weariness spread over him like a blanket, and evening fell. The trees looked like lace cutouts against the turquoise sky, and their leaves hissed gently as a warm breeze moved through them, bringing their strange, astringent scent.

His guts spasmed in fear as he caught a movement in the woods about twenty yards off to his left. In the near-darkness he couldn't tell size or color, or even whether he'd actually seen anything. The roaring of the gas stove—surprisingly loud for such a small thing—masked any sounds that might have reached him.

"Did you see something just then?" he asked.

"Where?" said Sybil. Hoyle pointed. She shrugged. "Probably a kangaroo."

"Where?" cried Ada eagerly. "I've never seen a kangaroo."

"Aren't you Australian?" said Hoyle.

"Do you think they hop around the friggin' Opera House?"

Hoyle shivered, and told himself it was because the air was chilling rapidly, now that the sun was gone. He dragged himself to his feet, the weariness doubly heavy following the adrenaline shot of a few moments earlier, and got his sleeping bag out. He pulled the bag up around his waist and sat down again, his back against his pack. Sybil, who had turned her headlamp on, handed him a bowl of food and a spoon.

"Thanks," he said, surprised. "I wasn't expecting table service."

"I'm not making a habit of it," she said. "Ada! Come and get it."

"What, no table service for me?"

"Yes, when you help make the food and set up the tent."

"I thought you were nice, for a minute back there," said Ada resentfully. "When you got the leech off me."

"Sorry for the misunderstanding."

Eventually Ada picked her way over to where Sybil's headlamp shone and got a bowl of food. "Is there one of those head-torches for me?" she said. "Eventually I'll need to go to the loo."

"Eat first, before the food gets cold," said Sybil.

"I didn't mean right *now*," said Ada. "You gotta put something in before something'll come out."

After that, they ate more or less silently and watched the moon come up.

When the clicking of spoons against bowls had stopped, Sybil gathered up the utensils. "I'll wash these tonight," she said, "but tomorrow I'll show you how to wash them without using much water. Then everyone does their own."

"Thanks," said Hoyle.

"Yeah, thanks," said Ada. "*Now* I need to go to the loo. Can I have a headlight thing? And where's the toilet paper?"

Sybil found the roll, unwound a length of paper, and handed it to Ada, along with a trowel and a flashlight. "Bury it when you're done, okay? The paper, not the flashlight. Torch, I mean."

Ada turned the flashlight on and walked, muttering curses, into the bushes. "Don't look," she called back over her shoulder.

Now that the stove was off, the quiet was profound. Hoyle tried hard not to hear the distant patter of Ada's pee, but his efforts only made him more acutely aware of every sound. He heard an owl of some sort, then the flapping wings of an enormous bat, up near the treetops. Then Sybil shifting her position where she sat. A branch breaking, the rustle of bushes as Ada made her way back.

"Hey, Sybil?" said Ada, when she'd made it back to the site. "Why are we here?"

"Some questions are just to big for humans to answer."

Ada gave an exasperated sigh. "No. Why are we camping here, right *now*?"

"We're after the Bloodwood Staff," said Sybil.

"What's that?"

"It's an artifact," said Hoyle, enjoying the feeling of knowing, for once.

"Huh?"

"A big stick, carved out of bloodwood."

Sybil added, "It's supposed to be fictional—just a story—but I think it's not."

"What's it do?" said Ada.

"Um, it's a stick. That's what it does," said Sybil.

"Is it valuable?"

"Probably not."

Hoyle remembered his termite-ridden house. "You told me we'd find riches."

"If you think back, you'll find I never said anything of the kind."

Hoyle tried hard to remember exactly what Sybil had said, and couldn't. It occurred to him to ask himself one more time why he had agreed to come with her.

"Anyway, why's it important?" Ada said as she sat back down.

"In the story, it's got magical powers."

"Like what?"

"That was never actually spelled out. But there are clues, hints, suggestions. Ingraham was sending a message to his readers. And I intend to figure it out."

"It's just a story, though," said Ada. "What makes you think there's a real stick?"

"That's a fair question," said Sybil. "I'm pretty sure that Ingraham, at least, thought it was real, and that his message was, 'Here's where you can find the staff.'"

"That just doesn't make any sense," said Ada. "Why didn't the guy just nick the staff and take it home himself?"

"That's part of what I want to find out," said Sybil. "It's a mystery!"

"Tell me the story."

"I'll have to read it to you as we go. It's kind of long."

"Make it a bedtime story. Nobody ever read to me at bedtime."

"Oh. Okay." Sybil sounded abashed. Hoyle could hear her

searching through her pack. Ada wriggled; when the light from Sybil's headlamp caught her face, he could see an eager, childlike expression that made him suddenly sad.

"Ah, here," said Sybil. The beam from her headlamp dipped down to illuminate the pages. "*After the Bloodwood Staff*, by C.G. Ingraham. Chapter One: 'In Which Ivory Accepts a Challenge'. 'The morning sun streamed across the dew-soaked fields that had been in the Ivory family estate for four hundred years. Ordinarily young Nestor Ivory, privileged second son of a jovial father and a gentle mother, was happy to be out riding on such a morning, but today his brow was furrowed. He had received a letter in the previous day's post that had troubled him deeply. His brother, Lord Nicholas, was still determined, upon receiving his degree from Oxford, to make his way to Australia.

"'Australia! Nestor had to admit the idea had more than a tinge of romance about it. And yet, was it prudent, with Mother so unwell, and Father needing more help every year managing the estate?'"

"*Bor*-ing," moaned Ada.

"Give it a chance," said Sybil. "It's a little slow at the beginning, I admit, but it picks up. I promise." She cleared her throat. "'He'd have to think of some way to convince Nicholas to stay, if simple filial loyalty were not enough. Nicholas was due on the midday train for a week's stay. He'd have plenty of time to wear his brother down.'"

Sybil read well, with animation and a lack of self-consciousness Hoyle hadn't heard in her before. Ada's fidgeting quieted, and Hoyle yawned as he stretched his legs inside his sleeping bag. As Sybil read, Nestor confronted his brother, who dropped the bombshell that their parents were going broke, which prompted Nestor to decide that to spare them his continuing university expenses, he'd nobly go with Nicholas to Australia.

"They're what!" cried Nestor.

"Nearly penniless, dear boy. Please try to pay attention," said Nicholas.

Nestor sank into the overstuffed chair. He ran his eyes over the shelves of leather-bound books, the expensive furnishings, the opulent Oriental carpet. "But how?"

"Do you think estates like this are kept up for pennies?" said Nicholas. "Your Oxford fees will be the final blow, I'm thinking."

"Surely not!" Nestor cried in horror.'"

Sybil broke off. "What's so funny?"

"What?" said Hoyle.

Sybil paused. "Nothing. I thought I heard you laugh, that's all. Time to go to sleep, anyway."

Chapter 6

In Which Things Go Badly Wrong

Hoyle sat bolt upright, frightened and confused by the sharp pain in his ribs. His face struck something cold, wet, and clinging. He tried frantically to push it aside, but he couldn't raise his arms. He yelped, then realized his arms were only trapped by the sleeping bag, the tarp was not actually suffocating him, and the pain was a rock he'd rolled onto as he slept.

As his breathing slowed, he freed one arm and lifted the side of the tarp. The sky was stacked bands of color: orange at the horizon, then green, turquoise, deep cobalt blue. A few stars still shone. The air was cold enough to sting his nostrils, and brought strange, aromatic scents. He listened, anxious lest he'd woken the others, but all was quiet.

A harsh, ringing squawk tore through the morning calm, then another, then dozens. Hoyle peeked out again: a flock of enormous white birds flew past—their cries literally deafened him for a moment. When his ears had recovered, he heard a freakish chuckling from further off; this, too, was soon joined in its ghoulish hilarity by dozens of others.

The woods were suddenly alive with noise: tweets, chirps, screeches, and drawn-out whistles ending with an abrupt swoop, like an old radio being tuned. Just above his head came a complex warble that Hoyle instantly decided was the most beautiful sound he'd ever heard.

"Wow," he whispered. He knew in that moment that it wasn't treasure or land-grabs that had driven all the old explorers—the real ones, the ones in actual history books—to go out into the wild. It was moments like this. He thought back to the northern Virginia suburbs he'd left, and his heart swelled with the glory and immediacy of this new morning, this new life.

A zipper whined, and with a rustling and scuffing, someone got out of the tent. Hoyle turned onto his other side and saw Sybil's boots.

"Morning, Hoyle," she said quietly.

"Morning."

"I'll put some hot water on. Tea or coffee?"

"Tea, please." He wriggled out of his sleeping bag. Even through his clothes (and he'd added several layers as the night had gotten colder), the morning chill struck him. He put his boots on and crawled out from under the tarp. Sybil had set up the stove and was boiling water. She glanced over at him.

"Did you check your boots for spiders?"

"*What?*"

"Shh. Ada's still asleep. If you haven't felt a bite yet, you've cheated death—for now."

"Are you serious?"

"Entirely. How'd you sleep?"

"Surprisingly well. You?"

"Ada thrashes in her sleep. So, no, I didn't sleep all that well."

"I do not," came Ada's muffled voice. "Besides, Jesus, you snore."

"Want some coffee?" said Sybil.

"Last time I heard anything like it," Ada continued, "I was living next to the railway line down in Rockdale. Coal trains all night." There was the sound of packs being pushed around, and the side of the tent bulged as Ada patted it in increasing frustration. "How do I get out of here? I'm claustrophobic, you know. I could panic."

Sybil leaned over and unzipped the door, and Ada crawled out.

"Zip up the door, would you?" said Sybil. "I don't want to deal with bugs getting into the tent. And for the second time, would you like some coffee?"

"Bugs? Aren't we going to pack up anyway?"

"Do you want to find out what the insects of Australia can do to you after they've spent all day rolled up in a tent, bored, angry, and hungry?"

Ada zipped up the door. "Hey, is that coffee? Can I have some, please?"

Sybil sighed and made some instant coffee in a metal mug. Ada sipped at it and made a face.

Hoyle took another mug from Sybil, this one full of way-too-strong tea. He realized it was so strong because she'd merely thrown some leaves in the bottom of the cup and poured the boiling water over them.

"No teabags?" he ventured.

"I don't feel like packing two weeks' worth of wet teabags around; do you? You can bury the tea leaves and they'll break down a lot more quickly. The bags last forever."

Hoyle steeled himself and drank, trying to avoid the leaves by slurping.

"If I'd known you did that, I wouldn't have brought you," said Sybil.

"If I'd known it was going to be non-stop sniping and nastiness around here, I wouldn't have come," Hoyle said in a flash of anger.

There was a pause.

"You don't know what nasty is like," said Ada into the awkwardness. "This is a fucking dinner party with the Queen compared to what goes on at my place. Count your blessings."

Breakfast was granola bars, which Hoyle ate grimly. Everyone took what seemed like forever to wrestle sleeping bags, mats, and the tent back into their respective sacks and clean up from breakfast. There was no cheery chatter; conversation was limited to Sybil's instructions and Hoyle's and Ada's brusque acknowledgements.

Hoyle remembered Ada's sly encouragement of the day before. Sybil sure wasn't showing any signs of "eyeing him off" today.

When Hoyle finally heaved his pack onto his already-aching shoulders, the sun was well above the trees. The enchantment of the early morning had vanished utterly, leaving him feeling sullen and guilty.

Sybil was busying herself with a map, drawing lines with a pencil and small plastic ruler.

"What are you doing?" said Ada.

"Plotting out our course. See, here, there's a place where three creek beds come together, and there's a round hill sticking up? That's mentioned in the book. That's where we're headed first. It's this way." She pointed.

Ada shook her head. "You can tell all that from those squiggles?"

"It's not so hard. Just takes practice."

"I could practice all year and not get it. You must be really smart."

Sybil shrugged.

"Hey, Hoyle," called Ada. "Do you know how to do this map thing?"

"Only a little."

"We better make sure nothing happens to her, then, or we're fucked."

Incredibly, this had never occurred to Hoyle. Apprehension surged through him as he had a sudden image of Sybil lying unconscious at the base of a cliff, with him and Ada staring, baffled and terrified, from the top. He blinked and shook his head and thought about anything else. Termites. Oh, how he hated termites. Crawling, squirming, breeding, chewing their loathsome way through book after precious, beloved book—hated them as hard as he could until the rigors of the walk could distract him.

Sybil led them all morning along fairly flat ground, but after lunch the way was far less easy. Hoyle struggled upward, pushing bushes aside and trying not to trip. Every cell in him shrieked for a nap, or at least a rest.

Behind him he could hear Ada grunting and swearing in a savage whisper. Ahead, Sybil plodded on. At intervals, as she'd promised, they took breaks, but it was not enough to feel reinvigorated. Sweat drenched his back, chilling him horribly whenever he took his pack off, so after a while he just left it on, bracing it on rocks or against trees at the breaks.

He was just about exhausted when the ground leveled off again. They came to an area with some open ground and a few trees; beyond them, the afternoon shadows were growing deeper.

"Let's set up camp," said Sybil.

"Oh, thank Christ," gasped Ada. She dropped her pack and sprawled next to it.

"Not today, you don't," said Sybil. "Today you get to learn how to put the tent up."

"Why can't Hoyle? He did a great job yesterday."

"Then Hoyle can sleep in it, and you can sleep outside under the tarp."

"What!"

"Take your pick."

"Don't bother," said a woman's voice from the scrub. "You won't be camping here tonight."

"Who are you?" called Sybil sharply.

"I'm Dianne. This is Marco. And Bruce, Hazel, Tommy, and Spike."

Spike. Hoyle began swallowing, again and again.

A half-dozen people stepped into the clearing.

"And why won't we be camping here?" said Sybil.

"We need to keep an eye on you."

"Why?"

Some of the six shifted their feet and glanced at each other, but Dianne's gaze was steady. "Don't worry about it. A bushwalker or two come through here every year. We watch all of them. Come on."

"Uh, no."

The six came a little closer. Hoyle's heart started to pound in a panicky, irregular beat.

"It's okay," said one of the men, not unkindly. "We've a hot dinner for you, and even a shower, if you don't waste too much water. And as soon as we can, we'll let you go."

"What determines that?" said Sybil. Hoyle was astounded at her calm. The tightness in his throat told him that if he'd tried to talk, it would have come out in a trembling squeak.

"Well, we don't really know," confessed Dianne. "Most of the time, we just watch people for a while, make sure they leave us alone. But you, we have to take back to the community."

"Community!"

"Yeah, there are—what, Tommy, seventeen of us now? Yeah, seventeen. Three went back to Sydney last week. They might come back, or not."

"Your own people can come and go, but you're going to force us to come with you," Sybil said flatly.

"We don't have a choice."

"Bullshit. You could turn around right now and leave us alone."

"It's not that simple," said Dianne. "Come on, follow me."

"No."

Dianne's shoulders slumped. In a voice that sounded genuinely regretful, she said, "Okay guys, you know what to do."

Hoyle found himself face to face with someone who said, "Start walking, or I'll bash you." The bleak simplicity of the man's request scared Hoyle far more than bluster and shouting would have done.

To one side, the other woman, Hazel, was trying to get Ada to pick up her pack.

"Jesus Christ," Ada was saying. "Can't you let me have a fucking moment? I've been walking for fucking *years*, mate. See here? See that mark? That's where the leeches got me. Big as fucking garden slugs, with teeth like this." She held her fingers to her mouth like fangs. "Must have taken a liter each out of me.

Greedy bastards. And do you know how much sleep I got last night? About ten fucking minutes—all right, all *right*, give me a minute. Jesus."

Scared, hungry, and already exhausted from the day's exertions, Hoyle found this last walk a torment. The light was fading fast, and the ground was getting more treacherous—at one point, Hoyle was forced to inch along a ledge less than a foot wide, a cliff face on one side and a drop of five or six yards on the other. His keeper sighed, exasperated, as Hoyle shuffled sideways along the ledge, clinging to outcrops with his fingertips and trying not to whimper.

Finally he heard Dianne saying, "Here we are. You can put your packs down here. Give me any pocket knives or anything like that, please."

Hoyle's keeper held out his hand and made a "Well?" face.

"I don't have a knife," he said. "Do I look like I'd know how to use a knife?"

The keeper nodded. "You've got a point. Still, hold your arms out, please." He frisked Hoyle and found a tiny flashlight Hoyle had gotten in Lithgow and stuck in his pocket. He turned the light on and off again and handed it back. "Cute," he said.

That word freed Hoyle from the immediate terror of being bashed, and as he relaxed a bit, he found there was still enough light to look around him. They were in a clearing ringed by about a dozen faded, tattered tents. Bright blue tarps were spread between trees as makeshift awnings. A few logs and large rocks made a circle in the center of the clearing, but Hoyle could see no sign of a fire ring. A few people were busy in the shadows; as he watched, one turned a headlamp on. He could just hear the sound of a gas stove, like Sybil's.

Dianne said, "We'll get you some dinner in a minute."

"We've got our own food," said Sybil coldly.

"Yes, but you're our *guests*."

"Are we?"

"Well, no, not really. But we'll feed you anyway. Otherwise we'd just have to give you food when we let you go."

"Why don't you just let us go now?"

"I told you. It's not that simple. Look, I've got a lot of people's best interests to balance. It's more significant than you think. Keeping my people safe, keeping you from either doing any damage or getting damaged, keeping there from being any ramifications from your wandering around here—"

"Ramifications?"

"Just—just come over and sit down, please." Dianne motioned toward the circle.

"It's getting cold," said Ada. "I want my hoodie." She started toward her pack. One of the keepers grabbed her arm. Ada gave a horrible shriek and crumbled to the ground. The alarmed keeper snatched his hand back, and in a flash Ada scurried over to her pack, unzipped a pocket, and grabbed her sweatshirt. She wriggled into it; her face, emerging from the neck-hole, had a triumphant look.

Hoyle glanced at Sybil, who had put her face in her hands and was shaking her head.

The keepers herded the three of them over to the circle. Hoyle saw nothing else to do, so he sat down. Sybil sat next to him. Ada remained standing, arms folded, managing to look both rebellious and powerless, like a teenager at the principal's office. After a few minutes, a young man came out of the shadows. He was precariously carrying three bowls, each with a spoon. He handed one to Ada.

"What's this?" said Ada.

"Satay vegetables with rice," he said. Then, with a touch of pride, he added, "I made it. Try it."

Ada looked at him for a long moment, then gave him a quick smile. She tasted the food. "It's really good," she said, trying to chew at the same time. "Mm." She theatrically enjoyed the next few bites as well, keeping her gaze on him and smiling.

"Um," said Sybil.

"Oh! Sorry," said the young man, and he gave the other bowls to her and Hoyle. It *was* good.

"What's your name?" said Ada.

"Oliver."

"Really? I love that name."

Oliver actually giggled. Hoyle was stunned that he couldn't see Ada's flirting for what it was: a transparent attempt to gain an ally in an enemy camp. But then, people only saw what they wanted to see. He felt a moment's anxiety: maybe he was no better, with his looking for signs that Sybil liked him. She certainly hadn't been all that affectionate today. But then, she'd been busy leading them through the wilderness. Surely that would put a damper on anyone's ardor.

"Hey, Oliver," said Ada, "what's going on here?"

Oliver sat down on a log, his back to Dianne and the others, who were gathered over near the packs and talking quietly. Ada sat down too, a little closer than Oliver had been expecting, judging by the expression of pleased surprise on his face. Sybil looked like she was still eating, but Hoyle could hear that she'd stopped chewing. Even from a foot or two away, he could tell she'd tensed up to listen.

"We're anarchists," he said earnestly. "And vegetarians."

"Cool," said Ada. "What's an anarchist?"

"Well," he said, settling in, "see, I'm an individualist anarchist. I believe that the individual knows what's best for him- or herself, and that any attempts at coercion, including but not limited to adherence to the social contract, are unnatural and abhorrent. Dianne, she's an anarcho-feminist. 'Patriarchy, patriarchy,' that's all she's ever on about. A bunch of the others are collectivist-anarchists, although that's not to be confused with anarcho-communism. All the difference in the world, really. Spike is an anarcho-capitalist, if you can believe it, but he's really good at fixing things, so everyone pretends not to mind ..."

Ada nodded, wide-eyed, as he went on. Sybil quickly got disgusted and resumed eating for real. Darkness became complete. Hoyle started to shiver—would they let him get his own jacket from his pack?

"Hey, Oliver," said Ada. "For anarchists, these people all seem to think it's fun to tell *us* what to do."

Oliver groaned. "I *know*, right? But, like, it's complicated."

"That's what that Dianne person keeps saying. But I have no idea what she means. And what damage could we do wandering around here? You're really good at explaining things, you made the anarchist thing all really clear, maybe *you* could tell me about it."

"Oh, I don't know," sighed Oliver. "It all seemed so *important* at first. So many people have so much more than they need—food, houses, money, education, power—and you start to feel guilty. Then you start to feel angry. But nobody you know listens to you, or cares. Then you meet people who are *doing* something about it—at least it seems that way at first. And so you start going to meetings, and it all makes so much *sense*. But—but we're not doing anything. I think maybe I could have made more of a difference back in Syd—" Oliver broke off. "Anyway, I'm glad you liked the satay. My mum taught me how to make it."

"Wow—all my mum ever taught me about cooking was to get takeaway Chinese. My childhood tasted like cashew chicken."

"That's awful," said Oliver.

"I *know*, right?" Ada stood, too, and touched Oliver's arm. "Thanks for dinner. You can cook for me anytime."

Hoyle could almost hear Oliver blushing in the darkness. "Um, sure." He stood up. "Good—good night."

After he'd gone, Hoyle murmured to Ada, "Don't you have any shame at all?"

Sybil said, "Leave her alone. She'd doing the right thing, for once. Neither one of *us* can draw that boy's attention, that's for sure. Just take it slow, though, okay, Ada? Pour it on too thick, and even he'll catch on. There's a reason they grabbed us, and a reason they say they'll let us go, but it can't be just yet. They're scared. And they're also very, very close to where the center of action was in the book. We might as well make the best of this and try to get some information. Although I notice he didn't say anything about those 'ramifications' Dianne mentioned."

"Right now I need to try to get my jacket," said Hoyle. "I'm freezing." His eyes had started to get used to the darkness, but even so it took him ages to stumble toward the packs. "Excuse me?" he said. "I'm cold. I want to get my jacket out of my pack."

The man who'd been guarding him on the way came over and stood next to him. "Go ahead."

Remembering various television shows where edgy thugs had overreacted, he said carefully, "I'm going to take that flashlight out so I can see what's in my pack. Okay? I'm just taking it out of my pocket. Just a flashlight."

The man grunted assent.

Hoyle got his jacket and put the light away. He took longer than usual to put the jacket on, to give his eyes time to readjust, and to give himself time to think. He'd found a tiny ridge in the side of the flashlight and suddenly remembered what had intrigued him so much about it in the camping store. It had a miniscule knife blade folded into the casing. As he picked his way back to Sybil and Ada, he decided not to say anything just yet. It would be like Sybil to insist she be the one to carry it, and Ada—who knew what she'd blurt out, if she were in a panic? Better to keep it to himself. Sybil wasn't the only one who could have ideas and fix things, after all. And he might get a chance to show her he was more than just a hanger-on. Daydreams of using the tiny blade to slash the vines holding shut the prison of green branches that the anarchists would surely build for them any time now, cut the bonds they would surely place on Sybil's wrists, and hack his way past the aghast guards entertained him until Dianne said it was time to go to bed.

Sybil wanted to set up her own tent, but Dianne made all three of them go in one of theirs. Anarchists took turns throughout the night guarding them; Hoyle only dozed and heard each change of watch. When dawn came, he woke fully, vaguely remembering random bits of conversation heard through Sybil's snoring. He thought he recalled Oliver saying something about "the big bloke" and bullies, but nothing he could piece together into sense.

Next to him, Ada stirred. "Jesus," she said, propping herself on one elbow and looking in awe at Sybil. "Who'd have thought that much sound could come out of that stubby little person? She keeps going, they'll let us go just to get some peace. Go, Sybil! Snore! Snore! Get us out of here."

"Shh!" said the latest guard. "People are still sleeping."

Hoyle was glad the guard couldn't see Ada flipping him off.

Sybil turned over, snorted sharply, and woke herself up. She looked around wildly for a second, then sighed. "Ada, for the fifth time since last night, could you please take your God-damned bony knee out of my back?"

"Too damn bad," said Ada. "This is my side of the tent. Hey, I'm hungry." She crawled over Sybil and Hoyle to shout through the door of the tent. "Hey! Hey! Where can I get some fucking breakfast around here?"

It was going to be a long day.

Chapter 7

In Which Oliver Offers an Opportunity

"I still don't understand," said Sybil doggedly.

Dianne cried out in frustration. "How many times, you stupid American? You have to stay here until the big bloke says you can leave."

"Where is this 'big bloke'? More importantly, who is he? And if you're so committed to anarchy, why are you taking orders? What happened to your self-determination? Your self-respect, for that matter?"

"It's not that simple, all right?" said Dianne. "I have to listen to that shit from Oliver all day, I don't want to hear it from you, too." Her patient demeanor had long since started to fray.

Hoyle had kept quiet all morning. The less the anarchists had reason to notice him, the more they'd get out of the habit, and he might see some sort of chance to use the little knife. He needn't have bothered; both Sybil and Ada were creating enough confusion to mask anything Hoyle could have thought of. While Sybil was spending the day arguing with Dianne and everyone else who made the mistake of letting her, Ada was staving off boredom by running around the camp like a puppy. She'd already kicked over a pot of food, broken a tent pole by falling on it, gotten into a screaming match with Spike about the quality of his tattoos, and come terrifyingly close to starting a wildfire by playing with the flint and steel Hoyle had bought in Lithgow, which she'd found when rummaging through his pack because she'd had "nothing to do."

Hoyle sat in the shade near the edge of the clearing. He noticed that a couple of the anarchists made it their business to stay close, one of them sewing a shirt, another writing intermittently in a notebook. When Sybil gave up her harangue and came over to him, they edged slightly closer, still pretending not to pay attention.

"Oof!" said Sybil, sitting heavily and stretching out her legs.

Ada's voice drifted from across the clearing. "If I *knew* what that was, I wouldn't have to *ask*, would I? You know, you should be careful of this edge right here—ow! Ow, Jesus, look, I'm bleeding. Stop laughing and get me a fucking Band-Aid. You know, you people don't have the slightest fucking idea about workplace safety."

The two anarchists glanced at each other ruefully.

"Maybe they'll let us go just so we can take Ada away," murmured Hoyle.

"If that were going to happen at all it would have happened five minutes after we got here," said Sybil. "It's not like she's hard to get to know."

"You are," blurted Hoyle. A cold flood of horror engulfed him as he realized he'd said that out loud.

"What?" Sybil laughed.

"Um … sorry. Nothing."

"No," said Sybil, with the same doggedness she'd used on the anarchists all morning. "Tell me. How am I hard to get to know?"

Hoyle hunched his shoulders up. "I don't know."

"Hoyle!" she snapped. "The main reason I never had kids is because I can*not* stand whining. Now sit up straight and *talk* to me. How am I hard to get to know?"

"Well—well, being like that is how."

"Better—I can actually make out what you're saying now. But I still don't understand it."

"All you do is give orders. This is the first time you've talked about your life at all. When you said why you don't have kids. I didn't even know up until now whether you even *had* kids. Or a husband. Or a boyfriend. Or a girlfriend. Or a cat. Or a goldfi—"

"I get your point."

"Well?"

Sybil frowned. "Well what?"

"Are you going to tell me about your life?"

"I genuinely don't understand why you want to know the messy details of one woman's messy life."

"How about because I dropped everything to come with you, apparently for no other reason than you wanted some company? Don't I deserve something for that?"

"Whether I tell you or not, you're still here. But if it means that much to you, okay." In a grudging sing-song, she said, "I'm fifty-two years old. I was born in Pennsylvania and moved to DC to go to college. After I graduated, I just stayed in DC. There was no reason to go anywhere else, and I had a job I could stand. I'm smarter than a lot of the people I've met. I read a lot. I like being on my own." After a moment she added, "I have a sister in Florida, and my dad still lives in Pennsylvania. How's that?"

"Still a little sterile, to tell you the truth."

"Sorry, I guess."

"What do you love?"

"You really are nosy today."

Hoyle shrugged and spread his hands. "After all we've been through together ..."

"It's just an odd kind of question, that's all."

"Why? People do things out of love all the time. Are you here," he gestured to the woods around them, "because you love, what? Books? Testing yourself? Danger?"

Sybil looked at him hard, long enough for him to start worrying he'd made her mad. Then she said, "Yeah, all right. A few years ago my best friend was diagnosed with early onset dementia. She was another one who'd been engaged a couple of times, but it had never worked out. Her parents are dead, and she hates her brother and sister. She's become convinced they're coming over and sowing weeds in her lawn at night when she's asleep, instead of that she's just forgotten to mow it for months on end. So a bunch of us have gotten together to help her stay out of assisted living for as long as possible, but it's getting harder and harder for her to cope. She can't use her computer anymore, can barely manage phone calls. This was one of the keenest, most vibrant, vital, engaged, intelligent, funny—" Her voice quavered. She took a breath and went on. "I got to thinking: if there's anything I want to do in my life, I'd better do it now. Things can happen. Not just dementia. Car crashes, cancer, nuclear-plant disasters. Next thing you know, you're dead. Or as good as. This is my defiance."

"Defiance?"

"Of death. Of uncertainty. Of wasted potential, wasted lives, wasted minds."

"Why the search, though? Couldn't you just travel around the world for a month or two?"

"The search is *everything*, Hoyle! *Everything*. There's got to be a reason, I've got to accomplish something."

"Like … a quest," he said, trying hard to understand.

"Exactly!" Her face lit up. "I knew you'd get it. That's why I asked you to come with me."

"But maybe I'm an axe murderer. You don't know."

Sybil snorted. "Yeah. You're the type."

"Hey!"

"I know, it's the quiet ones you have to watch out for. 'Bit of a loner. Kept to himself.' But really? You just don't give off killer vibes."

"What vibes do I give off, then?"

Sybil narrowed her eyes. "Let's see. You … listen to NPR. You wish you'd done better at college, if only because you wouldn't mind being a professor, it seems like a good life. You've been in love, but you lost out to someone with a more outgoing personality—you never followed up, because you couldn't see how she could possibly choose you. Right?"

Hoyle's stomach knotted. "Um, yes. Hey, wait, before you said your friend was 'another one who'd been engaged'—like you'd been, too."

"Nice counterattack, Hoyle. All right, I've had a couple of serious relationships. They didn't work out. And those, I *won't* talk about."

"Okay."

"Want to keep sharing?"

"Not right now, thanks."

Sybil leaned back against a tree, hands behind her head.

Hoyle's hands were shaking. He hadn't had a conversation like that with anyone for years—decades. It had felt like a wave curling slowly over his head and blocking out the sun, then slamming down to knock him off his feet. He dimly remembered a time when he'd been eager to feel that close to someone, but he'd lost the knack.

"Hi, guys," shouted Ada. She flung herself to the grass next to Hoyle, her elbow landing on his stomach. "Sorry, Hoyle. Whatcha talking about?"

"Just chatting," said Sybil. "Nothing important."

"Good," said Ada, dropping her voice to a conspiratorial whisper. "Because boy have I got some news for you. *They know about the stick.*"

Sybil's face went grey. "What makes you say that?"

"I heard someone having a go at Oliver, really mad, so I figured, anything that pisses them off, that could be useful to know. So I sort of eased my way over to listen. They were all wound up, they didn't see me. And the one guy, he was saying, 'Don't go being friends with them, you bloody idiot! Do you want to piss him off?' And Oliver got real mad—you'd never think a wussy little guy like that could *get* so mad—and he said, 'I'm sick of being bossed around. By you, by him, him and his damned—' What was it you called it?"

"Bloodwood Staff," murmured Sybil.

"That was it! That's what he said. And, see, here's what confused me. The other guy said, 'If he says go grab someone, and keep them around until he figures out what to do with them, then that's what we do. Remember what happened to—' And then Oliver kind of cut him off, 'Yeah, I remember. But maybe she was right. Maybe we should do what she did.' And then the other guy got real close and scary, and he said, 'I'd rather not have to find out, Oliver.' Then he walked away, and Oliver turned around too quick for me to get out of sight. He was dead scared when he saw me. I pretended I hadn't heard a thing—'What was that guy mad about, he looked pretty mad, is everything okay?'—and Oliver said it wasn't anything. So I was like, 'Oh, good, I wouldn't want you to be in trouble or anything. Did I do something to piss him off?' And he was like, 'No, no, really, don't worry.'"

She sat back with a satisfied air. Sybil, though, looked horrified. Worse than horrified. Hoyle got ready to catch her if she toppled over. But she shuddered, took a deep breath, and said, "Well. That changes a few things."

"Like what?" chirped Ada.

"I'm guessing Oliver meant this 'big bloke' they keep referring to. Whoever he is, he has the staff. And whatever it is, it's something that makes people afraid. If it were just a stick, they'd take it away, or hit him with a bigger stick, or something. It … does have powers after all. Ingraham …" Her voice died away.

"Was right," finished Hoyle.

* * *

Amid the evening bustle in the camp, they sat together, eating what they'd been served and trying to look like they were discussing the weather.

"We can spend the time until we escape finding out what they know," said Sybil quietly. "Besides, the more of their food we eat, the longer our food will last."

"It's not bad, either," said Ada.

"I'm not so happy about this," said Hoyle. "It's one thing to have some fun looking for an artifact. It's another to get involved with a psychopath and a political cult. We should get out of here as soon as we can, get back to Sydney, and get the police involved. We're out of our depth."

"You're out of your depth, you mean," snapped Sybil. "I didn't come all the way here to give up."

"It's not giving up," cried Hoyle.

Ada smacked him on the shoulder. "Shut *up*, yeah?"

He tried again, this time more quietly. "It's not giving up. You'll still find out. You'll have to lead the cops here, you'll have to be involved. It will all still be your adventure."

"Don't be stupid, Hoyle." Her voice was flat and final. "Once the cops are involved, I'm nothing. Again."

Ada snorted. "How could *you* ever be nothing? You're … you're a, what is it, a force of bloody nature."

After a second, Sybil muttered, "Thanks."

Ada took another enormous mouthful of food, chewed, swallowed. "I want to stay. I want to find out about the stick, too. And Oliver's a very nice guy. Fun to talk to. And he's—" She broke off, trying to cover it by gulping more food.

"And he's what?" said Hoyle.

"Never mind," said Sybil. "If she and Oliver are becoming friends, that's fine. He's obviously an impulsive boy, and he might let—Ada," she said sternly. "I've told you a hundred times, if you keep bolting your food like that, you're going to throw up. Where did you grow up, in a barn?"

Ada squawked, "You never said—" then caught sight of Dianne not exactly looking at them, but not exactly not, either. "You're not my mother," Ada shouted. "I'm sorry I ever came camping with you. 'Let's see what's up this gully,' you said. 'Come on, it'll be fun,' you said. And now look! I'm never going to get my award at this rate."

"What award?" said Hoyle.

"Ugh!" said Ada melodramatically. "Can't you remember any-thing? My Initiative Award. I was supposed to be leading us, remember? Well, that will teach me to be con-consultative in my leadership style."

"Sorry?" said Hoyle, completely mystified.

Ada dropped her voice again. "One time, when I was on the dole, they made me go to this approved training activity, and I had to learn about leadership styles and crap. Never thought it would actually come in handy."

Sybil gave her an approving look. Hoyle saw it and felt excluded, powerless. His thoughts echoed Sybil's leaden pronouncement: *Again.*

If Sybil wasn't going to see sense, maybe he could escape on his own. But he dismissed that thought instantly. He had no more idea than a goat how to use the map, even the GPS, no matter what he'd said to Ada. And the thought of going back across that ledge, all alone, no one to even know if he fell—well, just no. He was stuck. If Sybil wanted to stay until they found out more, then stay they would.

It was all kind of academic anyway, though, until there was actually a chance to escape. His best bet was to keep doing what he'd been doing: keep his head down, keep his eyes open, try not to be memorable or to give anyone—*anyone*—cause for concern. He'd gotten good at that over the years. Like Ada, he was mildly surprised that it was coming in handy.

Dianne actually approached them now. "Finish up, do your dishes, and then time to get in the tent, okay?"

"Are you really asking us if it's okay?" said Sybil. "Or is it just a figure of speech?"

Dianne sighed. "Does it matter? I wish things were different. But they're not. Eat. Wash. Good night. Don't waste my time. I have a lot to do."

Hoyle obediently scraped the last of the food from his bowl

and walked over to the water tank. Sybil hadn't had to show them how to wash dishes efficiently; Oliver had been happy to do so, especially as it had meant he could appear wise and capable to Ada. It was kind of cute to watch Oliver try to get Ada's attention. Granted, she wasn't really playing hard to get. She was pretending it was in accordance with Sybil's plan to get more information, but Hoyle suspected she was more than a little flattered herself to have the attentions of someone so good-looking, smart, and *nice*. Hoyle was pretty certain there'd been a shortage of nice people in Ada's past.

Oliver came over to wash his dish, too.

"Checking up to see how well I learned?" joked Hoyle. But Oliver didn't look in the mood for jokes. He was tense, even eager.

"Watch me tomorrow. I'll give you the signal," he said quietly.

"W-what signal?"

"To escape! Just watch, it'll be unmistakable. And follow me. Let the others know. I'm sick of this place. We can get out of here together. Sybil has maps and stuff. I know quick ways to get some distance, landmarks we can shoot for. It'll work."

"I—"

"Huh," said Oliver, suddenly pleased and buoyant. "You did do a good job on that bowl. Cool! Well, good night."

"Good—" But Oliver was already gone.

Chapter 8

In Which There Is an Escape

Hoyle turned the little knife over and over in his pocket. He had a headache from how his eyes kept darting around, looking at Oliver, looking frantically away lest he be noticed looking at Oliver, then, terrified he'd miss the signal, looking at Oliver again. He'd told Sybil the night before, while Ada tossed and muttered and squeaked in her sleep, that there was a plan to escape, and instantly regretted it as she began to grill him on the particulars. Which direction? Which maps? How would they be able to get all their gear all packed and ready to go without anyone noticing? What would they do after the food ran out? Hoyle had merely gaped helplessly.

In the morning, she'd found Oliver washing a large pile of laundry in a battered tub, and pitched in to help him so she could badger him for the information. Hoyle hadn't been able to watch, terrified that Oliver would crack under the force of Sybil's insistence, fall into hysterics, and get them all into trouble. *Even worse trouble*, he corrected himself. Over and over he tumbled the knife, until he knew every bit of it by touch, until it grew warm and sticky in his sweaty hand.

It wasn't long before Sybil was back. "He'd been within a whisker of calling the whole thing off," she murmured. "But I told him that if he wanted a shot with Ada, he wasn't going to get it while we were under twenty-four-hour observation. That worked. Oh, he genuinely thinks it's his idealism talking, but what is he, nineteen?" She snorted. "Did you know, this ragtag merry band

came out here for absolutely no specific reason? They just kept …
accreting … in a few run-down group houses in Sydney until, at
some unspoken tipping point, it occurred to someone that they
should come out here to plan their utopia. Oh, sure, there are
always disaffected intellectuals in any prosperous society—otherwise they'd be too busy trying to, I don't know, till a field or carry
water home from five miles away. But the sheer vagueness and
ineptitude of this group in particular is …" she looked around
at the chaotic campsite "… exceptional. The sooner we leave, the
better. Oliver said as soon as we're clear, he'll tell me all they know.
That's a lot easier and quicker than eavesdropping around here."

"So, um, what's the deal?" Hoyle said.

Sybil gave him a quick look; maybe she'd heard the quaver
in his voice. "The three of us act like they expect us to act, so
they get complacent. At some point yet to be determined," she
sounded disgusted at such slackness, "Oliver will arrange a distraction. When everyone is caught up with that, we'll slip away."

No knife fight, then. Hoyle couldn't decide whether that odd
feeling in his stomach was relief or disappointment.

Sybil went on: "We'll circle around to get back on the trail of
what we were looking for. I'm hoping we can shake them and still
do what we need to do before the food runs out."

"Didn't you mark where you wanted to go on the map? Didn't
they look at it when they captured us?"

"I like to keep my maps clean; I'm funny that way. I have the
route in my notebook."

Hoyle didn't feel any better. He shouldn't have been surprised
that Sybil wouldn't be shaken from her quest. How could someone so sensible be so … nuts?

Sybil reached out and touched his arm. "Hey," she said. "Thanks
for sticking with me on this. There's a lot more to you than—anyway, thanks."

Hoyle's face felt hot. "I don't want to let you down, that's all,"
he said.

"That's all? That's more than most people could come up with."

Hoyle felt an overwhelming need to change the subject. "Where's Ada?"

"I think she was waiting for me to finish talking with Oliver, if you know what I mean."

"Have you told her about …"

"God, no. I made Oliver promise not to, as well, that I wanted to be the one. Can you imagine?"

"Maybe I shouldn't have said we'd take her—"

"No, don't get caught up in that. She's earning her keep, in her own way. And besides, you were right: what were we going to do, leave her to get beaten up or worse? Even just getting her away from her mom for a while will probably earn us points in heaven."

Right on cue, Ada came bounding up to them. "Hey! You know what Oliver just told me?"

Hoyle blenched, and Sybil shushed her fiercely.

"Jesus, what?" she said. "He was only saying that he's never had a girlfriend. I just thought that was funny, nice guy like him. That's all." She looked back and forth between them. "What's wrong?"

"Nothing," said Hoyle quickly.

Ada's eyes narrowed for a second, then she shrugged. "Anyway, he says it's because he's been so dedicated to the cause, whatever that means. From what I can gather, his cause is to get rid of the government, and that's just kind of stupid. If there were no government, who would, like, dedicate bridges and stuff?"

Oliver had sidled near enough to overhear. "You know," he said earnestly, "that's a really good point."

"It is?" said Ada. "I was just talking out of my arse."

"No, see, one of the functions of government is to symbolically embody the essence of the people, and that can be expressed in things like bridge-opening ceremonies. We—that is, anarchists, *true* anarchists," he cast a meaningful look around the camp, "have to consider how that vital role will be fulfilled in a society without formal hierarchies."

"Uh-huh," said Ada brightly after a second. "Hey, Oliver, you said you'd show me a waterfall."

"Not right now," said Sybil. "The tent is a mess. I'd like everyone to put their stuff back in their packs so I don't keep tripping over it."

"Aw," whined Ada. "You're just like my mum. 'Clean your fucking room!'"

"Hey, Ada," said Sybil.

"Yeah?"

"Clean your fucking room."

With a murderous look at Sybil, Ada disappeared into the tent.

"That includes your sleeping bag and mat," Sybil yelled after her. "Everything! The mess is making me crazy."

"All right, all *right*!" came Ada's voice.

Oliver frowned. "That seemed a little … how can I put this? Unnecessarily dictatorial."

"Look, Oliver," said Sybil quietly. "I know it doesn't fit with your ideals. But how else am I going to get everything packed and ready to leave in an instant without the others getting suspicious? Get it?"

Oliver's mouth opened in an O of enlightenment, then collapsed into a frown again. "You mean you haven't told Ada about—" He dropped his voice to a harsh, melodramatic whisper. "The *plan*? How can she be a free agent, willingly choosing her participation?"

"Ada's a lovely person," said Sybil. "Smart, kind, full of life." Oliver nodded eagerly. "But she's got a mouth like Niagara Falls. Trust me on this one: you tell her what we're planning and in a moment of anger or carelessness it'll slip out. You really want her to be free? Don't tell her what we're doing until we stop to catch our breath a couple of miles from here."

"All right," said Oliver dubiously. "But I don't like it."

"Really. It's the only way. Now, I have to get to work packing my own stuff, and so does Hoyle. What is it you'd usually be doing right now?"

"Well, the washing is done, that's mostly my job, so I guess I'd be studying."

"What, at a university? From here?" said Hoyle.

Oliver snorted. "Those cesspits of hierarchy and coercion? No, I follow the knowledge where it leads me. Right now I'm reading up on the Futurists. 'War, the world's only hygiene'—lunatics!"

"Off you go, then," said Sybil. "We'll be watching you for ..." She raised her eyebrows, and Oliver nodded.

Hoyle and Sybil went over to the tent. "How's it going, Ada?" said Hoyle.

"Fine," snarled Ada. "I can't fucking fit everything into my pack. It all came *out* of the pack, why won't it fit back *in*?"

"Here, let me help," said Hoyle. "I'm good at packing. All those years of playing Tetris at work, maybe."

Ada guffawed. "You do that, too? I had this job once, pshyeah, for about a *week*, yeah? And I found out where the Tetris was on the computer, and I was like, 'No, wait, I'm about to get a high score,' and they were like, 'High score yourself back on the dole, mate.'"

Hoyle crawled into the tent. Ada's things covered the entire floor, and were draped atop Hoyle's and Sybil's packs as well. He started folding, then rolling, each article of clothing and stuffing it into Ada's pack.

He dragged a t-shirt out from under a pair of sneakers; with it came a notebook, snagged in the folds and pulled open by the sole of one of the sneakers. He was about to close it and push it back when he saw his name written on one of the pages. He'd only seen Sybil's handwriting once, on the note he'd found on his windshield, and that had only been one word. But this could easily be her handwriting. Why would she be writing about him?

Hoyle—shaping up okay, he read. Only okay? He thought he'd been doing a lot better than could be expected. Was that all? He scanned the page to see what else Sybil might have written about him—three words were not nearly enough to satisfy his sudden longing to be the object of her attention, if not perhaps her admiration. In the next instant he realized, mortified, that he was reading Sybil's private journal. He slammed it shut and pushed it over towards her pack.

But he couldn't unread what he'd seen. "Shaping up okay"—should he be grateful for that? What did he even want from Sybil? Was he only eager for her approval because of a chance remark from Ada? Or was he just bored, anxious, and strained to breaking, waiting for that fool Oliver to touch off the gunpowder? Which of Hoyle's inadequacies would be revealed then? What would be the retribution from the anarchists at the escape's inevitable failure? What did Hoyle think a one-inch knife could actually do?

He angrily started stuffing the rest of Ada's things into her pack.

"Hey, Tiger, easy there. That's all I've got to wear," said Ada, poking her head into the tent. "What's got you so upset?"

Hoyle decided sounding bored would keep him from sounding guilty. "I'm just tired of sitting around."

"I don't mind," said Ada. "It's like a vacation. They cook for us, they entertain us—"

"They do?" said Hoyle. This was news.

"Oh, yeah! Oliver's a barrel of laughs."

"You're joking, right?"

"Yeah. Poor guy. Real sweet, but so serious. And I don't understand half of what he's saying. Although I'll admit that what I *do* understand is pret-ty interesting. Did you know that you can have a whole bunch of people, and if they're all, like, brought up that way, they can look after themselves without any cops or nothing? I reckon that's Johnno's problem. He just wasn't brought up right. Not like me. I can control my base impulses. Oliver reckons that's what it takes. Although, if you ask me, there's something to be said for letting a few base impulses run loose once in a while." She chuckled wickedly.

"Good luck with that," said Hoyle. "Oliver is a very focused guy."

Ada went glum. "You're not wrong. Pretty soon I'm going to have to forget about being genteel and subtle."

"Is he your type?"

"Not my normal type. I figured an adventure would be a good time to branch out a little."

"I guess," said Hoyle.

"After all, is Sybil your type?"

Hoyle shushed her frantically; Sybil could be just outside the tent, listening to every word.

"Don't worry, she's off using the loo," said Ada.

"I don't have a type," said Hoyle.

"Sure you do! Everyone does. What kind of woman makes you kind of forget what you were doing while you stare after her? Or—hey, I never thought of this—what kind of man?"

"No, I'm straight," said Hoyle.

"Hey, it's fine with me either way. *You're* not *my* type, so it's all good. We're mates."

Hoyle was taken aback for a second until he remembered that "mates" only meant "buddies".

"Hey," said Ada. "You've done a really good job straightening up in here. Even Sybil ought to be happy. She'll be glad she's snagging a guy like you."

"Will you stop that?" snapped Hoyle. "Sybil and I are just … mates."

"Sure," said Ada. "Oh, here, you missed some stuff. This is mine. And this." She kept flinging clothes carelessly towards her pack. "Thanks. I'll leave you to it."

A second later, Sybil stuck her head in. Hoyle was suddenly, humiliatingly sure she'd heard every word. He bent over Ada's pack to hide his hot face.

"Good," said Sybil. "You pack your stuff up and then I'll do mine." She lowered her voice. "Then please have a snack, drink a fair bit of water, and go to the bathroom. It's all part of being ready. Oh, and Hoyle?"

"Mm?" said Hoyle, still busily packing the last of Ada's things.

"I'm lucky to have you along. I don't know of a lot of other people who would be smart enough to stay quiet until—well, anyway …"

She ducked back out of the tent. And Hoyle was blushing again, for an entirely different reason.

* * *

The tent was military-academy neat. Hoyle had fed, watered, and toileted himself. Ada had been sternly instructed to stay nearby, on the excuse that Oliver was planning something special for an afternoon snack and she wouldn't want to miss it.

"Where am I going to go, with those yobbos watching me everywhere, including the fucking toilet?" she'd said grumpily.

But Oliver had smiled wanly at her and said, "Please?" and she'd been won over.

A little while after lunch, Oliver wandered past where Hoyle and Sybil were each reading a book. "Get ready," he muttered through gritted teeth, clearly trying not to move his lips.

Sybil frowned. "You know what I hate? I hate it when the only vehicle on the road is a loose cannon."

"What?" said Hoyle.

"Never mind. Just be ready. Where's Ada?"

"Taking a nap in the tent, I think. She ate enough lunch to choke a horse, and she said it made her sleepy."

"Great," groaned Sybil, getting up. "I'll go see how she's doing. Ada!"

Hoyle suspected waking Ada up wouldn't go well.

It occurred to him that if the signal came right now, he would look like an idiot shrugging into his pack and running through the woods while trying to keep his place in his book. He edged cautiously toward the tent, wondering how long he should wait to see if Ada was going to explode.

"Ada! Ada, it's me, Sybil! Ada!"

About that long, apparently.

Sybil scrambled backwards out of the tent. "You try," she said to Hoyle, rubbing her cheekbone. "This is going to bruise up spectacularly. Watch out for her elbows."

"Ada?" Hoyle said gently, peering into the dim recesses of the tent. It was hotter than hell in there—how could Ada manage to sleep? "Ada, honey, time to wake up." He was surprised at the tenderness in his own voice. "Come on, Ada."

"Let her sleep," said Dianne from right behind Hoyle, who jumped. "She's a pain in the arse; we're all glad of a break. What do you want to wake her up for, anyway?"

"If she sleeps now, she'll toss and turn all night," he said, improvising wildly. "You have no idea."

"I used to be married to someone like that," said Dianne. After a second, she said casually, "She's spending a lot of time with Oliver."

Hoyle chuckled in what he hoped was an avuncular way. "Yeah. Apparently he's teaching her about anarchism."

"If he knocks her up, he'll want to do the right thing, take her to Sydney to look after her," she said. "The hospital people will want to know where he's been living, what his insurance number is, how he's going to pay for things, who's going to take care of the baby. I can't have that. Can't have people knowing we're here. You make sure she knows that."

"Why? You're not breaking any laws that I can see."

"You make sure."

She stayed close while Hoyle continued his efforts to wake Ada. Eventually Ada grimaced and moaned and said, "Jesus, what? Can't a girl get some sleep?"

Hoyle figured consistency was his best bet. "If you sleep too much now, you'll toss and turn all night."

"So?"

"You pack a mean punch in your sleep. You even clocked Sybil a minute ago when she tried to wake you."

"What'd she do, shake me or something? Yeah, I'm terrible when someone does that."

Hoyle figured she was probably awake enough now that he could risk being within striking distance. "Excuse me a minute," he said, and tucked his book into his pack.

He heard shouting. Then screaming, and metal things—pots?—being thrown.

"This is it," said Sybil. "Let's go."

"What?" said Ada, melodramatically groggy now that she sensed she might have to actually get up.

"Now," said Sybil. "Get your pack. Move!"

Ada and Hoyle scrambled for their packs as Sybil grabbed hers. Hoyle launched himself from the tent and looked around wildly. Across the site, a dozen people were clustered around two people rolling around on the ground and punching each other viciously.

"This way," came Oliver's voice from the woods nearby.

Hoyle blundered toward the voice, followed by Ada and Sybil. Oliver waited, bouncing up and down in agitation, an enormous pack on his back. As soon as they reached him, he turned and led them through thick brush.

"What?" said Ada. "What?"

"We're escaping," said Hoyle, who was last in line and already breathing hard.

"Not yet, we're not," said Sybil. "They've spotted us."

Hoyle looked back, trying to see past the top of his pack. Sure enough, one of the anarchists had gotten to the edge of the woods and was following hard.

Everyone started to run, leaving Hoyle farther and farther behind.

"Hey," yelled the anarchist. "Stop!"

Hoyle thought this was about the stupidest thing the anarchist could have said, but it gave him a wild idea. He reached into his pocket as he stumbled and ducked through the brush; yes, the little knife was still there. He took it out and opened the blade, then stopped and bent over to catch his breath. It wasn't entirely a ruse, but he made sure to make it very obvious that he wasn't going to start up again anytime soon.

The anarchist caught up with him quickly enough and grabbed for Hoyle's arm. Instantly, Hoyle wheeled and slashed. He felt the knife catch in something and yanked it free.

"Jesus! You cut me, you bastard," shrieked the anarchist. Blood ran down his cheek. Hoyle slashed again and again, wherever he could reach. The anarchist blocked a few with frantic, slapping motions; many more got in. Finally, Hoyle stabbed the blade up to its flashlight hilt into the anarchist's thigh—it made a sickening pop as it broke the skin—and ripped it down and out. The anarchist, utterly distracted by the pain and shock of being cut, never even saw Hoyle haul off clumsily and fling a punch of sorts into his jaw. It didn't knock him out, but between the punch and his horror at seeing his own blood pouring out of a dozen wounds, he didn't look like he'd be following all that effectively. Hoyle turned back and started to run again.

But which way had they gone? He didn't want to yell; it would be a beacon to any other pursuers. He had to stop again and scan the brush for any sign of movement. Wait—what was that? One branch moving in an utterly still thicket on a windless day. It was probably the only clue he was going to get. He plunged forward.

As soon as he got to the branch, Sybil peered over the top of the bushes. "Wow," she said quietly. "Saw that. Good work."

Hoyle didn't feel proud. He kept remembering how it had felt to plunge the blade into someone's flesh, and feeling like he was about to cry, or throw up. Probably both. There was no time now, though. He ran after Sybil, thinking nothing, and, soon, feeling nothing except the wild-eyed need to keep going, keep going, keep going.

Chapter 9

In Which Hoyle Makes a Decision

"So, yeah, they're all afraid," said Oliver, when they finally stopped for a real breather. "And nobody will tell me why. They talk about 'the big bloke,' and at first I thought they maybe meant Spike, but he's just as scared as the rest of them. I think Dianne's trying to protect me or something, which I very much resent. I can take care of myself."

"Don't knock it," said Ada. "If there's someone willing to give you a feed and chase the baddies away, I say let 'em. It's not like that sort of person is everywhere." She glanced at Sybil and blushed.

Hey, thought Hoyle. *I helped too.* The wave of resentment shocked him with its strength. And it wasn't just about helping Ada, either. He remembered for the thousandth time the feeling of that knife popping through skin into flesh. *One lousy "thank you" that Sybil tossed over her shoulder as an afterthought. They have no idea what that was like for me. None at all.*

Oliver was still going. "No, but it's my responsibility as a free human being to take care of myself—"

"Let's not," Sybil cut in. "Don't waste your strength on politics right now. Safety, food and water, shelter—politics is waaaay later in the hierarchy of needs."

"Maslow, right?" said Oliver. "That's what I'm going to get into after I'm done with the Futurists."

"Back to the big bloke," said Sybil. "Who talks to him?"

"Ruby used to. But then … um …"

To universal horror, Oliver's eyes welled up and sobs began to wrack his body. Ada, completely at a loss, put a tentative hand on his shoulder, then snatched it back as Oliver's sobs turn to wails at the gesture. A moment later he had draped his arms around her and buried his face into her neck. She stood, immobile and terrified, giving sidelong, panicky looks at Hoyle and Sybil. Sybil mimed a hug, and Ada cautiously raised her arms and encircled Oliver's heaving back without actually touching it. Sybil made an impatient motion, and finally Ada actually hugged him, and occasionally patted his back.

"I'm sorry, guys," he said at last, in a voice made comical by a clogged nose and by being muffled by Ada's collarbone.

"No, hey, it's okay," said Ada helplessly.

"Do we have any tissues?"

"Sorry," said Sybil.

"Oh, wait, there's toilet paper," said Ada.

"Don't you dare," said Sybil. "Unless you want to wipe your butt with eucalyptus leaves before we get through all this. Oliver, just turn away and give a big honk out of each nostril."

"It's okay, that's what we do in camp anyway," he said.

"Eeeeeeewww!" said Ada. "I was walking all over the place in that camp."

When Oliver had cleared his nose, Sybil said, "Okay, well, what was that all about?"

"Sorry. I'll try to keep it together this time. Ruby—she used to go see the big bloke all the time. He was like this hermit who lived somewhere not far from us. She used to go for walks all the time. I think maybe she was sorry she'd come out bush with us. I think she didn't feel like she belonged, not the way she'd hoped. She didn't say much in the meetings, was one thing that made me think so. And she spent so much time on her own. One day she went out for a walk and didn't come home until the next day. We were a little worried, but not so much, because, like I said, she was alone a lot. But we got more worried, because she came back from that one kind of different. It was creepy. Suddenly she wasn't friendly, or helpful, or even nice anymore. And she'd always been really nice, always listening to people. Even to me, and *nobody* in the camp does that. I might as well have stayed in Wollongong. Anyway, from then on she only listened to the big bloke."

He stopped and took a quavering breath.

"Go on," said Sybil.

"One day she came back from seeing him, and she was acting like—like a homeless person. Wandering around, never stopping, pulling at her hair, constantly talking. We couldn't tell to who. She didn't even notice any of *us*. Just after dinner, she ran off into the bush. We found her next morning with her—with her face—her face all bashed in. Dead. The bastard killed her!"

After a pause, Sybil said, "So now everyone's afraid of him. Who talks to him now?"

"Dianne. Apparently he doesn't want any of us leaving, because he likes his God-damned privacy or something and we might spread the word. So we're all kind of like prisoners. I hate it, but until you got here I couldn't leave, because I'd get lost and die."

"Don't they have maps?" said Hoyle.

"Sure, tons of 'em! That's why they didn't need yours. I just … don't know how to use them. Don't laugh," he pleaded.

"Don't worry, I don't know either," said Ada. This time she found it much easier to pat his shoulder.

"Why didn't they take our maps, to make sure we couldn't escape?" said Sybil.

Oliver blinked. "I never thought of that. Maybe they didn't think of it either. We're not the most practical people in the world, I guess. In theory we were out here to plan our political movement, sort of like on an extended retreat. Write the manifesto, draft the media releases, do some schematics for the website, all that stuff. Different set of skills entirely. Now, of course," he added bitterly, "we're here to do what the big bloke says."

"Something's not making sense," said Sybil.

"*Nothing's* making sense," said Ada.

"Why wouldn't the big bloke just let us go on our way? We wouldn't have known about you, or about him, so we wouldn't have been a threat."

"Oh. You have a point there," said Oliver.

"And there are probably a handful of hikers through here every summer, aren't there? Did he ever tell you to capture them?"

"Well, no."

"So what makes us different?"

"I don't know," cried Oliver. "Find him and ask him!"

"There's no need to be rude," said Sybil. "Govern yourself first, and then there's no need for a government, isn't that the idea?"

"Sorry," he mumbled.

"It's about time we got going again," said Sybil.

That's your answer to everything, Hoyle thought. *Every conflict, every question. Don't stop. Don't solve. Keep moving, and it won't catch up.*

* * *

That night's camp was somber. Oliver had managed to pack some extra food, and, to Hoyle's relief, another tent. While Hoyle hadn't minded sleeping with only a small tarp between him and the wilderness, it was quite a different matter now that he knew a hermit who bashed people's faces in was wandering around. Not that a tent was a fortress; he knew that. But even the illusion of a structure helped. A little.

Oliver still seemed distracted and upset after his outburst. Even Ada was subdued—probably thinking that she'd jumped from the frying pan into the fire, at least as far as getting bashed was concerned. Hoyle himself still felt badly shaken. He'd gone to wipe his hands with a damp cloth—the extent to which Sybil allowed the use of water for washing—and seen that his fingers were caked with cracking streaks of dried blood. He was now doing his best to keep to himself, lest he fall to pieces even more spectacularly than Oliver.

After dinner, even though he was exhausted to his marrow, he thought back to the hundreds of adventure stories he'd read and said, "Should we set a watch?"

"My watch is fine," said Ada. "It's seven o'clock."

"No," said Sybil. "He means take turns staying awake to hear anybody coming."

"Like that big bloke? No, thanks, I'd rather not see it coming when he bashes my face in."

Oliver made a tiny choking sound.

"Good one, Ada," said Sybil. "Any other insensitive comments you'd like to make at the moment?"

"I didn't—Oliver—hey, I'm sorry, okay? I didn't mean—"

"It's all right," said Oliver.

Sybil moved close to Oliver and said gently, "I'm sorry, Oliver, but I need to know: how long ago did Ruby die?"

"Just a few months. We actually haven't been up here that long. We'd been meeting up in Newtown once a week—"

"Figures," snorted Ada.

"Why?" said Hoyle.

"That's where all the artsy-fartsy people hang out," she said. "The ones who only listen to, I don't know, French jazz or whatever, and live off the money they get selling their stupid paintings on the street. And they all think their big ideas are so important."

"I like French jazz," said Oliver in a wounded voice.

There was a moment's silence.

"Go on, Oliver," said Sybil. "You'd been meeting."

"Okay, so, yeah. And a few people had this idea to go bush for a while, to clear our heads so we could think things through properly. Marco's uncle owns a house in Glen Davis; that's the address we use when we need one."

"Who buys your food?" said Sybil.

Oliver frowned. "I don't know. It just kind of shows up. Marco and Spike have a ute—"

"Sorry, a what?"

"A utility. Um, what do you call them in America? Pickups. They've got one hidden near a fire road, and once in a while they drive into a town and come back with stuff."

"If you can get out of here that easily, why didn't you report Ruby's death to the police?"

"We … don't tend to have a lot to do with the police. They lump anarchists with terrorists. Anyway, what were they going to do, bring her back to life? That's what Dianne said."

Sybil said, "I'm still trying to get a handle on who this big bloke is and what he wants. Why hold us at all? Why not either bash us or let us go?"

"The other morning, when they all went out to get you, Dianne told everyone that the big bloke wanted to talk to you. I don't know why he was waiting, though. Except that he never ended up coming to the camp."

"I guess he was busy."

She and Oliver began a lengthy and increasingly whimsical speculation about what a psychopathic hermit could be doing to occupy his time in the wilderness.

Hoyle said, "I'm turning in," and went inside Oliver's tent. His head was full of a dull apathy, into which spikes of horror stuck painfully at unpredictable intervals. He guessed this was post-traumatic stress or something.

He ought to be proud of himself. He'd done just like the heroes in the books: used a knife to get away from his captors. The books never told you about how the heroes felt afterwards, though. Maybe he wasn't tough enough. Maybe he hadn't done it the right way. He never seemed to do anything else the right way; why should violence be any different?

Like a turtle pulling into its shell, Hoyle slept.

* * *

It was just getting light when Hoyle felt someone shaking him awake.

"Hoyle?" whispered Oliver urgently. "We have to get up and pack. Right now. Sybil says. She was off having a wee when she heard voices."

Hoyle stifled a giggle at the image of Sybil hopping frantically back to the campsite, her pants around her sturdy ankles. The laugh woke him up fully, and he and Oliver had the tent taken down and put away in a flash. Oliver might be a whiny intellectual, but at least he wasn't entirely impractical. Hoyle glanced over towards the other tent. Ada was trying to collapse the tent poles to go into their stuffsack. They writhed and fought her like alien spiders, one end always springing back straight as she struggled to fold the other. Sybil stepped in before she hurt herself.

They set out into the shivery morning. Dew soon soaked through Hoyle's boots, making his socks chafe. There was only enough light to avoid the worst of the things there were to trip over, and all four of them stumbled often.

"Where now?" Hoyle said, as if he'd ever known at any point so far. But Sybil only gave him a warning glance. For the next hour, he did nothing but follow the heels of Sybil's boots, left, right, left, right.

"Sybil," he said at last. "If they were close enough for you to hear them, they would have heard us, wouldn't they? Who's to say they're not following us now?"

"Don't worry about it. They were too far away for me to make out the words, and they were shouting. They missed us, and now we're a moving target." She stopped walking.

The rest of them stood, staring blearily into space, as Sybil checked the GPS with her map and notebook. She nodded. "Getting closer."

"To what?" said Oliver.

"To the last recorded location of the Bloodwood Staff," said Sybil.

Oliver startled. "No, no, oh, no," he gabbled.

"What?" said Ada.

Oliver was shaking now. "The—" He turned on his heel and started back.

"Wait," cried Ada. "You'll get lost. You'll get bashed. There are leeches." She ran after him and dragged on his arm. "Oliver! Don't leave me."

"Do you know what that thing is?" he cried raggedly.

"What, the stick?"

"The Bloodwood Staff! That's what he used to bash Ruby. That's what Dianne said. She said a lot of other stuff about it, too, crazy stuff, scary stuff. Maybe it's all shit, but one thing's for certain: the Bloodwood Staff is evil!"

"What other stuff?" said Sybil.

"The big bloke says it's magic, according to Dianne. She's dead scared of him, everyone is, because he's got it. Ruby knew something was wrong. She *knew*. And he still managed to kill her. And now you're going to walk right towards him and the Bloodwood Staff? What the hell? What the hell?"

"If it's as bad as that, why shouldn't we take it from him?" said Sybil carefully. "Then he'll lose his power, won't he?"

"Jesus, how should I know?"

"We could stop the big bloke."

"Ruby couldn't. And she could do anything. How are we going to?" He flung his hand out in a gesture that dismissed them all.

Hoyle's apathy flared into anger. "How do you know what we can and can't do? How do you know one damned thing about us? Didn't we get this far?"

"Only because I set Spike and Marco up to pick a fight. If they hadn't started beating the crap out of each other, you would never have gotten away."

"If we hadn't—"

"Enough," said Sybil. "This way. Come on. We can't make any decisions until we have more information." She turned and started walking.

Ada shrugged and followed. Hoyle and Oliver stared resentfully at each other, then Hoyle, too, set off. A second later, he heard Oliver behind him. The mere sound of Oliver's footsteps made Hoyle seethe. Cocky little snot. And he had the nerve to give himself the credit for their escape! Hoyle could sort of understand Sybil not making a big deal of what he'd done. She had a lot on her mind, and she took it for granted that people should at least *want* to be capable and heroic, even if they couldn't quite manage it convincingly. And Ada—she probably had never had the chance to learn the difference between heroism and the daily sordid violence she'd grown up with. But Oliver, at least, should have recognized Hoyle's big moment, should have looked at him with admiration, not this sullen impudence.

He didn't want to be the hanger-on anymore. He didn't want to be overlooked, ignored, taken for granted, *dismissed*. Whatever the Bloodwood Staff was, whatever it took to stop the big bloke's reign of terror over a ragtag band of scofflaw fringe-dwellers, he was ready to do it. Tonight he'd borrow the book back from Sybil and find out for himself what clues it held. His headlamp had more than enough battery power to read all night.

Bolstered by his determination, he stomped, scowling, after Sybil and Ada. He did not once turn to see how Oliver was doing. Let the little shit keep up if he wanted to. Hoyle was done worrying.

Chapter 10

In Which a Proposition Is Suggested

Hoyle ate from yet another night's bowl of tasteless glop.

"Hoyle? You okay?" Ada put a hand on Hoyle's shoulder. He turned, and Ada leapt back. "Jeez, sorry!"

Hoyle shrugged. He'd be fine if everyone would just leave him alone.

It was two days since their escape, and according to Sybil, they were homing in on the location of the climactic scene in *After the Bloodwood Staff*. Hoyle had read the book twice now; the Hoyle who had worked in a cubicle and collected old books had kept up a running silent critique: "That was a really clumsy bit of plotting. But at least that character finally has something to do." The new Hoyle, dark and determined, pored over it for clues. He spent the time between dinner and bedtime comparing descriptions to the topographic map, and used the restless hour before falling asleep trying to piece together hints and references in the text about what the Bloodwood Staff was or did.

Ingraham had described it in detail: six feet long, with a paddle-shaped blade of wood on one end, filed to an edge of sorts. The deep red wood was weathered and scarred, and stained from the sweat and oil of countless gripping palms. But on its purpose, Ingraham was peculiarly silent.

And this Nestor Ivory. Younger son, following his brother into the Australian wilderness to help his parents sidestep the shame of bankruptcy. While Ingraham didn't come out and say so, Hoyle found it easy to imagine that such a character would be hungry for money, for his family, for himself. He'd be haunted by the insecurity of his position: even if his parents' fortunes were restored, he himself would get none of it. All would go to the brother.

The questions, then, were—first—what would Nestor Ivory do to give himself both unassailable prestige and a generous livelihood, and—second—how would the Bloodwood Staff help him do this? Would he bring it back to England and sell it? Ingraham might not have wanted such a mundane, self-serving ending to soil the romance of his story.

"Hoyle?" This time it was Sybil. Oliver had been keeping out of Hoyle's way, and Hoyle had already scared Ada off for the evening.

It had gotten dark enough that Sybil's headlamp shone painfully in his eyes.

"Sorry," said Sybil as he flinched, and turned her face aside. "Come on. Let's have a talk."

Hoyle felt just as he had when he'd been taken for coffee by his former bosses: suspicious, resentful, guilty, and fearful. "What have I done wrong?"

"Nothing. God, nothing! Hoyle, would you please—anyway, over here. Have a seat." She sat on a small sandstone outcrop, and he grudgingly came and sat next to her. She took a deep breath. "Will you please tell me what's the matter?"

"Why do you think something's the matter?"

"You're not yourself. You're not the man I met in the book barn."

"And who was that?"

"You were interested in things, in other people. You cared how they were feeling. Now, though, you seem all wrapped up in yourself. And you've been a complete shit to all of us. Ada's a nervous wreck."

"Why?" Hoyle felt real surprise.

"You were different from anyone else. For her, you were someone nice who actually liked her. And now, you're not nice and you don't act like you like her."

"What about you?"

"Like I said, you've been a shit to everyone."

"No, I mean, are you sad because you think I don't like you?"

"I don't have time for that."

Hoyle closed his eyes. "That's bullshit," he said wearily. "And one of the things that's making me cranky is how you keep trying to convince us that you're a fortress, a battleship, Joan of Arc, Queen Elizabeth the First. Do you know how many times I've heard you laugh since I met you? Once. Once."

"Hoyle, why are you—"

"You'd be a better leader if you actually acted like you valued the people who are following you. As far as I can tell, you asked me along because I wouldn't try to order you around, and because I liked books. People pick up on attitudes like that, and it starts to erode their enthusiasm, you know?"

Sybil's shoulders slumped; Hoyle could just see the gesture as utter darkness fell. "Okay. I see your point. I suppose it's too late to tell you that that's not why I wanted you along."

"Why, then?"

"I'm … not good with people. You've already noticed this, you've said as much. I'll make a confession to you. By this point in my life I've either alienated or written off as incompetent just about every friend I've ever had."

"I'm incompetent. Or I was when you met me. I guess I've picked up a few skills since then, like knifing people, and putting up a tent. But back then? I was a caricature of incompetence. Don't deny it—it was obvious. So, then. Why me?"

"I was getting to that. When I grabbed the book, your first reaction wasn't anger, or contempt, like most people's would have been. It was … surprise. You were someone who observed and experienced first, judged later. And then you were still willing to talk to me—socialize, even. It was amazing. You were amazing. So ready to take things at face value."

"You're about to say, 'Now, though …'"

"All right. Now, though, you're nothing but judgment. Nothing but contempt and condemnation. Are you sure you're not feeling this way about yourself, and just taking it out on us?"

"Why wouldn't I feel contempt?" Hoyle snapped. "For myself, for you, for all of us? We're pathetic. Every one of us. No wonder we haven't found anything. No wonder all we're good for is blundering, posturing, and mindless violence."

He reached into his pocket for the flashlight-knife, turned it on, got up and followed its indistinct spot of grey light into the woods. He'd originally just needed to get away from this conversation, but now that he had some privacy, he realized he needed to pee.

He was just finishing up when he heard a quiet voice in the darkness. "How is it going, old chap?"

Hoyle waved the flashlight wildly and spun in his tracks, but saw no one.

"It's all right," said the voice. "I'm not going to hurt you."

A suave voice, English, classy.

"Where are you?" Hoyle's own voice sounded harsh and nasal in comparison.

"Right here. But I'm going to stay hidden at the moment, if you don't mind. Trust me, there are good reasons."

"What do you want?" Could this be "the big bloke", who bashed people to death with a stick? Or were the woods coincidentally full of lone lunatics at the moment?

"I just want to talk for a bit. I've been overhearing—so sorry, terribly rude of me, but I needed to know what you're planning, you see."

"Why?"

"Well, of course, I need to look after myself. Nobody else is going to do it, are they? So I need to make sure you don't pose a threat."

Annoyance steadied Hoyle's voice. "Look, pal, who are you?"

"Me?" said the voice in soft incredulity. "Couldn't you guess? I'm Nestor Ivory."

"You're … pretending to be Nestor Ivory."

"No, old chap. I'm actually Nestor Ivory."

"Okay," said Hoyle carefully. "You're Nestor Ivory. I'm Hoyle. Pleased to meet you."

"You'll forgive me if I don't shake your hand."

"Of course."

"You're a very civil chap, I must say. I'm very interested in you."

"You are?" *Humor him*, thought Hoyle. *Don't set him off.* "Why's that?"

"I've been watching you all for quite some time. Sadly, I have been inconvenienced, and not in a position to approach you before now. But that was to my benefit, as it gave me a chance to get to know you. And you, my friend, are clearly the pick of the litter."

"'Pick of the litter'—what does that mean?"

"The boy is useless, with his fatuous ideas and wild, will-o'-the-wisp enthusiasms. The girl has possibilities—plenty of pluck, and a delightful tendency toward insubordination—but she has no self-discipline at all, and that's always a worry. That woman is simply dreadful in every way, and the less said, the better. But you! By Jove, I wish I'd had you at my back in that pub in Johannesburg."

"Um, I don't—"

"Don't stammer, man. It doesn't become you. Be the man I saw two days ago. Bold, desperate, daring. Why, you used that knife as though you'd been born to it. What is your trade, then?"

"I—I work in an office. Or I did. I got … fired."

"Lit on fire? Good God!"

"Sacked."

"Oh—bravo! Blew a gasket and finally told them what you thought of them, eh?"

"No."

"No? Well, I'm sure you're better off out in the wilderness, living a man's life, what?"

"Um, sure."

"What did I hear them calling you? Hoyle? Pleased to meet you, Mr. Hoyle."

"It's my first name. Hoyle Marchand."

"Odd sort of name. Although I suppose 'Nestor Ivory' is no better, eh?" A warm chuckle came from somewhere in the darkness. "Nestor. My parents thought the name might imbue me with saintliness. Ha ha!"

Hoyle longed to run back to the tents, but what if "Nestor" chased him? Even though he'd rapidly gotten into better shape than he'd ever been in his life, he had no illusions. He was merely a slightly less overweight, panting, pasty wimp than he'd been a week before.

"I can see you're thinking about running," said the voice. "Go ahead. I can't stop you. Not at the moment, anyway. I told you, there are reasons I'm hiding. And you're quite safe. Look, I can understand that this strikes you as a little uncanny, and it scatters your attention somewhat. But I'm starting to get quite tired of repeating myself."

"Sorry."

"Now, if you'd like to preserve your dignity, and—more usefully—avoid alarming the others, you might consider walking casually back to camp and saying nothing of me. What would you say, anyway? 'I had a lovely chat with Nestor Ivory whilst I was doing up my fly. Capital bloke.'"

"Mm. Yeah," said Hoyle. "You have a point."

"I've enjoyed our encounter, Marchand. I look forward to talking with you again."

"Okay," said Hoyle. "I'll just be going, then?"

"Damn it, man! Not so tentative. Assert yourself. Now, try again."

Hoyle deepened his voice and said briskly, "Good night, Ivory."

"Better. Au revoir!"

Alongside Hoyle's unease was something else: a small, surly, writhing feeling. "At least *he* appreciates what I've gone through."

And it was that, more than the fear of not being believed, that made him keep his silence when he got back to the others. He wanted to savor the feeling of being admired and praised, if only for just this one night.

If "Nestor" had wanted to hurt him, he would have. He was just a lonely guy living out in the woods because city life, human life, had gotten too much for him. He'd been drawn here, like Sybil, by the story of the Bloodwood Staff, and had decided that the solitude of the wilderness would soothe his scraped and battered soul. But that didn't mean the guy didn't need a little human contact once in a while. Telling Sybil and the others would only make them hound him. They wouldn't feel sorry for him. They wouldn't understand him.

Hoyle, though, understood. They understood each other surprisingly well, it seemed, he and this Nestor Ivory.

* * *

The next morning only cemented Hoyle's resolve not to tell. Every spat, every mishap, every labored sigh over this or that slight made him feel isolated and resentful. They should be grateful he was along, not patronize him. Not waste his time with bickering.

The sun was directly overhead and oven-hot when Sybil started leading them up a steep slope. They followed until the path leveled out. A ravine stretched out before them, broad, wild, and frightening. The ground dropped off a few yards ahead; Ada edged forward, peered over, and backed away in a panic.

"As far as I can tell, this fits the description," Sybil said. "This is the place where Nestor Ivory fought off the unscrupulous miners to claim the Bloodwood Staff."

Hoyle remembered the scene: Ivory crawling through the brush on a day much like today, his clothes and flesh torn by thorns, flies buzzing in thick clouds and landing on him in their hundreds to drink his sweat and blood.

Nestor caught sight of the staff, wedged under the sleeping body of a loutish miner. He crept closer, close enough to touch the bit of the handle he could see. Slowly, so slowly, he started to drag the staff free. He began to feel a flush of exultation—he was going to do it, he was going to keep his promise to Nicholas and reclaim the staff.

Just then, as if it had a will of its own, the staff began to glow, whiter and whiter. Nestor gripped it harder. It was just some sort of light, it didn't hurt. Only a coward would be afraid of a little light.

The lout woke with a scream and rolled off the staff: his clothes were smoldering and he had a horrific burn along his side. Nestor stood and wasted an instant marvelling at his own unhurt hand clenched around the staff, during which the lout scrambled to his feet and lunged at it. Nestor swung it like a cricket bat—however that is, thought Hoyle—and stove the lout's head in.

The lout's crass and brutish sidekick, hearing his companion's death-grunt, came running from the trees, where he'd been off for some undoubtedly sordid purpose. Nestor swung the staff again in a glancing blow to the sidekick's head, then punched the pointed wooden blade into his stomach. It penetrated easily, and Nestor yanked it free again, leaving a ragged wound in his opponent's body identical to the one that had been Nicholas's undoing.

Silence fell, and the staff went dark. Nestor had avenged his brother's death. He could bring the staff back to England now, where it would fetch enough money to save his parents from destitution and disgrace.

It hadn't made any sense to Hoyle. No matter how valuable to anthropologists as an artifact, the staff couldn't possibly have brought the kind of price that would restore a family's fortunes. The staff was essentially useless in England, no different from any of a thousand other staves, taiahas, and spears from across Oceania—and, indeed, anywhere in the world where humans had lived in the presence of trees.

Ah, well. Ingraham could do what he liked; it was his story. Maybe he was playing to a market that loved improbable plot devices. Writers always had to think of their readers, after all.

Oliver said, "Any reason not to set up here and have a real rest?"

"Yeah," said Ada. "Like three or four days?"

"We don't have all that much food," said Sybil. "But we can set up here and start the actual looking. No more hiking for a bit."

Ada hooted triumphantly and started setting up the tent, quickly and confidently now. She was laughing with Oliver about something. Her grin was open and joyful, not the artful cheeriness she'd shown back in Sydney. Watching her, Hoyle felt the gloom start to lift.

Sybil came and stood next to Hoyle. "Well! This is all right. Someone else doing my work for me. Took a lot of effort to get her this far, so I'm glad to see it paying off."

In an instant the resentment was back. Sybil always had to be the superior one. Even when he'd … done what he'd done with the knife, she had bestowed token thanks like a country squire thanking a peasant for holding the stirrup.

"Hey," she said. "What's up? You look really upset about something."

"No, just tired," he said.

"Hey, guys," called Ada, "me and Oliver are going to take a walk."

"Don't go too far," said Sybil.

"Okay." Ada waved like a child going off on a picnic, and she and Oliver set off.

Sybil waited until they were some way away, then said, "Who were you talking to last night?"

Hoyle went cold. "When?" he asked casually.

"When you were off having a pee. *Who were you talking to*?"

"Nestor Ivory."

"Very funny. Hoyle, this is our safety in jeopardy here. Have the anarchists found us?"

"No. Definitely not."

"Then who?"

"I told you."

"Don't mock me!"

"That's what he called himself, anyway. I couldn't see him, he stayed hidden in the bushes. He was just lonely. Just wanted to talk."

"Uh-huh. And it didn't strike you as an odd coincidence that he named himself after the very character in the very book—the utterly forgotten book—that we ourselves are using as our guide?"

"Um, I just figured there aren't a lot of reasons to be out here. Anyone else we meet has a fair chance of being here for the same reason we are."

"Look, Hoyle, let me clear something up. This is my show. My adventure. I'm the leader. I need to know everything that happens. It's the only way I'm going to, first, keep everyone safe, and second, find the Bloodwood Staff."

"This is my adventure, too. I paid for my own flight. I bought my own gear. I thought we were supposed to be some sort of team or other."

"Teams have leaders."

"Leaders aren't dictators."

"I beg your pardon?"

"You've been swaggering around, giving all the orders, never asking for more information, or opinions, or whether things are okay with anyone but yourself. Who got us away from the camp? Not you! You're not the only capable person. And I'm sick and tired of your thinking that you are, and treating everyone else accordingly." He stood up.

"That's right, storm off."

"Come and find me when you need someone to patronize and dismiss again. That's why you brought me along, isn't it?"

He started walking, not really caring where. On his way he passed Ada, her eyes wide.

"What was all that?" she said. "First fight? Good—that's progress. You guys were meant for each other."

"Oh, shut up," he said viciously.

Ada looked like he'd just slapped her.

He turned away from her, wretched and ashamed, and pushed through the bushes until he couldn't see or hear the campsite. He sat down, back against a tree, and wiped the tears from his eyes as they gathered and fell.

"Oh, now, dear, dear, dear," came the suave voice of last night's encounter. "What could the matter be?"

"I'm all right," said Hoyle.

"No, don't try to pretend. I heard everything."

"That's creepy. Could you not, please?"

"Not what, old boy?"

"Not stalk me."

"I told you, I'm interested in you. You have potential."

"Where are you hiding this time?"

"Really, if you have one fault, it's that you need to be told things several times. When I can show myself, I will. I promise."

"Yeah, all right, whatever."

"I detect a certain petulance about you today, Marchand. It's distasteful. Pull yourself together, would you? There's a good chap."

"Nobody's talked like that in a hundred years, by the way. If, indeed, they ever did."

"I confess I'm finding this part of the conversation tedious, so I'll move on. I'd like to make you a small proposal. If, of course, you feel up to it. I find I'm not as confident in you as I was last night."

Hoyle said nothing.

"Ah! Silence becomes you better than would frantic protests. Right, then. I know you're looking for the Bloodwood Staff; you've been very careless in your campfire chatter. I also know that your only guide is Ingraham's ridiculous pack of lies. I should have—well, never mind, what's done is done. And besides," added the voice, suddenly jolly, "that so-called book brought you here. Fortune has turned disaster into success. Ah, Ingraham, all your plans are confounded. You see, Marchand, I, too, wish to recover the Bloodwood Staff. But there's a difficulty. I can't actually get my hands on it."

"Isn't that what 'recover' means?" said Hoyle.

"No, I mean that even if it were right in front of me, I couldn't touch it. Not yet. A few things have to happen first."

"Like, a ritual or something?"

"Something like that," replied the voice. "My proposal is this: I guide you to where you can get it, and you help me with those rituals."

"Sybil wants it."

"Sybil can go hang."

Even though he'd been thinking much the same thing himself, Hoyle still found this animosity startling. "Well, um, I can't exactly find it without her, can I? She's bound to notice."

"It's easy to manage, Marchand. Think, for God's sake! You can pretend to be helping her while you feed her a red herring about where you think the book says it is. Soon you'll be able to just nip off and get it while she's looking elsewhere, eh?"

"I don't feel comfortable with that."

"All I ask is that you think about it."

The offer was tempting. Hoyle wouldn't mind being the one to show Sybil she wasn't the only hero. A quick fantasy arose wherein he emerged from a cave, triumphantly bearing the staff, and Sybil looked shocked, then rueful, then admiring.

"Ah, I see I have intrigued you. Think about it for now. There's time. You still have several days' worth of food, do you not?"

"I …"

"Of course you do. I know how much food you have. Now, head on back to camp, there's a good chap."

Hoyle sat still for quite a while, waiting for the voice to chastise him for not leaping to obey. But no word came. The woods were silent, except for the flies and the birds.

Hoyle returned without incident. Ada glared at him. Sybil frowned. Oliver looked from face to face, and changed his expression to match Ada's.

Hoyle's only friend, it seemed, was the madman Nestor Ivory.

Chapter 11

In Which Hoyle Looks for
Friendship Elsewhere

"I guess the easiest thing is to just systematically start looking," said Sybil. "The terrain is a little rough for a line search, but we can each take small patches."

"One thing," said Ada. "I have no idea what I'm supposed to be looking for. A stick, yeah? The bush is full of sticks."

"This one is carved. And straight. And the wood is reddish. All the sticks lying around here are grey and crooked. It shouldn't be a problem." She raised one eyebrow.

"And what happens when we find it?"

"I have absolutely no idea."

"If you want the willing consent of the masses," Ada said sententiously, "you have to make sure we're well informed by trustworthy sources." Oliver beamed.

"Cut the crap, Ada. And you," she turned to Oliver, "can stop half-teaching her your half-thought-out philosophies, okay? We have work to do, and only tomorrow and the next day before the food gets to the level where we have to start walking out."

"Don't worry, Oliver," said Ada. "The ruling classes are always threatened by … um … things that threaten them."

Hoyle had stopped even trying to have friendly conversations with anyone. He'd made one wan effort to apologize to Ada, which she'd ostentatiously ignored. Aside from that, he'd done his campsite chores, read a little of the camping book (he'd already learned through necessity and observation most of what was in it), and was now lying on his back staring through the leaves at the clouds going by. Sybil had reclaimed the Ingraham book for one last trawl for clues.

Sybil said, "All right, everyone, I suggest you do your best to get to sleep early. Tomorrow's going to be on the demanding side."

Hoyle felt tired enough to sleep right now. Well, why not? He'd turn in after a visit to the area of the woods he preferred as his latrine.

This time the voice didn't even wait until he'd finished peeing. "Listen, Marchand, here's what you—"

"Do you *mind*?" Hoyle asked peevishly.

"Oh, come now. We have no secrets from each other."

"Yes, we do."

"Ah. Well you have none from me, at any rate. But if it makes you more comfortable, I'll wait."

"Thanks a million." When he'd finished, he sighed and said, "All right, what?"

"Your manners are deteriorating."

"I'm tired. I'm miserable. And my only friend is a loony who's named himself after a fictional character in a bad book and refuses to show himself."

"We'll let that go for the moment, shall we? There's something more important to talk about. During this search tomorrow, you make sure you, yourself, start with the area over by the big sandstone outcrop—do you know the one I mean?"

"The one that looks like a sphinx?"

"The north side, if you can."

"Sure," said Hoyle.

"Right-o. I'll be on my way, then. If all goes well tomorrow, it won't be too long before you see me."

Back at the camp, Ada was washing some underwear, Oliver was reading a book in the last of the day's light, and Sybil was staring intently out at the landscape; Hoyle assumed she was refining the search strategy.

"Good night," he said to the party in general.

Each of them glanced toward him. Sybil said, "Okay."

The heavy, hopeless exhaustion that had dogged Hoyle all day overwhelmed him, and he welcomed the refuge of sleep.

* * *

Sybil woke them all when it was still dark. Once they were up and dressed, she pressed a trail-mix bar into everyone's hand. "Eat," she commanded. "And then drink some water."

Ada made a face as she took the bar. "Pencil shavings stuck together with dried flies."

"Thank you, that's enough," said Sybil.

Hoyle said cautiously to Sybil, "Mind if I start looking over there by that outcropping? I just have a feeling."

"No, we need to do this systematically. I'm going to brief everyone in a minute."

"It … I want to look over …" He faltered as Sybil stared at him.

"This is some kind of adolescent power thing, isn't it?"

"No!"

"You want to prove you're your own man. That you don't take orders from anyone, let alone me."

"I—"

"This kind of bullshit is why I never had kids. You know what? Just go. Go look wherever you want. I'll get Oliver to do your sector as well as his. You'll still need the briefing to minimize the chance that you'll do something stupid, but stay out of the way until then."

Hoyle wandered a few yards away and forced himself to swallow the granola bar past the lump of misery in his throat.

Sybil waited until everyone had finished their breakfast, then said, "We're at where I'm pretty sure is the last resting place of the Bloodwood Staff. After the fight scene here, the staff is not depicted as being anywhere else in Australia—Ivory just shows up with it in England, rich and happy, which is a ludicrous ending. I'm betting it never left this site. We want to find it. We'll search methodically—well, fairly methodically." She threw a poisonous look at Hoyle. "Each of us will take a sector and go over it slowly and carefully. When you're done, come to me and I'll assign you your next one. If you find it, signal me right away. Does everyone have their whistle? Two blasts, from me or anyone, means come right back to the camp, instantly, no matter what you're doing, no matter how close you think you might be to finding the staff. I am not kidding. Three means you're in trouble and need help. Does everyone understand?"

"Yes," they murmured in turn.

"All right, then. Ada, I'd like you to start there. Oliver, over there. Take up your stations."

"What about Hoyle?" said Oliver.

"Never mind, he's got his own ideas."

The "it figures" look on their faces made Hoyle's stomach hurt. He slunk over to the outcropping to await the full dawn.

"You showed remarkable strength of purpose, Marchand," murmured the voice. "Well done! Not that I would have expected anything less. You've shown yourself to be a true individual right from the start, and it's paying off now. Won't it taste sweet to be the one to find the Bloodwood Staff? You won't have to say a word; they'll know how they underestimated you."

"Yeah," said Hoyle shortly. "Just tell me where you want me to look."

"Oh, just around here," said the voice airily.

"Hey, why don't you just grab it yourself, if you know where it is?"

"And yet again I must implore you to trust me. This really is getting tiresome. Believe me when I tell you I have my reasons and stop asking fatuous questions, or else don't believe me and don't bother asking. No, no, Marchand, it didn't fly, it *fell*. Look down. And start walking. Back and forth. Cover the ground in a search pattern. About this far, then turn and do the next sweep. That's right."

Hoyle walked slowly and carefully, sweeping his gaze from side to side. "I'm looking for a reddish stick, about five feet long, right?"

"With a carved, leaf-shaped blade on the end, yes, yes. Don't talk, it'll distract you."

The eagerness in the voice was alarming. Hoyle shut up, worried about antagonizing a madman. Just because he hadn't been violent so far didn't mean he was safe.

The morning wore on, and Hoyle's nerves were starting to fray. A thousand times he startled, thinking he saw a straight stick, or a reddish stick, or a flat, wooden paddle poking out from among the leaves. A dozen times he reached for it, only to be disappointed on closer examination. Twice, he actually dragged a stick free and held it up, certain that this time he had it.

He heard a bored and irritated sigh. "You said to look," he said. "I'm looking. What more can I do?"

"You can *find*, you bloody idiot!"

Hoyle debated the merits of just turning around and going back to the campsite. It would thwart the loony's ability to intimidate him—four were stronger than one, and despite everything, he didn't think the others would ignore a genuine plea for help.

But ... the looks on their faces this morning. Contempt. They couldn't even be bothered to hate him, he wasn't worth hatred. He wanted to show them. Above all, he wanted Sybil to see that, after all, he was capable and strong. Despite his mistakes. Despite his flab, and his timidity, and his mildness. Underneath all that, he had a core of iron, he knew it was there somewhere.

His toes jammed painfully against a rock that had been hidden by leaves, and he lost his balance and fell. He wanted to get up, wary of Nestor's ire, but suddenly he froze, on all fours where he'd landed, his hands and knees throbbing from the impact. Because there, where the skid of his left hand had moved the leaves aside, was a patch of dirt. And poking through the dirt was a thin, straight reddish line. He started to scrabble with his bare hands, then with a stick until that broke, then with the rock he'd dislodged when he'd tripped on it.

"Be careful, can't you?" shrieked the voice. "That rock could—"

"No it couldn't," said Hoyle, now just as excited. "If it's been buried here for a hundred years, it's tough."

"It hasn't been, you fool! I'd been so diligent, taking such good care of it. It's not my fault she—" The voice stopped abruptly, and when it spoke again, its old, wheedling charm was back. "Just take care, old boy, all right? It's priceless. Hundreds of years old. It ought to be in a special room in a university or something. That's what we'll do with it, won't we, Marchand? Take it back to England—or, or wait, you're American, aren't you? We'll take it back to America, and you'll be famous. Won't that be capital! Just, please, be bloody careful!"

Hoyle moved his digging out from the line a few inches. If he could loosen the dirt on either side, maybe he could pry it out without the risk of gouging it with the rock. The shadows had gotten quite a bit shorter by the time he'd dug two trenches alongside the staff and started scrabbling with his hands at the dirt that still held it. He wriggled his aching fingers underneath it and started to jiggle the staff loose. Bits of gritty dirt crumbled away, and the staff began to move back and forth.

As he lifted it, his hands began to throb. His first thought was, *Arthritis? Already?* But the throbbing got faster and faster until the staff buzzed like a cicada. He looked around in a panic, as if the woods themselves could explain what was going on, and started to fling the staff from him.

"No," came a sharp shout that startled Hoyle out of letting go. "Don't do that. Stand still, damn you. Hold on!"

"It hurts," Hoyle cried. But the voice did not answer. The only noise in the world, swelling until it roared through the forest, was the sound of the staff. Hoyle's vision faded and contracted. Then his eyes went dark completely, and the roaring collapsed into a thick silence and a pulsing agony of headache. He felt himself starting to fall to a spinning earth.

Abruptly, it all stopped. The sun shone, the leaves shivered gently in a warm breeze, the birds made their odd Australian noises. Hoyle was gasping, but on his feet. He became aware of someone holding him up, an arm around Hoyle's waist, his own arm pulled across thin, bony shoulders. He was still gripping the staff, but he felt a tug on it as he tried to lift it for a better look.

"You just let me have it, old man," said the voice soothingly, but this time it was right next to his ear. Hoyle turned his aching neck toward the sound. A tanned, bearded face beamed at him and took his arm from around Hoyle's waist to take hold of the staff. "That's right, just let me—no, let go—Marchand, damn you, it's all right. Let go!" The man tugged again, and Hoyle let him take the staff. The man instantly stepped away from Hoyle, who staggered, then sat weakly down.

The man was absorbed in staring at the staff, tracing the carving with a dirty, broken-nailed finger, rubbing his thumb along the wooden blade, even inhaling the scent of the wood.

"Um," said Hoyle.

"Yes?" said the man irritably, without looking at Hoyle.

"You …"

"Have been following you since Newnes. Made those fools capture you—you'd been impossibly far from the right track until they took you to their pathetic little village. All to get the staff. At last!" The man spun in a triumphant dance, hooting as he turned. Then, still gripping the staff with one hand, he ran the other hand along his own chest, rubbed his face, stretched his fingers as wide as they could go, then balled them into a fist that trembled with the intensity of his grip. Then he opened his mouth and laughed, a ringing laugh that went on and on until he, too, gasped.

Finally, he said, "Oh, Christ, yes, it worked!"

"What worked?" asked Hoyle weakly.

"I had to take it from you, you see, I couldn't pick it up myself. You—" He stopped and looked imploringly at Hoyle. "You can see me now, can't you?"

"Y-yes," said Hoyle. He saw a slight man, dressed in worn khaki shorts and a shirt, and battered leather boots. His beard and hair were grizzled, but trimmed surprisingly neatly, considering his otherwise weather-beaten appearance. Although he looked like he'd be thin at the best of times, at the moment he was skeletal.

"Well, then, at last we can meet properly. Nestor Ivory."

"*The* Nestor Ivory?" he said with a thin smile.

The man frowned. "Do I still detect unbelief? Good God, man, look at me. Who else could I be?"

"Frankly, anyone," said Hoyle.

"I don't suppose it matters," the man murmured to himself, "now that this has done its work." He cast another loving look at the staff, then turned back to Hoyle. "But humor me, would you, old boy? Nestor Ivory. Loving second son of parents from the minor nobility, failed scholar, devoted brother." He laughed again at that, and Hoyle found he didn't quite like the sound.

"All right—Ivory." If he, Hoyle, was "Marchand," he guessed last names were what was expected. It was all very boarding school. This guy was really trying hard for verisimilitude, Hoyle granted him that.

"I say," said Ivory. Trying *very* hard, in fact. "I owe you rather a lot of thanks, don't I? Well, never let it be said that I didn't appreciate the assistance of my comrades. I don't know an appropriate way to repay you, I confess, but should one occur to you, I'll be more than happy to oblige."

"Sure. Thanks," said Hoyle. "Um, I'll just take that back to show Sybil and the others, shall I? Like we discussed?"

Ivory goggled. "You have to be mad. Give it back to you? And let that horrible woman take it? Let her even touch it? Absolutely not."

"But you said I'd get to show her. You know. That I found it."

Ivory scowled. "All right." He stuck out a hand to help Hoyle up. At the instant their hands met, Hoyle felt the buzzing, heard the roaring, for just a flash—then it was gone.

He and Ivory walked the hundred yards or so back to the campsite. He remembered he was supposed to use the whistle. He dug it out from inside his shirt, wiped the sweat off, stuck his fingers in his ears, and blew. A few minutes later, everyone came crashing through the brush. As soon as they saw Ivory, every one of them stopped dead. Then they noticed the staff. Sybil cried out and rushed forward. Ivory clutched the staff close and turned sharply away.

"Who is that?" said Oliver, pointing.

"Um," said Hoyle, feeling stupid. "Nestor Ivory. Ivory, this is Sybil. And Oliver, and Ada."

Ada laughed. "Nestor Ivory. I get it. Like the bloke in the book. And that's the stick?" She came up next to Sybil and stuck her head forward to look at the staff. "It's a little ordinary." She held out her hand. "Can I see?"

"No," said Ivory shortly.

"Uh-oh," murmured Ada.

But Sybil made an enormous effort and spoke quietly. "May I please look at the staff?"

Ivory hugged it closer, like a child.

"I won't touch it, I promise," said Sybil. "I just want to look at it."

Ivory thought it over. "All right," he said, and reluctantly held it out across his palms.

Sybil stepped close. She spent a long minute examining it, leaning from side to side to look at its entire length. Finally she stepped back. "When did you find it?"

"No, it was me. I just now dug it out of the dirt," said Hoyle.

"The first time?" said Ivory, ignoring him. "I've lost strict count, but I'd estimate about a hundred years ago."

"Very funny," said Sybil. "No, really."

"Really," he said flatly. "I am not *like* the bloke in the book," said Ivory. "I *am* the bloke in the book. I—am—Nestor—Ivory. And I've been waiting for someone like you—well, I'll be more specific. I've been waiting for someone like Marchand here for quite a while now. Oh, not the whole hundred years. Most of it went swimmingly, once I got the hang of things. But a short time ago, I had a … I suppose one could call it a mishap. But now that I have the staff back at last, everything will be much more to my liking."

"If I'm hearing you correctly," said Sybil, "you're asking us to believe that the staff has prolonged your life by, what, nearly a hundred years?"

"That's exactly what I'm saying. Well done!"

"Okay," said Sybil carefully. "What's so special about us—about Hoyle?"

"For one, do you know how utterly preposterous it is that someone would be rash enough, impulsive enough, flipping mad enough, to read that idiot Ingraham's pack of lies—and yet smart enough to notice that not one thing in that book made any sense at all and come looking for the truth? That alone makes him, to say the least, a tad unusual."

"That was me, not Hoyle," said Sybil.

"Ah," said Ivory with a knowing smile. "You're jealous already. Human vanity is the failing of us all, particularly in such adventures as these."

Sybil ignored that. "How do you know so much about us?"

"He's been following us since before the anarchists got us," said Hoyle.

Oliver was getting increasingly agitated. "He sneaks around in the woods. He's a pom, like Ruby said. And he's mean and nasty—look at him. He's—he's—" He screamed and lunged toward Ivory. "This is the big bloke," he cried. "He killed Ruby. He killed her!"

Chapter 12

In Which Ivory Tells a Story

Ivory flicked the staff around, catching Oliver in the stomach. Oliver collapsed, making long, moaning gasps as he tried to get his wind back.

"Stupid boy. I killed no one."

"I saw her," Oliver said in between desperate breaths. "I saw her with her head all bashed in. Who else is there out here? Who else could have killed her? Who else would have? She trusted you!"

"Before you fly completely off the handle," said Ivory coolly, "you could find out my actual story, couldn't you?"

Oliver was still having trouble standing up, but he staggered toward Ivory again. This time Ivory casually stuck out a foot and shoved him back. He fell, and stayed down, glaring at Ivory and trying to breathe. Ada ran over and squatted next to him, her hand uselessly stroking his hair.

"If I were a killer, I'd have killed you right then," said Ivory. "Self-defense, indisputably. But then you wouldn't involve the police anyway, would you? Neither you nor any of the other sad, hopeless, helpless people playing revolutionary in your pathetic little enclave. Because every one of you has done something to make you wish the police had never heard of you, haven't you?"

Sybil said, "All right, stop it. Tell me your actual story. First, *are* you the big bloke? You don't look very big."

"'Big' can refer to force of personality, as much as to stature. But no, I'm not 'the big bloke,' whoever that is."

"You're the one who told Dianne to capture them, I know it!" said Oliver, still curled in pain on the ground.

"Did you see me?" said Ivory.

"No, but—"

"Did you hear me?"

"No—"

"Then how the devil do you know I told this Dianne anything?"

"Well, someone told her. And who else is there?"

Ivory rocked back and forth on his heels. "I'm sure I don't know," he said mildly. "What I do know is that you have absolutely no reason whatsoever to accuse me of—who was it?"

"Don't pretend you didn't know her," wailed Oliver. "She—she—"

"She what, Oliver?" said Sybil.

Oliver turned to her, his face streaked with tears. "She loved him. And he killed her."

Ivory made a disgusted sound. "I couldn't possibly have killed anyone," he said. "I couldn't, for the very compelling reason that until Marchand dug the staff out and I could finally take it from his hand, *I had no body whatsoever!*"

After making this announcement, Ivory raised his chin as if expecting outcries of amazement at his miraculous recovery.

Instead, Ada, very slowly and scornfully, said, "Bullshit."

"Oh, it's quite true," said Ivory. "For quite a while now, I've been a voice on the wind, nothing more. I could see and hear, I could think and speak. But I could not act. I could touch nothing— not pick up so much as a grain of dirt. So digging out the staff— which I very desperately wanted to do—was out of the question. Is it any wonder I was so eager to find out more about you when I heard you talking about the very thing itself? It's hardly your fault your only guide was Ingraham's work of folly and lies. I wanted to help. We all wanted the staff. I knew where it was. You could get it for me." He turned to Oliver. "Young man, would you say those buffoons I've been watching in the bush were scared of 'the big bloke'?"

Oliver nodded.

"Then I ask you: could I, bodiless, powerless, possibly have been as frightening as all that? Would you have done whatever you were ordered to do? How could I have enforced my orders, whatever they were, were I 'the big bloke'?"

Oliver said nothing.

"However, he sounds like a right old rotter, doesn't he? Ordering people around—killing them, even. I'm surprised I've never run into him. Are you sure he even exists?"

"I've seen Ruby's body," said Oliver.

"Tell us your story," Sybil said to Ivory.

"Right. Well, then. This much of Ingraham's travesty was true: my brother and I came out to Australia because he'd heard of an artifact that could win us fame and fetch us a tidy sum into the bargain. It was that simple. Wanting to spare my parents the shame of not being able to pay my university fees? Ludicrous. They were quite comfortable. But they were wont to impose certain restrictions on our behavior, backed by the threat of disinheritance. This was our chance to win free of them. I should have asked Nicholas why nobody else, hearing the same stories, had ever gone after the staff and brought it back to England. But I loved and admired him—young fool that I was. If I'd known then that all our heroes are just as sordid and weak and petty as we are … remember that, boy, when you grieve for your Ruby. She was nothing special.

"Well. We followed rumors, from one nasty gutter-dweller to the next. We spent time in sordid back rooms in Redfern; stinking, fly-ridden shacks on Penrith farms; filthy, freezing pubs in Katoomba and Lithgow. We lost the trail in Newnes—for good, we thought. But winter had arrived in earnest, and we didn't want to risk the trip back over the mountains, on foot and exhausted as we were. So we settled in.

"It didn't take long for Nicholas to play his hand. Now that I had done most of the work in getting us this far—I was always much better at getting people to talk than he—he wanted me to head back to Sydney. 'For your safety,' he simpered. Obviously he'd uncovered a clue, and he wanted to follow it up with me out of the way. Of course, I refused. He would have to resign himself to my presence. And so he did—or so I thought. We hardly spoke of the staff at all over that winter.

"Nicholas became quite ugly. The little cruelties I'd seen in him in childhood, and which my parents and I thought had been trained out of him, resurfaced and redoubled. That winter was an endless torment. His normal brotherly joking became mockery and taunts, and finally degenerated into the most vicious, foul abuse any man has ever said to another. He stopped short of actually raising a hand to me, but not far short, and I was often in fear of violence.

"I made friends with the miners, among them a hanger-on named Ingraham. He relished the company of the rough and capable miners, but they had little time for him. I, in contrast, was not only garrulous, but both dashing and English, two things that held a rather awkward attraction for him. But he wasn't a bad sort, and with a pint or two in each of us we could manage to have a fairly jolly time. I confided in him—again, the folly of youth!—about the staff, and my brother's perfidy.

"Spring came, and Nicholas and I headed into the wilderness. I tried anything I could think of to plague Nicholas and prolong the search—the more distracted he was, the better chance I had of being the one to actually find the staff. I sabotaged his gear: thinning a bootlace so it would snap, fatiguing the spring on a folding knife so it would fail. And, all right, I confess I took a petty, vengeful satisfaction in inconveniencing him—a small bit of payback for the misery he'd inflicted on me. And when I found the staff, I'd be back to Sydney in a flash, and then to London, and Nicholas be damned.

"We'd been looking for three days when I found a split in some rocks that looked like a good hiding place, not far from where we'd seen some rock art earlier in the day; maybe the drawing was a signpost, maybe a warning, maybe nothing to do with the staff at all. But where men can go to make art, they can go to hide a staff.

"Nicholas was far away; I'd made it a point to keep well apart. I gave the crevice a few precautionary probes and taps with a stick. When nothing came slithering out, I reached in. My heart was pounding. It was as if I could hear the staff calling to me. I actually heard a voice: 'Ivory!'

"But just as my fingers closed on something deep within the crevice, I realized that the voice came from behind me. 'Ivory! There you are.'

"It was that crawler, Ingraham, blast and damn him, making enough noise to draw notice all the way from Sydney. I'd have to move quickly to recover the staff and get away from Nicholas. I knew it was already too late to sneak away. Nicholas's growing insanity had driven his senses to perpetual hypervigilance. I shouted at Ingraham to make him flinch as I seized the staff. Maybe I could outrun Nicholas and get to a position where I could at least defend myself.

"'Ivory!' Ingraham's petulant wail was followed by my brother's outraged bellow. In a moment he'd be upon us, and I knew from years of boyhood struggles that I was no match for him. I did the only thing I could: I ran. Ran for my life, back toward Newnes, toward Sydney, toward England.

"The staff was a desperate hindrance, snagging on trees and bushes, jamming against rocks when I let the tip drop in my haste. But I was damned if I was going to abandon it to Nicholas.

"Ingraham struggled along behind me, but my ears strained to hear another tread, determined, murderous: Nicholas. It didn't take him long to catch up; I'd been mad to think I could outrun him. With a flying tackle he brought me down. My arm exploded into white-hot pain. I rolled to trap the staff under my body, ignoring the agony, and with my other hand I scrabbled and clawed at his face like an animal. He pinned me with an arm across my jugular and began to press. Even as I started to black out—and I was under no illusion that he would stop before he'd killed me—I was galled by the thought that my last memory would be of his crazed face and hot, stinking breath.

"A moment later, light and sound rushed back in upon me, along with a ferocious headache and the smell of burnt cloth. Through the headache I began to feel a sharp pain all along my side. I sat up—although it nearly made me pass out again—and looked around in frantic confusion. Next to me lay Nicholas, with blood pouring from the side of his head. My first thought, though, was not for him—did he deserve my concern?—but for the staff. It lay along my side, pulsing with an odd light and giving out waves of heat. Obviously, it had burnt my clothes—and me— where I had been lying on it.

"Sitting a little way away, quivering and weeping, was Ingraham. 'Oh, God,' he whimpered. 'Oh, God, I've killed him. But I had to, didn't I? And then the staff, my God, the staff ...'

"Nicholas was dead. Now nothing could stop me from taking the staff to England. Forgetting its odd heat, I picked it up—and instantly dropped it with a scream.

"'I know,' said Ingraham through his tears. 'It started up like that while your brother ... was trying to kill you.'

"As he and I watched, and as Nicholas's lifeblood seeped into the dirt, the staff slowly cooled and grew dim again. I tested it cautiously; yes, I could pick it up now. I stood. I was in pain from the headache, the bruises and scrapes, and the long line of sting-ing burns along my side and across my palm, but that couldn't be allowed to matter. It was time to go. While we walked (and I blush to say I leaned on Ingraham's arm more times than I liked), he told me how the staff had begun to glow as my own life had hung in the balance, and how he'd taken advantage of Nicho-las's mad rage to creep up to him and swing a large rock into his head. It had taken several goes to deliver the killing blow, but finally Nicholas moved no more. The staff had blazed then, and Ingraham had thought to roll me off it before my clothes—or my flesh—actually burst into flame.

"Before long, I noticed the pain getting worse. Soon, I couldn't continue unless Ingraham all but carried me. He suggested that I might need water. We'd passed a stream about a half hour before, but we had no way to carry water, so there was nothing for it but to walk back. Oddly, I felt my energy returning at every step, and by the time we got to the stream, I actually felt better than I had since Sydney. I drank anyway, and we continued back toward Newnes. The pain increased again. It soon became clear that, in some way I couldn't understand, I was being forbidden to leave. Ingraham implored me to abandon the staff, but in the end he went back alone. He swore he'd come back soon with food, but I never saw him again. So much for his protestations of undying friendship. And I've been here ever since."

"What *did* you do for food?" said Ada.

"Not a damned thing," he said jauntily. "Whatever the staff is, whatever makes it tick, it gives eternal health, youth, and immunity from cold, thirst, and hunger."

"You could leave the stick here and go home," said Ada. "Don't tell me you're still trying to get one over on your dead brother. He's all, like, bones now."

"Oh, I thought of that," he said. "But it wasn't that simple. The staff had changed me—and not just in giving me eternal youth. I did try to make it back on my own after a time. If anything, the pain was worse. And my body was already starting to fade. I've been quite stuck. But at least now I'm corporeal, thanks to Marchand. Moreover, I have a very strong hunch that he's done me an even greater favor. The staff demands a servant, and it seems Marchand has taken on the job, leaving me free. Watching you stagger about as the staff made its claim was one of the loveliest sights I've ever beheld. I've spent nearly a century regretting my foolishness, and now it's time for me to return to England. In its own way, the staff has taught me much about human nature and how to manipulate it, and I'm sure it won't take long before I'm quite comfortably placed."

"Hoyle, what happened when you picked up the staff?" said Sybil, her voice sharp with worry.

Hoyle shook his head. He was having trouble finding words through the panic that was rising in him.

"We're leaving right now," she said. "Everyone back to the campsite to pack up."

"Well, *you* can go," Ivory said. "And so can I. But not Marchand. He's here forever."

Chapter 13

In Which Hoyle Must Learn

Some New Skills

There was a long, heavy moment, in which Hoyle had no idea what he was going to do next. He was aware of Oliver's horrified stare, Ada's rebellious scowl, Sybil's skeptical head-toss. None of these seemed like anything he wanted to do. It was only when he started gasping and wheezing with laughter that he found out he was panicking. He felt like he was standing next to himself, watching a pudgy, pathetic man fall to pieces. So much for the action hero, the wielder of knives, the finder of lost treasures.

As if through a pillow, he heard Ada saying, "Bullshit. Come on, Hoyle, let's go." He thought maybe she might be tugging on his hand, but it was hard to tell through his confusion. Was she yelling at him now? Why did everyone yell at him all the time?

He heard Ivory's voice, reverberating as though he spoke in a cathedral. *Marchand, for God's sake, buck up. It's not that bad. I've hardly minded at all.*

Ivory laughed, and the echoes piled up until Hoyle wondered if he really was going mad. *Look at you!* Ivory said. *What do you have to go back to?*

Hoyle tried to keep the thought from leaking out, but it was too late. *Nothing.* The word echoed like Ivory's laughter. *Nothing nothing nothing nothing!*

You see? said Ivory. *Do something noble with your life. If you let your friends try to get you out, you'll be putting them, as well as yourself, in danger. But if you agree to stay, they can return to their lives. Without you, they're safe. With you—well, the staff has its ways. This is your chance. Your moment to become a real hero, not just an eager, fawning imitation of one.*

Hoyle's face stung, and stung again. He flinched away, then realized he was sprawled on the ground, with Sybil slapping him.

"Come on," she said. "Time to go."

"But … Ivory said—"

"Never mind what he said." She seized one arm, Ada and Oliver seized the other, and they dragged him to his feet. Before he knew it, his arms were around their shoulders and he was being bustled toward the campsite. He twisted to look over his shoulder; Ivory was leaning carelessly against a tree.

"Oh, it's all right," he called. "Go ahead and try. I did. In fact, I'm going to have another go at leaving right now, and I'm sure I'll have rather more satisfactory results." With that, he started walking.

Hoyle lost sight of him almost instantly; being dragged along made it hard to focus. And something was worrying him. Something … was wrong. Wrong and getting more wrong with every step. The worry grew into fear, then terror. Suddenly he was screaming: "The staff! The staff!" Over and over the words tore from him, until they deteriorated into a horrible, hoarse wail that only stopped for Hoyle's hiccupping gasps before resuming.

"Leave it," hollered Sybil over the noise.

No, he couldn't. Utter loss carved through him. The agony of it made him sob and struggle and gave him strength. He broke away and stumbled back through the brush. He knew where it was, would always know. He threw himself down alongside it and lay his cheek along the wooden blade. Beautiful, cool calm flooded in as his wails became whimpers, and then ceased altogether. He lay there, heedless of everything but the relief, while the leaves waved overhead and the sunlight winked across his face.

He looked up to see three people standing around him. He blinked. They looked at him as if he should know them.

"Hoyle?" said one gently. "Come on now."

"Take the stick with you," said the second. "If it's that important."

"Guys," the third said, "I still don't like this."

"For God's sake, Oliver," said the first. "What choice do we have, other than to leave him here?"

"Why *don't* we leave him here? He seems happy enough."

"Leave me," Hoyle muttered. He worked hard to think of the words. "I'll be fine."

The first person snapped, "We'll do no such thing. I got you into this, and I'll get you out. Does *everyone* understand?"

Hoyle's thoughts were getting clearer. That one was … Sybil. And the middle one … what was her name? He liked her, she was nice to him. He frowned; sometimes she wasn't. In fact, none of them had been very nice to him recently. And it all came back: the bookshop, Sydney, camping, the fight in the woods, Nestor Ivory. And the staff. He reached for it, and once it was firmly in his grasp, he carefully sat up.

The others looked at him expectantly.

"Hi," he said.

"That's it?" said Ada. "After a scene like that, all you can say is 'hi'?"

Silence hung heavy.

"Um, what?" Hoyle said at last.

"Hoyle, we need to get out of here," said Sybil. "It's clearly not doing you any good, and the rest of us aren't having such a good time either. Let's try again. Take the staff if you need to. But let's try to go. We can get a fair bit of the way back before dusk."

"Ivory said I couldn't—"

"Pshyeah, like we're going to believe that twerp," said Ada. "We can at least check it out for ourselves, can't we?"

Hoyle shook his head, remembering the unreasoning terror and loss. "You go."

"I already told you, that's not going to happen, not without you."

Hoyle frowned. "But you don't even like me."

"Where did you get that idea?" said Sybil.

"For Christ's sake," said Ada, rolling her eyes. "Is that why you were being such a jerk?"

"You … well … you all—" Under their glaring outrage, he let his voice trail away.

"Look at the evidence, Hoyle, you idiot," said Sybil. "Here we all are. That kook who calls himself Ivory told us to go without you. *You* even told us to go without you. God knows we're eager enough to be out of here. Yet what do you see? Us, wasting time trying to get you to come with us. Why would we do that if we didn't like you?"

"Because … maybe … you felt sorry for me. Or something."

Sybil said, "Hoyle, listen to me. Listen carefully, because I have trouble saying this kind of thing and I won't be doing it very often in the future, if ever." She sat next to him and locked eyes with him. "I don't want to leave you here. I want you to come with me back to Sydney, and all the way back home. You've done more for me, with me, than any friend I've ever had. You trusted me when everybody else thought I was uncaring and harsh. Nobody but you has taken the trouble to see, whatever might be wrong with me, that at least I'm strong and I tell the truth. And I'm telling you the truth now: I really care about you, and I want you with me. Now please, let's go."

Hoyle was stunned, and suddenly even more afraid, horribly afraid. Now that he knew how she felt, that letting her down now would actually hurt her, the consequences were a thousand times worse. Not just a question of his own embarrassment and hurt feelings anymore. He had the power to really hurt her.

And God only knew how much power that was now. Ivory had talked about the staff changing him. Would he wake up one morning with the ability to kill with a thought? How much damage would he do without knowing until it was too late?

People dream about waking up with superpowers, he thought.

But it's a nightmare. Especially when you have no idea what they are.

"I—no, I have to stay here," he said, breaking eye contact with a convulsive turn of his head. "I don't know how dangerous this thing is, how dangerous I am."

"You can't be that dangerous, if you're anything like Nestor Ivory," said Ada. "He couldn't make anyone do anything, he had to trick you into taking the staff."

"That's a good point," said Sybil.

"Hey, thanks," said Ada in a surprised voice.

"But Hoyle is not Nestor Ivory. So Hoyle has a point, too: we don't really know what we're dealing with. Ivory's gone. Maybe it's a good idea after all to stay here for a few days until we know more. We have some food—and apparently Hoyle isn't going to need any for the moment, so that takes some pressure off. Okay, Hoyle, we'll stay here for a little while and see what's what before we head back. Okay?"

Oliver said, "What if the rest of the gang find us?"

"What, the anarchists?" said Ada. "I'm sick of them. Let 'em come, I'll show them just how self-actualized I can be with a big fucking rock."

"Last time they relied on surprise, and they were betting on the fact that they looked more intimidating than they are," said Sybil. "To tell the truth, they're just not that impressive when you get to know them. Are they, Oliver?"

After a second, Oliver smiled ruefully. "I guess not. I guess I should have taken a little more time to think things over before I came out here, shouldn't I?"

"We all do things on impulse sometimes," said Ada wisely.

Sybil said, "Ada, have you ever in your life *not* done something on impulse?"

Ada shrugged. "Can't think of an example, no."

Things were getting off track. "I can't go," Hoyle insisted. He had to make that clear.

Sybil said, "Let's wait until tomorrow to sort that out. Is that all right, Hoyle?"

"Sure," he said. But he was pretty sure he wouldn't be going anywhere.

* * *

Hoyle kept away from the others as they ate, chatted, slept. He wasn't hungry, wasn't tired. Lonely, though, he was that. And scared. But he had to ignore that. The idea was for him to experiment, see if he could find out anything that the staff did, or anything in himself that had changed. Except for the terrible need to have it with him every second, he didn't notice anything different about himself, but he admitted that he might not have the best perspective. So he let that question go for now.

Instead, hour after hour, he tried things he'd read about in stories: making things glow, or moving them without touching them, or trying to read the others' thoughts. All were spectacularly unsuccessful. As far as he could tell, the staff had been made solely for the purpose of keeping one gullible loser at a time pinned to a small piece of wilderness for no reason whatsoever.

It occurred to him that he only had Ivory's word that he couldn't leave. He'd found out the hard way that he couldn't leave the staff behind, but maybe there was nothing stopping him from leaving *with* the staff. And maybe its power would weaken as they got farther away.

There were some problems, though: how could he keep the others from accidentally touching the staff? And what if the anarchists came after them? How could he fight them without running the risk of enslaving them to the staff? He was hardly fond of them, but even they didn't deserve that.

The thought of the anarchists brought him around to the question of the big bloke. The more he pondered it, the less sense it made for Nestor Ivory to be the big bloke. Hoyle was now prepared to believe Ivory had been disembodied—where, after all, did weirdness end, once it had begun?—and therefore no threat to the anarchists. Whoever they were scared of, it wasn't Nestor Ivory. Was it the staff that drew so many freaks and misfits here, or was there yet a deeper attraction, of which the staff was just a manifestation, or a side effect?

Morning came, and the others got up. Sybil came over to him. "Find anything out?"

He felt suddenly shy, remembering what she'd said the day before. "Nothing much. I've found out a lot of things the staff *doesn't* seem to do, though."

Sybil sat down with contrived casualness, near but not too near. "Like what?"

Hoyle recounted his experiments. "And all I have to show for it is a headache," he finished. "I'm kind of unqualified for this sort of thing."

"None of us could do any better," she said.

"Maybe ..." he said after a moment.

"Mm?"

"Maybe I'm scared of finding anything, and that's why I'm not."

"Could be," she said. "Or could be that this is just the weirdest shit any of us have ever encountered in real life, and there are no rules." A smile appeared for an instant, and was gone. Hoyle tried to return it, without success.

Ada meandered toward them. Whenever Hoyle caught her eye, she looked away and pretended to peer at something growing near her feet, or checked for leeches. Finally she got close.

"Oh, hi," she said. "Sorry, didn't mean to disturb you, I was just ... oh, the hell with it. Look, Hoyle, I came over because I wanted to see how you're doing, but I'm shit-scared that some damn thing will, I don't know, possess you or something and you'll bash my head in like the big bloke did Ruby. So, like, are you going to?"

"No," said Hoyle.

Ada sighed. "Whew." She sat down heavily between Hoyle and

Sybil. "Now remember, you promised. I'm dying to know, right, so—are you hungry?"

"No."

"Sleepy?"

"No."

"Have you had to, you know, um, take a—"

"No."

"Wow, this might have its positive aspects."

"Ada," said Sybil wearily.

"What?"

"Not appropriate."

"I don't know why not. It's a whole new deal now. No point in being, what's the word? Oliver said it the other day. Oh, yeah, no point in being squeamish."

"It's okay, Sybil," said Hoyle. "I don't mind."

"Funny," said Ada. "This whole thing seems to have put you in a better mood."

"A matter of perspective, maybe," said Hoyle. "I guess I have bigger problems now."

"Um, anything I can do to help?"

Sybil stared, open-mouthed, at Ada, and Hoyle realized that this was probably the first time in Ada's life that she had actually *offered* to help someone. He tried desperately to think of something, lest he squelch her generous impulse.

"Um, yes, actually. I want to try something. Just stay there for a minute and relax, and see if you can tell me what I'm thinking."

"You're not going to burn my brain out or anything, are you?"

"Not that I know of."

"That doesn't make me feel very relaxed, you know." But she composed herself into a cross-legged pose and closed her eyes. "This is how you meditate. One of my cousins showed me. Not the Scouts one, another one. But he's also the one who thinks you shouldn't drink milk because it makes the cow your mother and that's unnatural, so I don't put too much faith in it."

"Ada, shh," said Sybil.

"Oh. Right."

Might as well give it a try, thought Hoyle. *Hot dogs. Ada, you want to eat a hot dog.*

"Anything?" he asked.

"Nope," Ada replied, eyes still closed. "Try again. Lots of people have told me I'm a bit thick; maybe you have to punch through a little harder."

Hoyle squeezed his own eyes shut. *Hot dogs! Hot dogs!*

"Nope," said Ada. "Oh, well. At least you didn't burn my brain out."

From a hundred yards away came Oliver's voice. "Aaaaarrgh! Why don't we have any bloody HOT DOGS?"

Ada's eyes snapped open, and she gave Hoyle a shrewd look. "Hot dogs, was it? Looks like someone's on someone else's wavelength."

"I don't get it, I'm a vegetarian!" wailed Oliver as he stomped through the brush in their direction. "I've never even liked hot dogs. Suddenly it's all I can think of. What is this? Am I pregnant?"

"I hardly think so," called Sybil. She murmured to Hoyle, "For God's sake, switch it off before he goes crazy."

"I don't know how," he whispered frantically.

"Just do it!"

No, no hot dogs. Everything's like it was before. You don't like hot dogs, they're disgusting.

Oliver stopped in his tracks. "It's ... I don't ... wow, that was weird." He shook his head like a wet dog, and said, "Hot dogs aren't actually why I was on my way over. I've been thinking, and the more I think, the less sense it makes that that Ivory guy was the big bloke. Who'd be scared of him? Were any of you?"

Ada frowned. "Not really, I guess. Pissed off, more than anything."

"Maybe a little," said Hoyle. "He seemed to hold all the cards.

And look what I'm stuck with now. So he really was dangerous."

"But we only found that out later. Before that, he wasn't *scary*. The others were all *scared* of the big bloke."

"Shit, Oliver," said Ada. "How many more loonies are there out here that you haven't told us about?"

"No matter how many there are, we need to get out of here," said Sybil. "Hoyle, do you feel like you're ready to try leaving here with the staff? We'll just do a little trial walk, okay? Not too far until we know."

Terror rose inside him, but he struggled to ignore it. "Okay. Right now, please. I don't want to sit brooding about it."

They got to their feet, and Sybil took out the map and her GPS. "That way. We'll just go very slowly, see how Hoyle reacts."

Hoyle carried the staff vertically, clutched close, both to keep it from touching any of the others and because he felt better that way. They set off.

Hoyle's breath started coming in gasps almost immediately.

"That may just be nerves," said Sybil. "Can you tough it out?"

Hoyle nodded and tried to steady himself. It wasn't long, though, before he started feeling nausea squirm in his stomach. *Psychosomatic, psychosomatic*, he chanted silently. But the symptoms came on relentlessly: headache, shaking limbs, all-over aching, and the same growing despair and panic as the day before. He struggled on, step after step, hearing his own weeping through the roaring in his ears.

He turned and ran back and let himself collapse at the spot where he'd been sitting.

No, he wasn't going to be going anywhere.

Chapter 14

In Which Hoyle Is Left to

His Own Devices

They sat in the darkness as the night approached. They'd spent all day avoiding a discussion of what had happened.

Finally Hoyle took a deep breath and said, "You'll be out of food soon. You can't risk going back to the anarchists for food—they'll feed you, sure, but they've probably learned a lot about how to guard prisoners. You're just going to have to leave me here and go back to Sydney."

"What if—" began Sybil.

"I appreciate that you don't want to leave me. But I'm not in any physical danger, and you are."

"We don't want to *protect* you, you dickhead," said Ada. "We're your *mates*. Mates don't leave mates to, um, be immortal and that. Out all alone. In the bush."

Sybil said, "Exactly."

Hoyle felt a rush of relief that they wanted to stay, but was suddenly aware that Oliver had remained silent. "All right," he said, before Oliver could start arguing. "Thanks."

"Just so you know," said Ada, "we weren't looking for your permission."

"But what are we going to *do*?" said Oliver, with a touch of whininess.

"The way I see it," said Sybil, "we have three main tasks. First, we have to find a way to … disconnect Hoyle from the staff.

Second, we have to disable the staff so nobody else gets trapped. Third, we have to avoid the anarchists, the big bloke—whoever he is—and Ivory long enough to get back to Sydney."

"What makes you think Ivory is still here?" said Hoyle. "He seemed pretty bent on getting away."

"If you can't leave, I'm betting he can't leave," said Sybil. "It can't have been as easy as all that to foist the staff off on someone else."

Oliver said, "But now won't he need food and shelter and—"

"Not important."

"It's important if he starts stealing *our* food," said Oliver.

"Hoyle can guard it while we sleep."

"Oh," said Hoyle. "Yes. I can." Ada could be right, this whole situation might have advantages, here and there.

"So," Sybil continued. "As I was starting to say quite some time ago, what if we use tomorrow to look around for any clues, artifacts, tracks, any sort of information that might help us get a better picture of what's going on here, and what the staff is? Oliver, I want you to spend some time writing down everything—everything—you remember about the staff, the big bloke, and Ruby. I know it's going to be painful, but it's important. Okay?"

"Uh-huh," murmured Oliver.

"Ada, you and I will do the looking. Hoyle, I'd like you to use tomorrow to keep trying to figure the staff out. Now, sleep. Hoyle, thanks for standing watch."

"No problem."

Hoyle noticed, amused, that Ada and Sybil were going into different tents; clearly Ada and Oliver were taking advantage of Hoyle's wakefulness to bunk together. But Oliver was still sitting there.

"Hoyle?" he said.

"Mm-hm?"

"What's it feel like?"

"What does what feel like?"

Oliver fumbled for words, then said, "Th-that. The staff. Being connected to it. Do you feel, like, electricity? Or something? Power? Do you feel powerful?"

Hoyle frowned. Did he? "No, not powerful. You sort of have to know what you're doing to feel powerful, don't you? Even electricity can't *do* anything unless you know how to *make* it do something."

"So, what do you feel?"

"So far, most of the time all I've felt is scared. And kind of … horrified. Like when someone tells you really bad news and you have to try and understand it." He gave a hollow laugh. "Right before I left, I lost my job and found out my house had termites and most of my books were ruined. That seems really straightforward now, I could handle that. Nowhere near as complicated as being enslaved by a magic stick that makes me yearn for death when I disobey."

"Yeah, but, like—hey, try and do something."

Hoyle remembered how alarmingly easy it had been to make Oliver want a hot dog. "Not tonight. I'm tired. I don't know what will happen. It's dangerous."

"Oh. Okay. It's just—it would be cool to know."

"Yeah. Well, good night, Oliver."

"Good night."

Hoyle stared out at the forest, listening for Nestor Ivory.

Do I feel powerful? How would I know? I don't know what powerful feels like.

* * *

"What, exactly, are we looking for?" said Ada. "This adventure sure has a lot of looking in it."

"*This* time," said Sybil, "we're looking for anything that isn't normal."

"None of this looks normal to me. Streets and buildings and broken bottles and that, that's what's normal."

"Just do your best. You'll do fine, you're smart."

Ada looked taken aback. "You reckon?"

"Of course," said Sybil casually. "Now, let's get to work."

Sybil and Ada set off together, and soon Hoyle could see them walking slowly side by side, eyes scanning the leaves and brush at their feet.

Oliver sat by the tents, back against a tree, writing in Sybil's notebook. Sometimes he would look over at Hoyle, watching him for a minute or two, then go back to writing.

Hoyle was having another try at figuring out the staff. At least, that's what he was intending to do. But the task was overwhelming him to the point of stupor. *I seem to know how to make Oliver want to eat a hot dog, and that's the sum of it*, thought Hoyle resentfully. Once again, he was revealed as totally inadequate to this adventure's demands. He sat, eyes closed, as the flies buzzed around him and the heat of the day began to build.

The insects made a droning, atonal chord that ebbed and flowed. Soon it covered the sounds of Ada's and Sybil's voices, the rustling of the leaves, the scratching of Oliver's pen. He felt like he was floating in a buzzing sea that was the warm, rich color of the sunlight through his eyelids.

Through the buzz he began to hear a whisper—at first it was only a vague spitting and hissing, but soon it resolved into something that almost sounded like speech, like words he couldn't quite figure out. He strained to hear them, and gradually they became clearer.

"That's it … let go of everything and just listen."

"Oh, God, now what?" Hoyle said.

"Shhhhhhh! Listen. This is hard enough as it is, old boy."

Hoyle's eyes snapped open—Ivory! Rage flooded him, and his hands clenched to strike.

"Not quite. Not quite. I mean, yes, but no. *Nicholas* Ivory. First-born and heir."

"Jesus Christ, is there no end to you freaks? Go away, okay? Hasn't my life already been ruined?"

"Yes, old boy, I saw it all happen."

"What do you want?"

"I finally had Nestor, nearly had him. Year after year of careful work—*that* close to snuffing out his miserable life. Then you, you bumbling, fatuous fool, you had to find the staff. You had to pick it up, accept the power. You had no idea how to control it. He knew he could siphon it from you and regain his body—the body I've spent a hundred years wearing away, at great cost to myself, so that he would finally float away forever. You stupid, stupid man." The venom in his voice was terrifying.

"Why couldn't—"

"Why couldn't I kill Nestor right out? The same reason I can't kill you, unless I take another hundred years at it. You're the servant of the staff."

"I told you—I don't want it. Take it."

"I missed my chance," said the voice bitterly. "Nestor ensured I'd be distracted at the crucial moment. It's only in the transfer that the power can be accessed by someone else. Nestor figured that out before I did, I'll grant him that. I'm just going to have to find another way. For example, you didn't let your friends touch the staff. That was wise. And foolish. For now they have no protection."

Hoyle wasted no more words. He leapt up, grabbing the staff without thinking, and ran through the bush to find the others. "Sybil! Ada! Oliver! You have to go now. Pack up and go *now*," he cried. "Come on, move, move! Get back to camp, pack up."

He found Sybil first. "Ivory's brother. Nicholas. He's here, too, and he's even meaner. He wants to get revenge on me by hurting you. Loyalty or no loyalty, you have to go now. You're his only hold on me, the only way he can hurt me."

"Whoa, whoa, whoa," said Sybil. "Nicholas Ivory? Where?"

"I really don't feel like wasting time trying to make you believe me. Just help me round up the others, pack your stuff, and get out of here."

Sybil stared at him for a long moment while he fidgeted with impatience. "All right," she said at last. "If it were just me, I'd take my chances and stay with you. But Ada and Oliver are another matter. Come on, they were over this way, last I heard them."

When they were all together, Hoyle went over it all again.

"I don't get it," said Ada.

"It doesn't matter," said Oliver urgently. "The big bloke is after us."

"Oh, you, you see the big bloke behind every tree," Ada said disgustedly. Oliver wilted.

"No, Hoyle is right, and so is Oliver," said Sybil. "It's not just a question of keeping him company anymore. Time to go."

"So you're just going to leave him?" said Ada.

"No, *we're* going to leave him."

"It's all right, Ada, he can't hurt me," said Hoyle.

"You're just trying to be brave, but really, you want us to stay," said Ada. "Deep down."

"No," said Hoyle frantically. "What will it take before you—"

"Let's *go*," said Sybil.

It took about twenty minutes for them to pack up the camp, Hoyle standing guard, ready to use the staff to flail, poke, bludgeon whatever form in which Nicholas Ivory would appear. He watched Sybil take a bearing, as he'd watched so many times before. He swallowed hard to stifle the mixture of tenderness, gratitude, resentment, and fear that threatened to make him cry. Then Sybil and the others said a brusque goodbye, promised they'd wait for him in Sydney, and set off without him.

* * *

Hoyle sat on a fallen tree, the staff across his knees, as the sun went down. He spent the time thinking of each of them in turn. Ada, brave and brash and ready for anything, yet—even after the life she'd had—still eager to be friends if you took the risk to care about her. Oliver, desperate to figure everything out, to do important things—Hoyle remembered being like that.

And Sybil. She was so strong and capable, it had taken him forever to start seeing how she cared about people. She'd taken Ada under her wing, and Oliver. *And me*, he thought. But it wasn't like that now. She'd wanted to stay by him not to protect him, but to be his friend. And she'd believed him instantly when he'd said they were in danger—she didn't debate, or double-check, or present her own theory. "You need to go," he'd said. And she'd gone.

He thought back, embarrassed, to how intrigued he'd been at Ada's sly hints that Sybil was attracted to him. How easily he would have settled for that. Instead, he had something far better: her trust. Her respect. Her friendship. Loneliness welled in him, adding to the fear and frustration he already felt. He longed to have her with him, to lean against her determination and competence—not to shelter behind her, but to battle alongside her against this power that he didn't understand.

He had to find some way to defeat the staff and get back to Sydney, back to Sybil and the others. It wouldn't be enough just to break the staff's hold on him; he wanted to destroy it forever. And hopefully the Ivory brothers would fade away for good, once its power no longer fed them.

He looked with disgust and hatred at the staff, and felt it pulsing against the palm of his hand. The shock of realization hit him: that's why the staff needed a servant. To feed it hatred. It gave its servant just those powers it would need to stir up loathing and animosity: wickedly clear insights into others' thoughts and feelings, the force of will to influence weak minds. He knew, suddenly, why he now perceived so much about his friends that had escaped him before. Why it was so easy to make Oliver crave a hot dog. He breathed a sigh of relief that he'd been quick enough to send them away, before he'd made them hate him. Before he'd started controlling them, using them, despising them.

The staff had no need to make him cherish it. It was enough, more than enough, that he couldn't escape it. The power of his hatred only made the staff stronger, in a hideous cycle. But humans hated; the story of humanity was the story of wave after wave of rage and fear, mistrust and contempt, between individuals, nations, and every size group in between. How was he going to starve the staff of hatred, weak and fearful and spiteful as he was?

He forced himself to face his failings as evening came on. He must despair: he was not brave enough, nor good enough, to defeat the staff. His only choice was to stay here and try, for the next how many hundred years, to keep the staff away from anyone else.

His powerlessness brought on the tears yet again. *I am really, really tired of crying*, he thought. But he could not stop, and the sound of his sobs rang through the nighttime woods. Finally they ebbed, and he looked up to see stars in constellations he could not name. Except for the birds and animals he heard moving or calling, he was alone.

"Ah, capital," said Nicholas out of the darkness. "They're gone. Thanks, old boy, you've done quite the right thing, at least for my purposes. Now we can get to work."

Chapter 15

In Which There Is a Setback

Hoyle tried several times to speak. Finally, he managed to say, "What?"

Nicholas said, "You can't leave here. I know that all too personally. But if you help me, I think I can. Which means I have one last chance to stop Nestor before he gets back to Sydney and it's too late."

A hand came out of the darkness and seized Hoyle's hand where it gripped the staff.

"Ahhhhhh," said Nicholas.

Hoyle tried to pull away as he felt energy pulsing through him in a disquieting rhythm. The pulses started to hurt, and Hoyle heard his voice squeak in weak, panting cries. Finally, using a part of his brain he hadn't known about, he lashed out in desperation. Nicholas cried out, and Hoyle wrenched his hand away.

"You bastard," Nicholas gasped. Hoyle could see that he was taller, broader, and much more handsome than his brother. No wonder Nestor had felt overshadowed. And Hoyle guessed that Nicholas would have been unused to challenge, once Nestor had begun rebelling. It had clearly been a volatile mix, the two of them wintering in that cabin in Newnes. Hatred would have seethed, making both of them perfect fodder for the staff.

Nicholas interrupted Hoyle's thoughts by making a lunge for the staff.

"Stop it," Hoyle cried petulantly. He lashed out again with his thoughts, but an instant later dropped to the ground, clutching his pounding head.

Nicholas laughed. "You caught me unawares the first time. But the staff taught *me* a few tricks, too. And I've known it far longer than you. You might as well let me have it."

"I've already offered it to you, you idiot," cried Hoyle, although shouting made his head hurt even worse.

"I'll take you at your word, then. I'm warning you, Nestor couldn't do it. But he's less than a man, always has been. Shall we see whether you're better?"

Hoyle no longer cared whether anyone else thought he was brave. He hadn't been able to stand having the staff wrested from him—would things be different if he chose to relinquish it? He didn't give a damn about stopping Nestor, but he could be free, he could go back to Sydney, back to Sybil. "All right," he said.

Nicholas said, "Don't fight me. It will feel like I'm ripping out your soul. There is no pain like it. Nestor and I learned that quickly, as we struggled for it, back at the beginning. Be very, very still and let me take the staff. Lie down here, in the clear area. You'll thrash around, and there's no point in giving yourself a concussion against a tree."

Hoyle lay down obediently.

"Let your hand just rest on the staff for a moment. Stop gripping it."

Hoyle's hand ached. He actually had to sit up and use his left hand to carefully pry loose each finger of his right. Then he lay back down.

"Think of release, think of peace, think of deep, untroubled breaths," droned Nicholas. "Close your eyes, remember your life before this place. Remember calm days and laughing nights."

Hoyle tried, but he couldn't call any to mind. *And that's what I get for living the life I have*, he thought bitterly. *And now I'm finally having adventures, like I always wanted, finally not being so ordinary, and look at me: lying on the ground, pitiful, weak.*

"No," cried Nicholas, making Hoyle jump. "Not like that. Calm, blast you! Deep breaths. A child could do it."

"You're not helping," snapped Hoyle. *Holy crap, I'm even a failure at doing nothing.*

Nicholas sighed. "Let's try it again. This time, just close your eyes and lie still. Can you do that?"

Hoyle did as Nicholas had said, feeling his stomach rise and fall as he breathed deeply. The staff lay at his side, warm and buzzing slightly, like the speaker from a stereo in the silence between songs. The buzzing spread from his hand up his arm to his head, and up and down along his spine. It was not unpleasant—soothing, even. He relaxed into it, letting it fill him. The instant he began to think about losing the staff, about missing Sybil and the others, about anything, the buzzing receded, leaving him feeling empty and mean. He soon caught the knack of focusing only on the staff, and how it sang through his body.

In an instant, everything contracted to a pinpoint of shock, then exploded into agony. With the tiny piece of himself he was still aware of, he thought, *Let him take it. Be free of it! Without it, you can—you can—*

He trembled as his torture went on and on, wracking him as it seared white-hot across his body.

He did not notice the sun rising, did not hear the birds waking. He was trapped in a roaring hell of loss and pain.

* * *

When Hoyle finally was able to think, look around him, and move his aching limbs, the sun was at its mid-morning height. Flies were crawling on his face; he raised a feeble hand to brush them away.

"Nicholas?" he murmured, but with a feeling of sick despair he realized he still knew where the staff was, and that it was close. Nicholas had lied. Hoyle was still a slave—all his suffering was for nothing. Less than nothing, because Nicholas had regained the staff, and what might he do with it?

Hoyle shook as he tried to stand, then gave up. He'd have to rest for a while longer. He pushed his brain to keep thinking. Nicholas would doubtless be on Nestor's trail. Maybe the connection had been weakened, and Hoyle would be able to leave.

But which way? He no longer had any idea. He didn't know how to track Sybil and the others. He couldn't even remember where the sun had been when they'd set out from Newnes. If he stayed here, he would probably die—there was no knowing how much of the staff's power of preservation he still retained. If he started walking, there was at least some chance that eventually he'd find water, and maybe even a fire road or a power line.

He still had his pack, and in his pack was still his compass. He'd pick a bearing and just stick with it as closely as possible. He tried hard to remember the map: which direction had they taken from Newnes? About sixty degrees. That meant the back bearing was … um … two hundred and forty degrees? Better than a random guess, anyway. He put his pack on, took the bearing, and started to walk.

He found hiking much easier now; whether that was because the staff had lent him stamina, he'd gotten fitter in general, or he no longer cared about petty discomforts, he didn't know, but it was a welcome discovery. The day wore, and he made his slow, resigned way through the scrub and trees that stood between him and, perhaps, liberation. He kept waiting for the anxiety of leaving the staff to start up, but it never did; that, too, was a nice surprise.

It was only when, as he walked along a gully with a sullen little stream at the bottom, that he started to realize why: in the mud was a footprint, and leading up the hill from it, a faint trail in the brush. The weight of his pack settled onto his hips as his shoulders sagged. He had been working his way back to the anarchists' camp. He didn't miss the staff because he'd been following it. And Nicholas.

If the anarchists came here to get water, they'd be along sooner or later. He needed to sneak away right now. Even though he was pretty sure his usefulness to Nicholas was at an end, the anarchists might still be eager to please him by capturing Hoyle. And Hoyle didn't want the delay, the danger, or the torment of having the staff so close, but inaccessible to him.

He began moving much more carefully, trying hard not to make noise or leave footprints. He labored up the gully to where the trail resumed, stopping every few steps to listen. He heard nothing for another half hour's walking, but as he crossed a large clearing with little bushes and weird, hip-high mounds of tan mud, he turned his head sharply toward the trees—there were voices. He ducked behind one of the mounds and took off his pack to lower his profile. A slow, cautious look showed him two of the anarchists walking about fifty yards away.

"Why can't we just let him go?" said one—Spike, Hoyle remembered. "We go back, say we saw some tracks, but couldn't find him. Then the big bloke will be happy, and this guy's mates will think he took off to Sydney looking for them, and that's it. And it's probably the truth, anyway. Let the poor bastard get away, Marco. Hasn't he been through enough?"

"But the others—if he's gone, they're not hostages anymore, just prisoners. And you know what the big bloke is going to do to them."

"Yeah," said Spike grimly. "You're right, then—we have to keep looking. I don't want their blood on my hands."

The others—Sybil, Ada, and Oliver had been recaptured. Hoyle's heart sank. He circled carefully, keeping the mound between himself and the anarchists, and trying hard not to make any noise. Were they heading out, or could he follow their path to get back to the camp? He had to do something. They'd gotten away once; they could again, Nicholas or no Nicholas.

Staff or no staff.

Hoyle swallowed. He had no choice but to follow the anarchists. He marked their direction, then, once they were too far away to hear the noise, rummaged in his pack to grab anything small enough to carry that might be useful. Even with the new stamina and coordination the staff had given him, he couldn't move quietly or quickly enough with his pack on.

He darted through the woods after the anarchists. He no longer stumbled and skidded, but ran from cover to cover with a confidence that felt good. He started to feel like everything would work out. He'd help his friends escape, they'd get away from both Nicholas and the staff, and he would be free. They'd go back to Sydney. Maybe Ada and Oliver would want to come to America. Ada would like America. And Sybil would stay his friend, they'd be friends forever. And on Sundays they'd go looking for second-hand books together.

He followed the anarchists, sunk in his daydreams, until he nearly ran onto them. Evening was falling, and they had made their way back to the camp; Hoyle could see the clearing a little way away. He let them get ahead, then followed them with renewed wariness. Near the camp, close enough to hear the anarchists talking, he found another of the tan dirt mounds to hide behind. He let his breathing quiet down, his heart slow. He'd learned over the last day or so the benefits of using the odd capabilities that the staff had given him.

Could he sense the staff anywhere close? Nicholas? Sybil?

A moment later, a heaving wave of pale, distorted insects poured from the mound.

Hoyle suddenly realized what they were.

Termites. They'd chosen that exact moment to swarm.

He leaped up, frantically scraping them off his body, shrieking with disgust and fear. He was vaguely aware of people running up to him. He forced himself to stop, even though he could still feel termites crawling on him.

A voice called out from across the clearing. "Run, Hoyle! Jesus Christ, run! Run, you dipshit!"

Hoyle was surrounded. And whatever powers the staff was

giving him, he didn't think they included actual flight. "Too late, Ada," he called back.

"Too right, old boy," said Nicholas. He was empty-handed, but Hoyle could sense the power of the staff radiating from him. "Come along. We'll just pop you over with the others for now. It's not a permanent solution, but it will do."

Chapter 16
In Which the Anarchists
Descend into Anarchy

"Why do I have to do it?" whined Tommy, the one Dianne had assigned to guard duty. "I'll tell you one thing, I'm not going to put up with being knifed again." He cast a murderous look in Hoyle's direction. Ada, who was sitting next to Hoyle, waved cheerily.

"Jesus, Hoyle," she muttered out of the corner of her mouth. "You've pissed off every single person here. It's like your super-power."

"Ada, please don't. I'm not at my best right now." That wasn't strictly true. He felt more vibrant, more restless, than he ever had in his life. He wanted to be making things happen, solving problems, saving his friends, destroying—

Destroying the staff?

He was starting to be afraid of what that would mean: a return to his timid, soft, passive self. Did he really want that?

But I'll be trapped here. Sybil and Ada will go back, and my only friends will be these anarchists. Who hate me. Oh, and Nicholas. Who hates me.

He noticed Nicholas staring at him, a strangely wistful expression on his face. Hot, exhilarating rage boiled up inside Hoyle, and without conscious thought he rocked forward, ready to leap to his feet and punch him.

Oh, no, old boy, came Nicholas's voice inside Hoyle's head.

Don't even think about it. The staff protects you, but it also means you can never surprise me.

Ada said, "Easy, tiger. You look like you want to punch someone out."

"I do."

"That guy, Nicholas, right? Look, Hoyle, one thing I've learned a lot about is who's going to win a fight. I can tell even before the first punch. Take it from me and settle the fuck down." She looked intently at him for a moment. "On the other hand, you're … you …"

"Yes?" said Hoyle irritably.

"You're not your old self, are you?"

"Would you be?"

"No, not like that. You're … tougher."

"That's a good thing, right?"

"Not in your case."

Hoyle turned away.

"See?" Ada continued. "You're just not very nice anymore."

Hoyle frowned. "Where's Sybil?"

"No, don't change the subject."

"Okay, I'm not very nice. Blame the staff." Whatever the staff was, wherever it came from, whatever it did. Who knew what it was capable of? Was whoever made it good, or evil, or something else entirely? If he knew the answers, he might be able to figure out what to do. As it was, he just had to let it keep doing what it did. Just keep … waiting. The passivity of it all disgusted him.

"No," said Ada, "I'm not going to blame the staff. I'm going to blame you. Even before the staff, you were shitting everyone. Why?"

Hoyle shrugged. "Maybe that's my true self. Maybe that's why the staff won't let me go. It knows I'm just its type."

"Well, sure, if you think that, it's going to be true. I spent a long time thinking I was a bad person, but then you and Sybil—so, anyway. Yeah."

Hoyle turned back at the catch in her voice. She was rubbing her eyes.

"Hey," he said, feeling helpless.

"Just stop being a jerk, okay?" said Ada from behind her hands. "I have enough jerks in my life."

Spike's voice rose from across the compound. "No! Look where your 'leadership' got us. Ever since Ruby died, you've had one bad idea after another. I'm sick of following you down into failure again and again."

"Are you saying you could have managed things any better? What about *him*?" shouted Dianne, gesturing toward Nicholas. "Even Ruby couldn't do anything about *him*."

"And what is he? Some poor, sad nerd who wanders around in an explorer costume, that's all he is."

"Spike, for God's sake, have you forgotten what he did?"

"Killed Ruby? I'm not afraid of him anymore. Hear that, big bloke? Do your fucking worst!"

"I didn't," shrieked Nicholas suddenly. "I didn't kill her."

"Then who did?" Spike's voice was thick with rage. "Who did? Of course it was you." He rushed at Nicholas—and went straight through him to sprawl in the dirt.

Several voices cried out.

Spike struggled to his feet. "Yeah, you're quick, you bastard. But I can still—" He threw himself at Nicholas again.

"Spike, stop," someone cried, too late: Spike fell again. Blood seeped from his nose. Everyone else stared at Nicholas.

Long moments passed, then Ada said, "Holy shit, are you, like, a ghost?"

Nicholas said dully, "I don't know what I am."

Hoyle felt his brain whirl. He'd been afraid of Nicholas, but it had all been a bluff.

Nicholas raised his head and stared into Hoyle's eyes. *Don't be too sure*, came the thought. *I can't touch a thing except the staff, it's true. A hundred years in its service, and I'm just about at the end of being able to even make you see and hear me. Why do you think I needed you to find the staff? I knew exactly where it was, I heard it, I felt it, just as you feel it. But could I move the stones and dirt to pick it up? Not even the leaves, old boy, not one leaf could I brush aside. The staff is the only thing left that I can feel now in all the world. Nestor and I both needed your hands to get it for me.*

A wave of dark-grey despair rolled from Nicholas, and Hoyle made a little mewling sound at the overwhelming bitterness of it all.

Yes, said Nicholas's voice in Hoyle's head. *That's what it's like. That's what you have to look forward to. Any wonder I'm desperate to escape it? But that's not the only reason I want to leave. I'm after Nestor as soon as the staff will let me go, because if he can, he'll try to shed that despair by forcing it on everyone he meets. He's an animal, Marchand. I have to find a way to get out of here and stop him. Like Nestor, I thought if the staff had another servant, we would be free. Apparently it's not that simple. And apparently there's some difference between Nestor and me, because he got away, and I didn't.*

Hoyle shook his head, trying to free it of Nicholas's oppressive emotions. *Then why are you still here? Why don't you just ... throw the staff away and beat it?*

Because I'm a fool. Because I should have known the staff wouldn't let me go. Or you. Or Nestor, but damned if I know where he is, the little bastard.

"If the big bloke is just some sort of ... shared delusion, there's no reason for me to be here," said Spike. "None! I'm going."

"Me too," said another voice. "At least in Sydney I'm not worried about getting bashed like Ruby."

"I am," said a third, "but it's still better than here."

Everyone scattered across the campsite and began packing up gear. Everyone except Dianne, who stood watching the colony disintegrate, her eyes wide with horror and despair.

"Wow," said Oliver. "It's like the fall of the Berlin Wall around here."

At that moment, Dianne threw back her head and let out a wild, desolate, animal howl.

Everybody froze.

The howl went on and on. Dianne gulped a panicky breath, and it started again. Long, tearing sounds, horrible to hear, until her voice went ragged, and then hoarse.

Sybil strode purposefully up to her and shook her. "Dianne!"

The wails were now mere air rasping past Dianne's ruined throat.

Hoyle ran to Sybil. "Are you nuts? This is your chance. You can go, and nobody will stop you. Go! Just go. Christ, Sybil, go, get Ada and Oliver out of here. The only danger here now is that Nicholas may still be able to hurt you, even if he can't touch you."

Dianne started randomly hitting out towards Sybil, but Sybil deftly blocked the blows. Yet another thing she was good at—was there no end to them?

Sybil stepped out of range, and Dianne stood, silent at last. Sybil stared at Hoyle with an odd, dark intensity. "I'll be back."

"I'll wait," said Hoyle, as gently as he could.

"Okay, Ada, Oliver, let's go," shouted Sybil. "Now, now, now. Move."

"What about—" said Ada.

"Move." Sybil was implacable, and once again, Hoyle watched them disappear into the bush. Dianne had sunk to the ground, and now sat rocking, silently and ceaselessly. Within a half hour, the camp was deserted, except for Nicholas, Hoyle, and Dianne. The anarchists had left food, water, and utensils for Dianne ("We're sick of her, but we're not monsters," one had commented right before he left), and most of the tents were still set up. Hoyle stood awkwardly near Dianne, who stared dully. Nicholas was nowhere to be seen.

"Nicholas?" called Hoyle.

"Yes, what?" Nicholas stepped from the bush into the campsite.

"You didn't even *try* to stop them going. What does that staff really do, if it doesn't make you able to boss people around?"

"I never controlled them at all, you idiot. All that talk about the big bloke? That was a fiction concocted by this wretch." He gestured contemptuously at Dianne. "She's the one who wanted to keep everyone here. She used the occasional sightings the others had of Nestor and me—mainly me, as there wasn't much left to see of Nestor by the time they got here—to terrify them into staying. 'Oh, we can't go, the big bloke will get us.' You have no idea how much I do wish I could throttle her. Do you know how far she was willing to go to keep control over the others? As far as murder itself. I didn't kill Ruby, she did."

Nicholas waited a moment for that to sink in, then continued. "Doesn't look much like a killer now, does she, old boy? But I can assure you, she was willing to do anything—*anything*—to keep what happened just now from happening. What you see, Marchand, is a terrified despot whose worst fears have come true. And, as with all despots, you see what's left when her power disintegrates. And I could do nothing at all in return—until you found the staff. And now, what could I do worse to her than has already happened? Look at her."

Hoyle frowned. Despot, he could believe. But … killer? "She seems pretty shook up for just losing some lackeys. In fact, she doesn't look angry or anything I'd expect. She looks … horrified. Like now something really, really bad is going to happen and she can't stop it."

Dianne raised her head, and her eyes slowly focused on Hoyle. "Can't stop it," she rasped. "Can't stop it. Can't stop it."

Hoyle asked carefully, "Can't stop what, Dianne?"

"You know. I know you know. You're with them, with him." Dianne twitched her chin toward Nicholas. "Ruby, she wanted him, too. Only ever thinking of herself. Oh, so handsome, so dashing, so tragic, him and his damned stick. Them and their tragic doomed love. Ruby only ever thought of herself. She never cared what would happen if she left, if anyone left. I was keeping them all safe, keeping myself safe, keeping the secret safe. And now there's only me. And no secret. They'll take it with them and spread it. All over Sydney. All over Australia. All over, all over the world, all over. And then do you know what will happen, stupid fat American? The hate will follow. You won't be stuck here anymore, fat man. You'll be able to go anywhere the hate goes. And the stick will capture more and more. Why do you think they put it here? So, so far from Sydney. And Australia so, so far from anywhere. They should have thought, they should have known there would eventually be tracks instead of roo trails. And then roads instead of tracks. Cars instead of feet. And boats and then planes to bring more and more feet to Australia. They should have known that human beings can't stand the thought of anywhere too far for them to reach and to trample and to take. But him," another spasmodic jerk of the chin, "he got this far and then he was stuck. And then we got here, and, oh, God, we didn't know. Ruby, stupid booby Ruby, fell in love. *I* knew what would happen. *I* knew she would try to run away with him. But he was better off here. I was ready. I saved us all. I knew he couldn't leave without her. Wouldn't, couldn't, couldn't, wouldn't, it didn't matter, it couldn't matter. I could stop *her*. So I did. I could and I did. And everything would have been fine, they were all fine with staying here. Here trying to make their fucking new society. Until you got here—the vector that would spread the plague at last. Didn't you wonder, fat man, why they were so useless? So dissolute? Where all their drive had gone? Why were they so aimless? Well, guess, fat man. Guess. I kept them that way. I did it. I broke their hearts and sapped their dreams. I killed Ruby. Why? To save every single idiot on this planet."

Is this true? Hoyle asked Nicholas silently. The last thing he wanted to do was to speak out loud and remind Dianne that Nicholas was still there.

Which part? came Nicholas's thought, wry and bitter.

All of it, any of it!

Dianne grew still. "He's here, isn't he? No, don't bother

answering. And I still can't hurt him. Because the stick still exists. If I touch it, I'll be like him, like you, full of hate. And I won't even want to destroy it anymore."

Hoyle said, "I'm not full of hate."

Dianne snorted.

"No, really. I'm not. And—"

"And what, fat man?"

"And I want to destroy the staff."

"If Ruby couldn't do it, if I couldn't, if *he* couldn't, what makes you think you can? What makes you different from *him*?"

Hoyle felt a sudden quickening of interest from Nicholas; the intensity of it confused him into silence. Dianne's eyes narrowed in contempt; shame shot through him. But he was different from Nicholas, and from Nestor. He saw now, very clearly, all the ways Sybil and Ada had been showing him, all along, that they loved and valued him. He was no ordinary person, if he could gain *their* trust. He was something special, because they thought he was. That staff hadn't known what it was in for, messing with Hoyle Marchand. He stood a little straighter, and felt a power ringing inside him that had nothing to do with the staff.

"I know the difference between loving something and craving it," he said. "I know the difference between caring for people and possessing them. I know what it's like to be ... *better*, a better person, for seeing a friend's smile. I finally know what it is to feel happy sitting next to someone, just because they're glad you're there. I understand how you could literally rather die than see that someone hurt or afraid. That's why I can do what he couldn't."

A look of surprise slowly emerged on Dianne's face. She rubbed her eyes, wiped her hands on her shorts, and flicked her hair back. "All right, then," she said. "You'd better hope that's enough."

Inside Hoyle's head, Nicholas murmured, *Good luck, old boy.*

Hoyle couldn't decide whether he sounded sarcastic or sad.

Chapter 17

In Which Things Sound Much Easier
Than They Turn Out to Be

"Are we sure it's a question of actually destroying the staff?" said Hoyle.

"What else could it be?" Dianne said scornfully. "Ruby thought a healthy dose of *amor vincit omnia* would do it, and look how effective that was."

Maybe we would have found out how effective it was if Dianne hadn't bashed Ruby's brains out, came Nicholas's thought, heavy with barely controlled rage and bitterness.

Will you please? thought Hoyle desperately. *Unless you've got an actual suggestion, trying to cope with your own baggage as well as my own is exhausting.*

Baggage—meaning?

Oh, right. The 1980s had never happened to Nicholas. *All someone's bad emotional habits. They slow you down and make everything hurt, like carrying a … a steamer trunk on your back. And I have enough of my own.*

Yeeeeess, thought Nicholas. *I know.*

Dianne had been waiting this exchange out. "It's rude to whisper in front of other people. Moreover," she added meaningfully, "it makes other people trust you even less than they already do."

It had been like this all day: an endless cycle of futility, frayed tempers, and suspicion. Hoyle felt waves of sickness each time the thought that he was talking to a murderer came to him again.

And it came to him every time Dianne showed any temper, which was often.

He and Dianne—Nicholas was refusing to participate in the discussion—had managed to agree on a few premises: the staff was evil. The staff was designed, or wanted (Hoyle favored the former, Dianne the latter), to return to high-population areas and increase its influence, using human beings as its vector. Its influence consisted of increasing conflict and hatred, which would form a positive loop that would generate yet more conflict and feed more power into the staff. Neither Dianne nor Hoyle wanted this to happen; it was less clear whether Nicholas had an opinion.

In fact, Hoyle wasn't really sure what Nicholas wanted. Their connection let him feel Nicholas's presence and flashes of intense emotion, but not to discern any thoughts that Nicholas didn't want him to know. That didn't help their efforts to work together. After the hundredth squabble, Dianne broke down in gulping sobs, and Hoyle watched her helplessly. All his glorious resolve had been eroding, and he felt the last of it wash away as Dianne's tears dripped down her face.

"It's too late," said Dianne. "We're already too full of hate. Listen to us! The staff has already won."

"It hasn't," Hoyle said, feeling frantic. "Look, you can't stand me, right? And God knows there's no love lost between you and Nicholas." Dianne actually turned her head and spat. "But isn't it something amazing that we are still trying to work together? Isn't that even more important than it would be if we were friends? We're fighting the staff, all right." His spirits began to rise as he realized he'd stumbled on an important point. "And you bet it's doing its best to keep screwing things up. But we're still trying. It's not winning. It's—it's the opposite of winning."

That would be ... losing? said Nicholas archly.

"I'm really not enjoying it when you make these snarky comments in my head," said Hoyle. "I would like you, please, to talk out loud. Dianne can cope."

Dianne spat again.

"Dianne can cope," repeated Hoyle. "Can and will. Because her other option is to face up to the fact that she killed someone for no reason at all."

"Thanks a lot," she said. "I'd clean forgotten what I'd done. It doesn't haunt me at all, not for one single second."

"Nestor is the key," said Nicholas out loud, quite suddenly. Hoyle and Dianne both jumped. "Somehow—*somehow*—he was able to leave the staff behind. It's no good wasting more time trying to outwit the staff. We need to look at someone who did. As much as it pains me to say it, my toad of a brother is the key."

"Can you tell where he is? Like you can with me?" said Hoyle. "Are you sure he's actually gone? Maybe he tried and is ashamed to admit he failed. Or he's afraid of you."

Nicholas paused, with a distant expression. "I sense him, but very faintly. He's weak, he wouldn't be able to hide himself from me. Not after all this time. You try."

Hoyle searched. There was Nicholas, a brassy and cold presence. And there was the thick, sickening pulsing of the staff. He reached—what was that flicker? It felt thin and elusive, but with a sourness that reminded him of the staff. Nestor, no doubt. "I sense him. He's really nasty."

"That's him, all right. It's not just the staff, either; he's been nasty from the nursery."

"Whatever," said Dianne. "Your family issues are irrelevant."

"If they help me understand him and figure out what he's going to do next, no, they're not," said Nicholas peevishly.

"He's the vector," said Dianne. "Everything I did, it was all useless, worse than useless. I didn't even know he was there. The staff was looking after him, wasn't it? He was its favorite."

"Why did it want me, then?" said Hoyle.

"Do you really think it won't take anyone and everyone it can get, old boy?" said Nicholas. "You, me—it wants to hedge its bets. Certainly, Nestor was its most likely choice. This is all irrelevant, though. The question is not 'Why Nestor?' but 'What's he doing now?'"

* * *

Nestor ran easily through the woods toward Glen Davis. That poor, sad lump of a so-called man had taken a bit more prodding than Nestor had wanted to give, but he'd eventually stumbled and bumbled and done what Nestor needed. And now Nestor was reveling in the feeling of wind and sun—even the scratching of twigs and the occasional bite of an insect filled him with glee. Finally, he had a body again. Finally, he could make real the dreams that had pounded within his heart for so long. Finally, with the injection of that buffoon Marchand's life force, such as it was, he would show his brother just how little it mattered that Nicholas had disembodied him. And, even more, how little it mattered that Nicholas had been so unutterably stupid as to fall in love. Nestor snapped his fingers. Just *that* much.

Nestor had felt the staff pushing him back toward Sydney, but something had always made him wait. Maybe it was his certainty that once he was stupid enough to go back to Sydney, the police would have found him easily. But as the years had gone by, and the likelihood of anyone remembering what had happened grew less and less, he'd found himself more amenable to the staff's promptings, and even more resentful of Nicholas. Always telling Nestor what to do, just as he'd done in the nursery, and at school, and at Oxford. But Nestor had started to listen more closely to the staff. When he did the things the staff wanted—distasteful as they'd been, especially at first—he felt clever and capable. He felt more than the equal of Nicholas.

Why should he leave? The staff was keeping him young, giving him power, saving him from the endless nuisance of eating and shitting. The staff would tell him when the time was right. He knew he'd be able to hear it forever, and wherever in the wide world he traveled. There was no urgency, not yet.

But then those idiotic Australians arrived, and everything changed. They were dismayingly resistant to the tricks the staff had taught him, the ones that had let him have so much fun slowly driving Nicholas mad. He didn't know whether it was their fatuous enthusiasm that insulated them from his wiles, or whether they were simply stupid. And his irritation knew no bounds when Nicholas decided to fall in love with one of them. By no means the prettiest of them, either, but Nicholas had always had odd taste in women.

The memory of that horrible day when everything had gone wrong still had the power to unnerve him. He would have thought, after what had happened back in England, that a little bloodshed wouldn't bother him. And, indeed, that hadn't done more than cause him a moment of dismay. The worst had been the moment that Nicholas had made to swing the staff against a rocky outcropping—and, crazed as he was, there was little doubt that he could have swung it hard enough to shatter it—and Nestor had caught it at the cusp of the backswing. A hundred years of Nicholas's rage and loneliness had overwhelmed him like a monstrous wave, and in the chaos the staff had dissolved his and Nicholas's physical forms, leaving them to wander, wraithlike, on the fringes of the campsite, hating each other, yearning to walk inside a body again. But there was no power left; the conflict had spent it all.

The people at the campsite had already learned to be terrified of both Nicholas and himself, thanks to the very handy paranoia of that Dianne woman. There was no way they could be tricked into touching the staff. The months went by.

Then—newcomers! Clueless and compassionate strangers, who could easily be tricked. And now, restored in body and spirit, with his reluctance to leave gone like a puff of smoke in a stiff breeze, Nestor was off at last to the city, to do what the staff wanted—and what he himself wanted. More deeply satisfying tricks, more control over more people. This was going to be good fun.

* * *

"Which brings me to my main point, which is what the fuck?" raged Ada. "That ghost bloke wasn't going to do a thing to us. If he could, he would have. We need to go back—Hoyle needs us!"

"For the hundredth time, he's fine," said Sybil. "We're not going to help him by staying in the woods."

"Well, then, how are we going to help him, huh? Tell me that!" Ada crossed her arms defiantly. "How does leaving him alone there help him?"

"We're not going far. In fact, we're staying here in Glen Davis."

"Huh?"

"That other brother, Nestor, he's just as stuck as Nicholas and Hoyle, right? So we'll wait here to see if we can find him. I'll bet he has more answers than Nicholas would like to admit."

"Why didn't we just stay with him? Hoyle is all alone, no friends, just a couple of loonies." Ada was near tears.

Sybil turned to Oliver. "Some of the others are heading back to Sydney. Maybe you should go with them."

"Of course not," he huffed. "How could you even think I would leave? This could be my destiny, helping sort all this out. Haven't I already been useful?"

There was a moment's silence before Ada said enthusiastically, "Sure!"

Oliver nodded in a satisfied way.

"In that case," said Sybil, "we need to start talking to people here. Maybe they've seen or heard something relevant."

"I'm no good at that stuff," said Ada.

"Me neither," said Oliver.

"So much for your being helpful," said Sybil.

"He has other skills," said Ada.

"You know what?" said Oliver. "You're the first girl who ever said anything nice about me without starting it with 'at least.'"

"That's so sad," said Ada.

"Tell me about it," said Oliver.

"All right," said Sybil. "Don't go anywhere, and don't do anything stupid."

"What do you call doing something stupid?" said Ada.

"At the rate we've been going, just about anything carries the risk of being stupid."

"You really ought to think about being more cheerful," said Ada. "I'm serious."

"Mm," said Sybil. "I'll be back in a while. There aren't too many people here, so if I take more than about an hour, come looking for me."

"Why?" said Oliver uneasily. "Are you expecting something to go wrong?"

Sybil rolled her eyes. "When are you going to learn the importance of a backup plan? All right, I'll see you." She started walking toward the closest of the tiny, weather-beaten houses.

A few of the anarchists were still wandering vaguely around the village. "Hey, Oliver," called one. "Denny should be here in a little while. We're heading to Bathurst. You sure you—"

"Yeah, thanks, I'm fine here," Oliver yelled back. He frowned. "So the famous Denny is finally driving in. He's nuts, did you know that?"

Ada opened the rear car door and flung herself along the back seat, her legs sprawling outside. "What makes him so nuts?"

"He comes and goes, and every time he shows up, he starts ordering everyone around. He's someone's uncle or something, but nobody's ever admitted to being the niece or nephew in question. I know I wouldn't. I guess he's got a good heart and everything, but still …"

Oliver opened the front and sat glumly in the passenger seat, sighing loudly.

"Now what's wrong?" said Ada.

"I wish I could be doing something. No matter what, I always end up sitting around waiting for other people. Or getting ordered around."

"Well? Why don't you just do something?"

"There's always someone telling me not to. And they always sound so convincing. Like Sybil."

"Shows what you know," said Ada. Oliver found himself staring at her lips as she talked. "She's just as fucked up as the rest of us," she was saying. "She looks at Hoyle like she's looking at—I don't know—at the Opera House or the Harbour Bridge or something. But she doesn't do anything. So really, she's kind of chicken. Everyone's got something they're scared of."

"I never notice things like that."

"Yeah, I know. If you did, you wouldn't keep believing people all the time. What people say means shit. The only thing that matters is what people do. Like, how they look at people. Or whether they go off and fucking leave someone in the bush."

The sound of a car being driven vigorously intruded on their conversation.

"That's Denny," said Oliver. "He needs a new fan belt; hear it?"

"I don't know anything about cars," said Ada.

A mud-caked SUV pulled up. A grey-haired, sunburned man in glasses leaned out the driver's side window. "Hey, um …"

"Oliver," said Oliver. "Hi, Denny."

"You're the one who's always trying to cook people dinner, right? You should stop being so emotional about it. They don't like your food, so what? Tell them to get stuffed. No point crying about it."

"Sure, Denny," said Oliver uncomfortably, glancing at Ada.

Denny went on obliviously. "They've called me in to save the day. *Again.* How many are ready to go?"

"Oh—um, I don't know."

"Well, either round them up or get in so I at least know where you are. Bloody hell, you lot are heaps more trouble than you're worth. Well? Get in!"

"No, thanks, I already have another ride," Oliver said.

"Suit yourself," said Denny, scowling. "If you change your

mind, let me know. I could probably get you a job in Bathurst. Mate of mine runs a bakery—well, no, maybe you'd be better off working somewhere else."

"Hey," said Ada. "I like his cooking."

"Really?" Denny's voice scaled up in astonishment. "Hey, Oliver, keep hold of this one. It's not often you find a pretty girl who's got no sense of taste."

He drove off; after a few seconds, he turned the engine off and they could hear him talking to some of the anarchists a little way away, but they couldn't make out the words.

"Hey, Oliver," said Ada. "Am I really pretty?"

"Of course you are," said Oliver, shocked.

"Oh." A few seconds later, she added, "Wow."

"Beautiful, in fact."

This left Ada entirely speechless.

They sat in the car, feeling the awkwardness beat between them. They heard Denny's car start up and drive towards them.

"I guess Denny's found everyone he needs," said Oliver.

The car was about to pass them when it stopped with a jolt. Two of the anarchists jumped out, ran to Oliver, and dragged him into Denny's car. Before Ada could do much more than crawl out of the back seat, the car was gone.

"Oliver," she screamed. "Oliver!" She started to run after the car, but realized how stupid that was before she'd gone more than a dozen strides. Where was Sybil? She could fix anything. Ada threw her head back and bellowed as loudly as she could: "Sybil! I need you. Sybil, help!"

Sybil came running. "What is it?"

"Those bloody anarchists—they took Oliver!"

"What—why?"

"I don't know! We have to follow them. They're going to Bathurst."

"But Hoyle—"

"You said he was fine. You said he wasn't in any danger. Oliver doesn't have a magic stick. They bully him, push him around—he's like a little kid. He can't take care of himself. We have to go find him. We already know they take hostages, and they have no idea of what's right and wrong."

"And if Hoyle needs us while we're gone?"

"He won't. He's nothing like he was a while ago. He knows how to look after himself now. You know I'm right—he doesn't need us like he used to. Oliver does—let's *go*!"

Sybil stared into the woods in the direction of the camp, then back at the dust that was still hanging in the air from Denny's hasty exit. Ada bounced on her toes in an agony of impatience.

Finally, Sybil said, "How far is it to Bathurst?"

Chapter 18

In Which Oliver Gets Into
Even Deeper Trouble

Sybil knew better than to give the map book to Ada. She spent a few minutes figuring out how to get to Bathurst, and they were on their way. As they pulled onto the main road, she said tensely, "Actually, this is why I never had kids."

"Why's that?" said Ada.

"Because when they're in trouble, it hurts worse than anything in the world." She sighed anxiously. "Will you remember this Denny's car, and what he looks like?"

"Until the day I die. Or he does," said Ada grimly.

"Whoa," said Sybil.

"There are people all over Sydney who have learned not to mess with me."

"Uh-huh. Because you killed them?"

"Well, no, that was a figure of speech. But I'll make sure Denny will remember me, all right."

"Mm-hm. How big a place is Bathurst?"

"Compared to Sydney? It's a fly-speck."

"Have you ever been there?"

"Um, not recently."

"Ada …"

"All right, no. But didn't you see how small a dot it was on the map? It'll be a piece of cake to find them."

"Did Oliver mention Denny's last name?"

"Are you kidding? I don't even know Oliver's last name."

"You don't?"

"He doesn't know mine, either, so we're even. Really, the subject never came up. We had other things to talk about." Even in her distress, Ada sounded smug.

"We should be in Bathurst in about an hour."

"An hour? Anything could happen."

"And it probably will. Look, just keep your eye out. This car doesn't go too fast, but maybe Denny's doesn't either."

"It looked pretty beat up, I have to say."

"Especially look out for gas stations."

Ada snickered. "Gas …"

"Petrol," said Sybil, annoyed. "Petrol stations. He's got an SUV, so he'll be running out of … petrol … sooner than a little car like this would. I have to watch the road, so it's up to you to check the petrol stations."

After Ada gave three false alarms that had Sybil stomping on the brakes until the car skidded, Sybil said, "You know what? Never mind."

"Sorry, all right? I'm just edgy. My boyfriend has been kidnapped."

"Your what?" Sybil's mouth twitched.

"I mean, I don't even know why they want him. Nobody liked him there, he said so. He should never have gotten mixed up with them. He needs to be among his own kind."

"Who are his own kind?"

"We are!"

"What? You, me, and Hoyle? We're not a kind. There aren't three people more different on the face of the earth."

"That's where you're wrong, mate. You know what we have in common? We don't mind if each other's not perfect. And *that*," Ada declared, "is why we're not like other people. *That* is what makes us a … a … team."

Sybil drove in silence for a while.

"You okay?" said Ada at last. "Wait! There. I just saw them. This time for real. No, really. Turn around. Turn around!"

Sybil slowed the car as abruptly as she dared; the road had gotten busier approaching Bathurst. She pulled off onto the shoulder. "Which side?"

"The other one. Turn around. Hurry!"

Sybil eased the car into a U-turn and drove back to where Ada had seen the SUV. Ada jumped out of the car and, before Sybil could stop her, ran over to the SUV. "Oliver! Oliver! Oli—" She stumbled to a halt.

Sybil ran up to her, grabbed her arm, and started pulling her back to the car. "Are you nuts?" she whispered fiercely.

Ada did not resist. "He's not there," she said weakly. "It's the right car, I know it is, I remember that broken tail light. But he's not there."

"Maybe he's in the bathroom, did you think of that? Maybe they're just getting a coffee. And if they see you, they may drive off too fast for us to follow."

"They're not getting a bloody coffee and they're not in the toilet, all right?"

"How do you know?"

"Because they're in the car. And Oliver isn't."

"Oh, Christ, Ada, did they see you?"

"I don't think so. I think they're dead."

Sybil turned and ran back to the SUV. "Ada, go to the gas station and tell them to call an ambulance, right now. Move!" She made her voice as sharp as she could, hoping to cut through Ada's shock.

Sybil opened the driver's side door; in the driver's and front passenger's seats were two men she didn't recognize. Both were motionless.

She took the pulse of the one at the wheel, finding nothing after several tense seconds. She ran to the passenger's side to do the same for the other man. As she checked, she glanced into the back seat; it was empty except for some scattered papers.

The other man had no pulse either. Well, she could only help one at a time. She dragged his body out onto the ground and started CPR. One of the workers from inside the petrol station came out, took a second to figure out what was happening, and dragged the driver out of the SUV to begin CPR as well.

"I phoned the ambos," she grunted as she did the compressions. "Three, four …"

The two of them kept going while Ada wandered nervously around the gas-station parking lot, peering along the road in either direction and out into the fields as if Oliver would come nonchalantly wandering into view. By the time the ambulance and police arrived, Sybil was aching and breathless, more than happy to relinquish her place. The police were establishing a crime scene, and one of them had started interviewing the gas-station worker. Ada sat on the ground, back against the wheel of Sybil's car and head buried in her arms. Sybil came over to sit next to her.

"Now look upset, okay?" said Ada. "If we look upset they won't ask so many questions."

"I'm too exhausted to look upset. They'll have to settle for me looking exhausted."

"Well, I'm upset. I've had to watch you kissing a corpse for God knows how long—where did you learn CPR? You know lots of shit, don't you?—and I still don't know where Oliver is."

"At least he wasn't in that SUV. That doesn't seem to have been a particularly healthy place. And I was not 'kissing a corpse', if you don't mind. I was trying to save a life."

"We can't go until the cops talk to us, you know that, right?" said Ada.

"I know."

"I'm hungry."

"You're going to have to tough it out. Unless you want me to get you a candy bar from inside."

"The cops don't like it when people wander around. We should stay put. Also, it probably won't be long before the reporters get here. We definitely shouldn't say anything to them."

"You know a lot about this sort of thing."

"Yeah, well. I don't come from a real nice neighborhood. Looks like out in the country isn't as nice as everyone told me, either."

"No," said Sybil.

"At least there are no leeches right here."

"At least that."

"I hope Hoyle's okay."

"Mm," said Sybil.

Ada lay her head on Sybil's shoulder. Sybil reached across and drew her closer. She felt Ada's tears soaking her shirt, but Ada made no sound.

* * *

"Stop your bloody whining," snapped Denny. "You have no idea what a big favor I'm doing you. And for Christ's sake, sit still, will you, you little shit? Jesus, Craig, you want him to kill us all? How am I supposed to drive with him throwing himself around like that?"

Oliver felt, not for the first time, a stinging cuff from Craig, who was with him in the back seat. Each blow had been harder than the last. And, indeed, this time Craig really meant business; Oliver saw stars. It wasn't going to stop him, though. Nothing would stop him until he escaped and made it back to Glen Davis, back to Ada. He wasn't about to desert Sybil and Hoyle without a fight, either. He was full of roaring rage, and it felt terrific. Let Denny yell, let Craig hit him. They had no idea what they were getting into. No idea. Once they stopped somewhere, then they'd see. Oliver would show them he wasn't just a soft, weak intellectual. No, he was a tough, determined intellectual.

When they got to the main road, Denny picked up speed.

"Hey," said the guy from the front seat. He was someone Denny had brought in, not one of the anarchists from the camp. "Not so fast."

"She'll be right," said Denny. "I always know where the cops are. It's a talent I have."

"Uh-huh," said the guy. "It'd better be. Oh, and do you also have a talent for keeping an eye on the fuel gauge? Because, uh ..."

Denny glanced down. "Shit. This thing drinks petrol faster every time I drive it. All right, there's a petrol station coming up in a while."

The guy said, "Maybe that's where we should—"

"Shut up," said Denny.

"I'm not so sure anymore that you know what you want to do. That geek in the back seat—you say we need him, but you haven't said what for. You say we need to head back to Bathurst, where everybody fucking knows you, instead of Sydney, where you can do what you need to do without anyone noticing. Instead—"

"Shut up."

Oliver's rage vanished, replaced by a wave of cold horror. Why would they need him? Nobody ever needed him. Something was even more wrong than he'd thought.

Denny took one hand off the wheel and wrestled a phone out of his pocket.

"What's that?" said the guy sharply. "Who are you texting?"

Denny didn't reply.

With a new part of his brain he hadn't known he had, Oliver knew Denny was calling for reinforcements, now that the bloke in the front was making trouble. This made him feel even colder. There was going to be a fight. He found himself wishing desperately for Ada, Sybil, and even Hoyle. Even if they didn't always know what to do, they always did *something*. He needed to be like them. He needed to do *something*, like when he'd helped them escape. But even that wasn't much. Maybe he could escape by himself this time. But the SUV was barreling at a hundred kilometers per hour along the Great Western Highway. Besides, if he so much as twitched again, Craig might hit him so hard he wouldn't be able to do anything anyway. He'd have to be cagey. Wait for his moment.

"I swear to God, Denny, if you're texting your little mates, I'll—"

"All right, all right, I'm putting the phone away, see?" said Denny. But from the back seat, Oliver could see he'd already sent the message. He'd probably had it ready-drafted, just waiting for that one touch of the screen to send it.

Craig spoke up: "How much longer to the petrol station?"

"Why? Gotta wee?" said the guy in the front seat in an unpleasant voice.

"Yeah, as it happens, arsehole. Or I could just wee in your briefcase back here. Why don't I do that?"

"Because I'll fucking kill you if you do, you useless fuck."

"Hm," said Craig. "I wonder what's in this briefcase. I wonder …"

"Don't fucking touch it!"

Craig made a show of taking a handful of papers out. The guy turned savagely and reached into the back seat, quick as a snake, to grab a handful of Craig's hair. He yanked, hard and hatefully. "Put those back."

"Sit down and shut up, both of you," said Denny. "I've had it with you."

The guy sat back down, glowering.

I'll bet you have, thought Oliver. *But you needed them to come and get me. One of the others must have told you I was back in Glen Davis. But I was about to go back to Sydney, and you'd never find me then, your bad-tempered mate there was right about that.*

But … Oliver was nobody. Denny hadn't even remembered his name. He'd had no idea why Craig had suddenly dragged him into the SUV, why they'd driven off, taking him away from Ada.

Ada would be really worried. She might even try to come after him. The rage came back at the thought of any of them hurting her. She was so little, so easy to hurt. And she talked like she was so tough and cheeky, but he'd held her close in the moonlight, he'd kissed her. He knew just how terrifyingly easy it would be to hurt her.

He had to do something. For himself, and even more, for Ada.

He writhed in frustration. Craig dropped the papers he'd been holding so he could hit Oliver again. Luckily, this hit wasn't as bad as the last one; he guessed that Craig had been preoccupied with teasing the guy in the front seat, and he hadn't been poised for violence.

Oliver chastised himself. He had to stop letting his brain go off on tangents like that. If he had somehow become important—important enough to kidnap—he'd better stop being such a dreamer and start paying attention to things. He'd never figure them out otherwise.

He heard the turn signal clicking and felt the car slow. They were turning into the petrol station. Denny pulled up to a bowser.

"Right," said Craig. "Time to wee. You need to look after the kid," he said to the guy in the front seat, then opened the door.

Oliver tried his own door, but of course Denny had thought to put the childproof lock on. And the guy in the front was already out of the car and standing next to Craig's door, ready to jump into the back seat if Oliver tried anything.

Another car pulled in to the bowsers. Denny's shoulders raised a fraction, and Oliver knew: this was it, the car with Denny's mates.

Denny got out to fill the tank, slightly too carefully ignoring the people in the car behind him. This was the country, after all; Denny should have at least given them a quick nod, not stonily pretended he didn't even see them.

Sights and sounds were pouring over Oliver in a torrent—he was noticing everything: the clicking and humming of the bowser as it pumped, the smell of the petrol, Craig's footsteps as he came back from the loo, the rattle as Denny tapped the nozzle to get the last drops into the petrol tank.

Denny went inside to pay. When he came back, he said to the guy in front, "Hey, I'm getting a bad headache. I can hardly see. Can you drive the rest of the way?" He held out the keys.

"Sure," the guy said, and got into the driver's seat.

"Hey, Craig, you get in front, okay?" Denny said. "The glare off the road is really killing me. Jesus, I hate these migraines. It's okay, I'll look after the kid."

"You can't even remember my name," screamed Oliver. "What the fuck!"

Everyone ignored him.

The woman who'd been pumping petrol into the other car came over. "Hey, guys," she said. "I can't believe this, but I'm five dollars short. How embarrassing is that! Do any of you have five dollars you can spare me?"

"Yeah, sure," said Denny, and got out his wallet. He fumbled it, muttered, "Damn it," then got out a five-dollar note. He pressed it carefully into her hand. "This headache is making me a little shaky. You got it?"

"Yeah, thanks, mate. Thanks a lot. I really appreciate it."

Denny suddenly had something in his hand that wasn't his wallet. He dropped his hand to Craig's shoulder. Craig yelled, then stood, puzzled and silent. A moment later Denny was guiding his limp form down into the passenger seat, then placing his feet inside and closing the door. Meanwhile, the woman had done the same thing to the other guy. She opened up the back door. Oliver batted at her arms frantically, but she grabbed first one hand, then the other, and held them implacably.

Denny said, "Should have gotten rid of them as soon as we had the kid. He told me to expect them to give me shit. He always knows what people are thinking. Gives me the creeps."

Oliver felt a searing pain in his arm, and his head rolled with sudden wooziness. With that new part of his mind, he thought, *He. That's Nestor.* He tried to yell again, but darkness fell.

Chapter 19

In Which Hoyle Gets a

New Job Description

Dianne had wandered off into the bush, probably to get some water. Nicholas and Hoyle kept talking, trying to figure out something, anything, about the staff.

"If the staff wants to take over the known universe, why does it also want to stay here?" asked Hoyle.

"I don't think that's the staff, actually," said Nicholas. "Whoever put it here had some fairly serious power of their own. It's the fight between them that tears us to pieces when we try to take the staff with us."

"Have you ever tried to figure out who put the staff here? Were they white? Aborigine? Space aliens?"

"Don't laugh—it's as plausible a theory as any other. Although bloodwood is native to Australia, which argues against space aliens."

"But not compellingly. Maybe they took a local artifact and trapped some kind of malevolent force inside it, then took off in their space ships, leaving us to deal with it."

"Now you're just being silly."

"Have you asked the staff?"

"I try not to converse with it, lest it strengthen its hold."

"Well, I'm maybe not so vulnerable, as I was tricked into servitude—as opposed to the Ivory brothers, who seem to have gone willingly."

"You're being unfair."

"Shh." Hoyle closed his eyes and searched for where the staff lay, pulsing ceaselessly, sickeningly, always connected to him. *All right*, he thought. *What can you tell me?*

As if it had been waiting all this time to be asked, the staff sent a rush of images painfully through Hoyle's head. He was high above the earth, looking down at the Wollemi National Forest— the spot where the staff lay quavered nastily in the rhythm Hoyle knew all too well. All around it, circles spread out. He couldn't see them, but he felt them, as if his mind were a hand running over the rings in a section of log. They were ... different from the power in the staff: cold and stinging, but clean. They made a sort of moat around the staff, keeping its loathsome emanations contained.

Hoyle looked more carefully. The lines were distorted, damaged, at spots that made a track south and west to Glen Davis, then back east, heading unmistakably toward Sydney. Whatever was making the trail hadn't gotten very far. Hoyle knew it was Nestor.

He could see himself, and Nicholas: dull dimples in the energy field around the staff. Not a very flattering image, he had to acknowledge. He tried to look for Sybil and Ada, or even Dianne, but no luck.

But why are you here? What are you for? he asked the staff. His head was starting to ache ferociously, but he didn't want to give up now that he was getting some answers. If only he'd thought to ask before. Why hadn't Nicholas?

His musings were drowned out by a new series of images and sounds.

Voices spoke in a language he didn't know, but the concern in their tone was unmistakable. They fell silent, as one began speaking in a careful, rhythmic way that suggested a ritual. Hoyle sensed that the ritual was putting those lines in place. He felt outrage stirring in him; how dare they constrict his power, bind it to this place? Emotion swelled in him and made a roiling redness in front of his eyes: fury, resentment. The outrage was exhilarating, and it fed and fed upon itself until it formed the very beating of his heart. How dare they keep him from—

No!

He wrenched his emotions away from the staff and focused on the voices again. They sounded worried, yes, but cool and sane. Such a relief, so different from the churning, distressing excesses of the staff.

Hey, he called to them, silently, impulsively.

The voices stopped, and he felt the sudden weight of their scrutiny—like a dentist's lead apron settling on him.

Hello, he added awkwardly. *Um …*

He was being gently urged to be silent. The feeling of being examined was becoming acute.

Something odd happened in his head, and he heard their voices again, but this time he understood.

An interesting champion, said one. The tone was wry, but not unkind.

Hoyle's heart started to pound.

Not what we were expecting at all, said another.

Hoyle felt himself hyperventilating. *Um,* he said again. *Um …*

You're wanting to protest. You're wondering if we've mistaken you for someone else. So far you're doing everything right, despite— well, despite not being what we expected.

So maybe I'm really not the—the champion. Maybe you need someone like—

Like Nicholas? Or perhaps … Nestor?

Hoyle's guts cramped in quick loathing.

Exactly. But that's irrelevant now. Let me start again. First, we're here and not here. We did what we could, long ago, to constrain harm and foster the chance for redemption, but we can no longer take an active role in the doings of the staff. Time in its presence does that to all of us, eventually. The staff gained power from us, until we had none left. But we felt it was worth the sacrifice, because over the centuries, we have been able to—

Centuries? It only took a hundred years for Nicholas and Nestor.

The process was somewhat accelerated in their case, as they spent themselves in brotherly conflict. We've been able to contain the staff, keep it isolated, and minimize the damage it's been able to do to anyone stumbling by. But now we can't even do that anymore. We didn't foresee what wanderers your kind would be; we thought our isolation virtually complete. But to be human is to wander—to seek. If we'd known ...

It's not the staff keeping me here—it's you! The staff—

—doesn't want to stay here at all. We've been weakened by trying to keep so many people from leaving. Nestor was quick to sense we were overstretched and slipped away. A new way must be found. And you must find it.

I'm telling you, I'm not your champion.

You are all there is, and so you are our champion.

So ... you're not going to try to tell me that all my life I've had hidden magical powers and only needed adversity to bring them out?

No. You're relentlessly ordinary. But you are here. Listen carefully: there are three servants of the staff. You are one, Nicholas and Nestor are the others. No one else now embodied has touched it with their bare skin. While even one of you continues to serve it, it can remain strong and continue to feed on and poison people's hearts, then use them in turn to conquer more, in an endless cycle of gluttony and lust for power.

So, the staff actually wants things? It has, like, a mind?

No, it's entirely mindless. But it was made carelessly, and its properties twisted as they were used, until it became hateful to us. But we could find no way to destroy the staff, and so chose to quarantine it.

In other words, Australia is your toxic-waste dump.

And now one of the servants of the staff has gone back. The resulting suffering of thousands and millions will be … worse than heartbreaking, worse than horrifying. Convince Nicholas to go with you. Find Nestor. Redeem him from slavery. Perhaps the three of you together can destroy the staff at last.

Perhaps?

If we'd had all the answers, we would have destroyed it ourselves.

Can you at least give me some pointers about how to get started?

If we could do more than speak with you, we would also follow you in our hundreds—

Hundreds? And you couldn't do anything? How are three supposed to?

Take our place. Save us all from what the staff will make us become.

For a long, tense moment, Hoyle did nothing, thought nothing. The silence grew inside him. A memory flickered: Sybil, back at the bookstore, saying, "There's no one else."

No one else.

Hoyle thought matter-of-factly, *Okay, then. Time's a-wasting.* He called out loud, "Nicholas?"

"There you are," said Nicholas, also out loud. He sounded relieved far beyond what Hoyle would have thought commensurate. After all, couldn't Nicholas tell where he was, just as he could sense Nicholas's presence?

"I couldn't sense you. I wondered if you'd gone off to follow Nestor, and I'd be left here alone with Dianne. Nestor, in his nastiness, was at least entertaining."

Nicholas stepped out from the bush and sat casually on the ground, his limbs sprawling. Hoyle envied him his good looks and graceful, insouciant air. It wasn't hard to imagine how Nestor had ended up with such an inferiority complex or whatever it was.

"So, yeah, going after Nestor," Hoyle said. "Who knows what kind of damage he'll wreak out there. And if he could leave, maybe something's changed, or worn out, or been overtaxed or something, and we can leave now, too." He found himself deeply reluctant to mention the voices to Nicholas. "Wouldn't you like to get out of here, finally? Come on, let's go. Let's try."

"Leave the staff here?"

Hoyle went cold. He hadn't thought about that. Which would be worse, to leave it here for the cycle to start all over again, or to take it with them, desperately hoping nobody accidentally touched it or insisted on knowing what it was? "Maybe we can try to burn it."

"Have you ever tried to destroy it?"

"No."

"I have." The flat finality in Nicholas's voice was chilling.

"I guess we can, um, wrap it up or something."

Nicholas said nothing.

Hoyle's temper snapped. "You want to go after Nestor or not? If so, let's go. If not, quit pretending you're worth a damn to anyone, including yourself."

"But I'm not," said Nicholas. "I'm still just—what was it? A ghost. Worth nothing."

"God damn it," muttered Hoyle in profound irritation. On pure impulse, he aimed a bolt of whatever energy he had inside him at Nicholas. *Not a ghost anymore. Stand up and be a man.* Nicholas yelled from shock and fear, but Hoyle didn't let up. He forced more and more power into Nicholas, making him substantial.

Once he could see a shadow from Nicholas's body, he let up. He was exhausted.

Nicholas stared at him. "How did you do that?"

Hoyle couldn't be bothered speaking. He gave a tiny shrug, all he had energy for. Funny, though, how he could use the powers the staff gave him to start bringing the staff down. But he did not exult. He longed to be normal again.

He would never have predicted how much he yearned to take a shit.

Chapter 20

In Which the Search for Oliver Continues

For lack of anything more concrete to do, Sybil and Ada told the cops that Oliver was missing, answered questions, and agreed to stay in Bathurst for the next couple of days. It only took a few minutes of driving around the town to find a hotel. Sybil found Bathurst's broad streets, wrought-iron lampposts, and varied shop fronts and houses far more appealing than the dingy and claustrophobic Lithgow. Just the feeling that she could stretch out and breathe again made her start to feel a little more optimistic.

Once they'd checked in and Sybil had phoned the police station with their contact details, they sat awkwardly, one on each bed. Ada ran through the television channels, over and over, until Sybil snatched the remote from her.

"I want to drive around and see if I can find Oliver."

"You know it's essentially impossible that he's still in Bathurst, right?"

"Then we'll ask people if they've seen him. Get clues."

"We're not driving around Bathurst randomly asking people if they've seen Oliver."

"What if we're next?"

"You think the kidnappers will come after us? Why would they?"

"Why would they get Oliver? I'm all stupid over him, and even I don't think he's the kind of guy who's, like, a mover and shaker. So maybe they want him purely because he was up at the campsite. And so, so were we. And people saw us come out with the rest of them, back at, what was it, Glen Davis. Or maybe one of the anarchists sold us out to try to divert attention from their own escape. Or maybe you and I are really special and we don't even know why—how come Hoyle gets to be the only one with magic powers? Or maybe—"

"Okay," said Sybil. "But I for one have never felt less magical. And as much as it galls you, we're going to try an experiment: we're going to wait and see for a while."

Ada whined. "I *hate* wait and see. Can I have the remote back again, please?"

"Are you just going to keep scrolling through the channels?"

Ada gave a brilliant smile and held out her hand for the remote. "Of course not." Sybil sighed and handed it over, and Ada immediately resumed scrolling.

There was a knock on the door. Sybil and Ada froze and looked at each other sidelong.

"Who is it?" called Sybil.

"Room service."

"We didn't order any."

"The front desk forgot to give you milk for your coffee."

"That's all right, we don't drink coffee."

There was a pause, then, "All right. Sorry to disturb you."

Sybil listened hard for receding footsteps, but heard none. She looked at Ada in quick concern. Ada, too, was tense and suspicious. Sybil pointed to the television and put a finger to her lips. Ada slowly brought the volume down. There was a muffled cry from outside the door. Sybil was already reaching for the phone when they heard the key in the lock and the door burst open. A man pushed past the hotel employee; he had a gun in his hand.

"Your turn," he said. "Let's go."

Sybil leapt to her feet and started dithering. "Oh, God, I'm so scared. Please, please put that gun away. We'll do anything you say, I'll do anything." Her voice was high and panicky, and her hands were flapping.

There was a soft crack as the remote, flung by Ada as he'd been distracted by Sybil's act, hit his nose with brutal accuracy. Before he could recover his composure, Sybil kneed him hard in the groin, twice, then, as he doubled over, grabbed his head and drove her knee upward once more, into his face.

Sybil snapped back to her usual brisk manner at once. She glanced around the room and out into the parking lot, then back down at their fallen attacker. He was utterly still. "Now," was all she said. She and Ada grabbed the backpacks they hadn't even opened yet and walked, as casually as they could, out to the car. There was no sign of the hotel employee; Sybil hoped she was all right.

Once they were driving, Sybil said, " I guess I shouldn't have doubted your instincts for mayhem."

Ada gave a satisfied "hmph."

Sybil said, "If I drive out into the country, there will be no one to hear us when we yell for help. No matter how dangerous Bathurst is, we're no safer anywhere else."

"But if we're going to find Oliver, we're going to have to be brave, Sybil." After a minute she said, "This driving around Bathurst is really boring. And Oliver's in trouble, in case you didn't remember."

"They wouldn't have bothered taking him if they didn't need him alive," said Sybil.

"He's so meek," fretted Ada. "They could tear him to pieces and he wouldn't even think to ask them to knock it off. Or if he did, he'd say please."

* * *

"I can't keep drugging him," said Denny over all the hoarse yelling and crashing sounds. "It's bad for him, and besides, that stuff costs real money."

"We've got to do something. He's tearing the place apart, and all of us are scratched, bitten, and kicked about as much as we want to be. Why can't we just slam a cricket bat into the back of his head?" And indeed, the woman who had just come out of the other room had a swelling around her eye and several angry welts down her cheek.

"Too risky. Brain damage."

"I'd be very precise."

"Once we get him to Katoomba—"

"And when will that be? Soon, I hope. Why not all the way to Sydney, do the final handover, and be done with him? Spoiled little shit."

"Actually, he's not a bad sort. Always seemed kind of like a puppy amongst the jackals, up there," said Denny.

"Poetic. But he seems to have picked up a lot of nasty habits. I hope they're ready for him in Katoomba."

"It stops being my problem then."

"The problem never stops, you know that. Every time you think that maybe this time you'll have done enough to finally satisfy them, they come up with a new complication. And now that they've got this new bloke, that creepy little pom—what's he need the kid for, anyway?"

"All I know is what I told you. Something about his brain. It's different in some way that means we can't belt him, or just haphazardly drug him."

From the next room, Oliver was hollering, "And you're ugly. And you have bad breath. And if you hadn't tied me up, I'd beat the crap out of you. But I can still kick. Come closer, you coward!"

Denny yelled, "Remember what I said—don't hit him."

"Yeah," screamed Oliver. "Don't hit me, you fuckers!"

"Puppy?" said the woman.

Denny shrugged. "People change."

* * *

"So that's why we have to find Nestor," said Hoyle. "It's not just a family squabble anymore."

"I think you have me mistaken for a good man," said Nicholas.

Hoyle's despair threatened to overwhelm him. "But they—"

"First, I have no idea who these voices are. Second, if they can talk to you, they can bloody well talk to me. I'm a servant of he staff too, am I not? Third, where are they from? Fourth, where are they now? Fifth—"

"All right," snapped Hoyle.

This conversation had been going on for what seemed like hours. Hoyle spoke out loud to start, finding it exhaustingly intimate to speak by thought; luckily, Nicholas followed his lead. Besides, speaking gave Hoyle the comforting illusion that his mind was his own. But Hoyle was starting to panic.

He did his best to calm himself and focus his energy. "Centering," the person at the workplace-productivity retreat had called it, years ago. Hoyle almost laughed; he'd been a very different person then, shuffling dully from day to day in his tedious and inconsequential job, with the biggest excitement in his life the find of some moldering book or other about someone else's adventures.

Never mind that. He breathed deeply, surprised yet again at the new depth and ease of the action. The staff had made him a better slave, stronger and fitter. But he wasn't seduced. He'd go back to his wheezy, bumbling self in a moment if it meant he could be back with Sybil again. *No—focus now. Breathe.*

It took him three or four more tries to realize that the skittering of his attention from topic to topic was, itself, probably the work of the staff. It knew what he was trying to do: convince Nicholas to go with him after Nestor. He renewed his effort, hardening the edges of his awareness like a wall, making a quiet place, thinking only of his breathing. When he finally felt stillness, he carefully sent out as clear and bright a thought as he could: *This thing has to be done, Nicholas. And we're the only ones who can do it. Can't you—can't the man Ruby loved—do this one thing to stop the evil that's already ruined us from going any further?*

As he sent it, he did something he hadn't done before: he

deliberately reached out, not just to sense Nicholas's presence, but to welcome it. The way he'd learned to welcome Sybil's gruff camaraderie, Ada's insouciance, even Oliver's gentle gee-whiz curiosity. *Come on, buddy*, he thought in a sudden, giddy rush of hope. *Come on, mate. We're in this together. Yes, I am mistaking you for a good man. I'm deliberately mistaking you for a good man. Make me be right.*

Hoyle opened his eyes; he hadn't known they were shut until now. Directly in front of him, Nicholas met his gaze, his own eyes hollow.

Hoyle trembled, but refused to put the wall back up. The staff had opened up this channel between his mind and Nicholas's; let it be the staff's undoing, then.

"I didn't set out to hate him," said Nicholas bleakly.

"I know," said Hoyle.

"It started so long ago. He had a temper, right from the start, quick to interpret everything in the worst possible way. If he called to you across the playing field and you didn't hear, you had obviously snubbed him on purpose. If you made a light-hearted joke, it was a hurtful insult. I tried my best to be a good older brother. I knew what I was supposed to do: teach him, protect him, give him a good example. But year after year, he grew in spite, if not in stature, and I stopped pitying a little boy and started despising a pitiable man. I may or may not be a good man, but I tell you now: this effort is doomed and damned before it starts, because Nestor is a bad one."

"Even so," said Hoyle, "we've got to try."

"The staff will stop us. It won't let us leave here without it."

"Well, then, we'll just have to take it with us."

"It will enslave everyone we meet."

"Not if we're careful."

"Once Nestor has it—"

"That's fine, don't you see? All three of us together, that's what needs to happen."

"You have no idea of the risk you're wanting to take."

"And staying here is better? With him on the loose? Maybe if we catch up with him, we can at least restrain his worst excesses. Instead of, um, making them worse."

Nicholas attempted a laugh. "You're referring to me there, aren't you? I made him worse. All right, I did."

"Did you ever try to talk to him about it?"

Nicholas frowned, his mouth open. *Wow*, thought Hoyle. *He genuinely has no idea what I mean by that.* He wondered how many of those eager explorers of a century or two ago had simply been running from pain and humiliation and remorse. *Not that people are all that much better now*, he thought. *But at least—* at least what? At least nowadays people talked about things? He thought back to that horrible time right before he'd found the staff. Maybe things hadn't changed all that much after all.

"Let's go," said Hoyle. "We can find something on the way to wrap the staff up with." He walked unerringly to where it lay, picked it up, and started down the trail toward Glen Davis. He knew this time he'd be permitted to leave. "Nestor may have stopped on the way to pull the wings off some flies; maybe we can catch up."

He did not check to see if Nicholas was following. He could feel that he was.

Chapter 21

In Which Trails Begin to Converge

Hoyle and Nicholas walked easily and quickly through the woods. Hoyle was worried they'd get lost, but Nicholas had been wandering here for a century, and led confidently. They spoke little, rested less, until they got to Glen Davis.

They'd expected the little town to be essentially empty, the anarchists having scattered. But from a few hundred yards away, Hoyle could already hear police radios, anxious voices arguing, and the occasional car coming and going. They stopped and watched.

Carefully, now, came Nicholas's thought. *We'll get closer and find out what's up.*

They moved slowly forward. Nicholas clutched Hoyle's arm. Four people in bright orange overalls and helmets were walking carefully in single file along the trail. Hoyle guessed they were some sort of search-and-rescue detail. He and Nicholas eased back behind some rocks.

"This is stupid," said one of the searchers, who looked to be about nineteen. "Why would they take him back into the bush? Didn't Ashleigh say—"

"Shut up," said the leader. "Jesus Christ, I got to talk to the training officer. Who signed you off for land search?"

"You did," said the kid sullenly.

They said no more.

As they moved off, Hoyle said silently, *Who do you think they're looking for?*

Nicholas gave a mental shrug.

The sun was starting to set. Hoyle and Nicholas stayed in the woods until the police and searchers left, then walked through the town, keeping to the shadows.

There was no sign of Sybil.

Hoyle told himself that made it easier. He and Nicholas could head straight out after Nestor, with no cumbersome explanations, and without putting Sybil, Ada, and Oliver in the way of more danger. But he couldn't make the dull shock of their desertion go away, no matter how many times he went over it to himself.

"Before we start back to Sydney," said Hoyle, "I need to find something to wrap the staff in."

Nicholas nodded, and Hoyle started searching for beach towels, horse blankets, anything. He eventually found and commandeered a sheet hanging from a clothesline, and they faded back towards the woods to spread it out and wrap the staff thoroughly.

Hoyle was trying to ignore how much he yearned to carry it. *What is this, Lord of the Rings?* he thought irritably, then was sorry he had, because he already felt enough like Gollum without the comparison being explicit. Even if he managed to destroy the staff, would it bring him down with it, like the Ring? *Be careful what you wish for,* he thought. *You wanted an adventure? You wanted to finally do something meaningful? Well, here you go. How do you like it?*

It took them a day and a night to get to a tiny village called Mt. Victoria, and another four hours to make it to the significantly less tiny Katoomba. The road rose relentlessly, and even with his newfound stamina, Hoyle was finding the pace demanding. He was grateful for the distraction when Nicholas began offering isolated snippets of conversation: comments on the weather; occasional reminiscences about other treks he'd done; musings on now Hoyle was still so much more corporeal than he; and speculation on how long before Hoyle would be completely consumed by the staff's need for energy. Hoyle did not encourage this last one, but he quite enjoyed listening to the stories, and by the time they'd reached Lithgow, Nicholas was unstoppable.

"It's amazing how far you can walk with a broken foot when you have to," said Nicholas. "I was this close to taking my knife and slicing the end off my boot, the swelling was so bad. And the throbbing! Lord, the agony every time my foot came down. But I figured the boot was probably the only thing holding the shattered bones in my foot together at this point, and I struggled on. But when I found I was being trailed by a pack of opportunistic jackals—me with no gun and no hope of being able to run—I knew I'd somehow have to make a stand."

Hoyle wasn't sure how much to believe, but he didn't care. For the first time in a long time, he was enjoying himself, and he warmed to Nicholas for taking the trouble.

"Nicholas?" he asked during a pause in the stories.

"Mm?"

"What about Ingraham?"

Nicholas laughed sharply. "Him! Pathetic hanger-on. As soon as Nestor spurned his advances, I'm assuming he ran in humiliation back to Sydney."

"Nestor said Ingraham killed you because you were choking Nestor to death. And that as soon as he found out Nestor was stuck where the staff was, he ran away."

"As far as I knew, Ingraham never knew anything about the staff. Although—" Nicholas frowned. "If he did, it would explain why Nestor tried so hard to chase him down. That was when we found out about being trapped, when Nestor nearly killed himself in his efforts, never mind my doing it."

Hoyle nodded thoughtfully. "Did you?"

"Did I what?"

"Try to kill him?"

"Why does everyone think I go around killing the people I love? No, all right?"

"Sorry."

As if to himself, Nicholas added, "Despite everything, he was my brother."

They walked on in silence.

"Do you think we're gaining?" said Hoyle after a while. Nicholas, after all, was in his own way closer to Nestor than Hoyle was, and might be able to sense him more clearly.

Nicholas narrowed his eyes thoughtfully. "Maybe. There's a certain tang of nastiness in the air that could possibly be getting stronger."

"Your talking like that isn't going to make it any easier to get him on our side when the time comes."

"He's not *that* close," said Nicholas. "He can't hear us."

"No, I mean it's giving you bad habits. You need to start thinking of him differently. The more often you tell yourself he's nasty, the less able you'll be to work with him. And we need all three of us to figure out how to make the break and starve the staff. Habit, it's all habit. Start making new habits." He wondered scornfully how he'd gotten so wise all of a sudden. Well, it didn't matter if he was really wise, he just had to sound wise.

Nicholas mumbled something dismissive, but Hoyle really did hope Nicholas stopped being so damned negative. It had gotten old some miles back. That was another reason for keeping Nicholas telling stories: it distracted him from brooding about Nestor.

Nicholas had also been distracted by Lithgow; he hadn't seen it in a hundred years, and while Glen Davis hadn't changed all that much, just a few modest structures added, Lithgow was an unnerving and unsightly conglomeration of haphazard buildings, roads, wires, noise, trucks, lights, and thousands of people.

"Can't be any worse than the jackals, can it?" said Hoyle brightly.

Nicholas glared at him.

* * *

Oliver sat, glowering and rebellious, on a hard wooden chair in a bare room. Nestor lounged against a wall, puffing sensuously on a pipe.

"Can you please not smoke around me?" said Oliver.

"No," said Nestor. "A hundred years, it's been, and for several of those I didn't even have lungs. I'm damned if I'll let your woman-ish sensibilities keep me from a well-earned smoke."

"You're damned anyway, as far as I can tell," said Oliver. "You're just plain mean, and that's all there is to you."

Nestor smiled. "Thank you, boy. That quite a compliment, and a sign that my efforts to achieve greatness have begun to yield fruit."

"Greatness." Oliver snorted.

"Don't scoff," said Nestor smoothly. "Greatness. And you will help me achieve it."

Oliver snorted again.

"Oh, you will. You won't be able to help it. You, too, are spe-cial—unique, in fact. I found out through the powers of the staff, and through the unwitting help of that buffoon Marchand. Gads, what a relief to be rid of him. Simpering idiot."

"What do you mean, I'm special? I'm never special."

"You are uniquely attuned to the staff."

"No I'm not."

"Oh, yes, you are. When that fool Marchand was playing around, trying in his own weak, ineffectual way to figure out how it worked, he stumbled upon your gifts. The staff found you exceptionally responsive."

Oliver's eyes opened wide. "Hot dogs."

"Oh, so you do remember," said Nestor. "Yes, indeed. It's just as well you didn't find the staff yourself, because I probably never would have been able to exploit you the way I did Marchand—the staff would have consumed you utterly."

"Con-consumed me?"

"It has no will of its own, it's not alive. It only does what it was designed to do. And as far as I can tell, it's designed to consume. Most people are able to put up a bit of a fight; you'd have been gobbled up in a heartbeat. On the other hand, when a strong-willed man can channel its—well, for lack of a better word, we must say 'desires'—it, and he, can accomplish so much more than when it's just left to its own devices. I serve the staff, but the staff also serves me. As you and your unique gift will serve me as well."

"A, no, and B, you haven't got the staff."

Nestor smiled. "What would you like for dinner, boy?"

"Oh, God, I'd love a hot d—" Oliver began to shake. "Nothing, thanks."

"You see?" murmured Nestor.

"I won't let you," said Oliver. "I'll stop you."

"No," said Nestor in a kind voice. "You're my friend, aren't you? You'd do anything for me."

Oliver struggled to speak. "No. The staff is way far away from here. You can't be using it. You can't be making me do things."

"Do you think things like time and space matter now, stupid boy? Do you think I don't know that your fat friend Marchand is looking for you right now? And that my beloved elder brother is with him?"

"If time and space don't matter, why do you need me here? Let me go."

Nestor looked at him sharply. "Not a bad question, boy. But you haven't touched the staff, you see. I can control you, but I need you with me. We're not linked in that way."

"Damn straight we're not," cried Oliver. His head dropped to his chest. "I'm really hungry."

"I could get you one of those, what was it, hot dogs."

"No."

Nestor's voice softened again. "Come now, boy, stop denying it. You admire me. You want to help me. Don't you?"

Oliver said nothing.

"Don't you?" insisted Nestor. "You were jealous that I'd chosen

Marchand. You wanted to be the special one. But now you *are* special. You tried so hard to resist, you fought so hard—brave boy! Where did you learn to kick like that? But you're tired now. You deserve a rest. You don't have to fight to prove you're special—I know you are, remember? It feels so good to believe me, doesn't it? Don't make any decisions now, boy. There's time. But don't forget—I'm the only one who's ever seen how very, very important you are." He turned and left the room, and Oliver heard the door lock.

"I'm hungry," said Oliver to the empty room, and started to cry.

* * *

"You were amazing," said Ada as they drove. "Where did you learn all that karate stuff?"

"You pick things up along the way. Besides, you were pretty good yourself. Where did you learn to throw like that?"

"One of my cousins. He didn't show me how, exactly—I watched him. And that's not easy to do while you're running away from him, let me tell you. The breakthrough came when I snuck up on him chucking rocks at stray cats. I caught on real quick, and to this day I bet he thinks one of the cats was sneaking around behind him to throw the rocks back in revenge. Hey, where do we go next?"

"What about going west?"

"There is fucking nothing between here and Perth, as far as I know."

"That's not true. I looked at the map. There are lots of towns west of here."

Ada snorted. "Sure, if you mean Dubbo. Giraffes are cool, they have blue tongues and everything, but that's no reason to take Oliver there."

"Giraffes?"

"There's a zoo in Dubbo. I think it's in Dubbo. Maybe it's in

Parkes. Or there's something else in Parkes. But I'm betting they're heading back toward Sydney. Like I said, a thousand places to hide. Only hitch is, their thousand is probably different to my thousand. Still, we'll be safer there than here. And there are too many flies here."

Sybil could only agree, especially about the flies. "All right." She drove back to the main road and headed toward Sydney. Before long they were in the mountains.

"Can we stop in Katoomba again, please?"

"Why? We've already seen the Three Sisters."

"I got a feeling."

"Or you have to pee."

"That too."

Sybil sighed. "All right. I guess we could top up the gas tank, too."

"And some dinner?"

"Oh. Um, sure."

"Don't tell me you forgot we hadn't had any dinner."

"Sometimes I forget to eat when I'm stressed."

"Wow. I thought you didn't get stressed. I mean, I knew you were fooling that guy in the hotel room, I knew you weren't falling apart. You never fall apart, even a little."

"What kind of bizarre thing is that to think? Do you think I don't care about people, that I don't worry about them? What kind of monster would I be then?"

"Sorry," said Ada, suddenly subdued. "Didn't mean to insult you."

They drove on as night fell. Sybil said, "Here—we'll fill up, and it looks like they have a restaurant next door."

Sybil bought the gas, then they parked in the restaurant lot and went inside. The grey of its walls were rendered even more undead-looking by the buzzing and flickering fluorescent lights. Smears of ketchup were hardening on the tables, and flies circled and lit, crawled through the ketchup, then circled once more. Ada looked at Sybil with a quizzical "Is this all right?" expression, and Sybil shrugged. They ordered hamburgers, fries, and soda, and took a number on a metal stick over to one of the less filthy tables.

"Right," said Ada. "Excuse me." She walked to the back of the restaurant, where a sign saying "Toilets" hung on the wall. What an embarrassing word—"toilet." Sybil couldn't get used to how Australians just said it right out like that.

A minute later, Ada hurried back, wiping her hands on her jeans. "Hey, guess what?" she said as she sat down and leaned forward. "I just heard a clue."

"Quietly," said Sybil. "What was it?"

"Back near the toilets there were a couple people at a table, and I heard one of them saying, 'That weedy little pommie.' Who else could it be but Nestor?"

"Why?"

"Well—that's him. He's a weedy little pommie, never saw a weedier one."

"What's a pommie?"

Ada raised her eyebrows. "Don't you guys call them that in America? It means someone from England. So, you see?"

"But this is a big tourist area, right?"

"Well, yeah, but so what?"

"So there are probably a thousand or more English people here at any given moment. And at least a few of them have to be weedy, right? Coincidence."

"I told you, I have a feeling."

"Okay, I'll admit it's very slightly better than nothing. But only very slightly. There's a rack of potato chips over near there—can you go and pretend like you're trying to decide which one you want and listen some more?"

"If I pick one out, will you buy it for me?"

Sybil sighed. "Yeah, all right. But you know you're getting fries with your burger, right?"

"We've been eating camping food for a long time. I could eat five or six burgers. Some salt and vinegar crisps will go down a treat as well. Round out my meal just perfectly."

"Quit wasting time, then." She handed Ada some change.

Sybil was impressed; with absolutely convincing nonchalance, Ada wandered to the rack and perused the offerings. She read labels, she picked up packets and put them back, she made faces at ones she pretended not to like (and, indeed, who could like something called—what was that? "Burger Rings"? Who would want beef-flavored potato chips? The thought was revolting).

The server brought their dinner. Ada put down the packet she'd been scrutinizing, dashed back to the table, and started eating with an animal intensity that Sybil found alarming.

"Whoa, whoa, you'll make yourself throw up," she said.

"No I won't," said Ada between bites. "Even though this is a really shitty burger."

"Then don't eat it. I'm done with mine." The half-eaten burger lay on her plate, its slick of glistening grease slowly congealing to cloudy grey.

"Too hungry."

"Did you hear anything?"

"No." Ada screwed up her face. Sybil wasn't sure if it was in disgust at the lack of data or the burger. "They just kept going on about someone who got drunk at a party or something. 'Poor guy. Kept going on and on about chompsy, chompsy, chompsy. Not that it does him any good.'"

"Wait—what?"

"What, what?"

"They said 'chompsy'?"

"Yeah."

"Not—'Chomsky'?"

"I don't know. Maybe."

"Anarchist philosopher Noam Chomsky."

Ada's eyes got wide. "Anarchist—"

Sybil nodded. "Finish up. We need to be ready to follow them."

Ada swallowed the last of the burger and shoved a handful of fries into her mouth. Then she grabbed her soda bottle, nodded back at Sybil, and stood. Together they sauntered casually to their car, then sat in the darkness.

Ada said, "Do you know how to tail someone?"

"Don't you just drive along behind them and turn when they do?"

"Not according to the movies my cousin watches."

"Okay, so what do you do, then?"

"I don't know. I always got bored during those scenes and went over my auntie's house—she had cake."

"You're not helping."

When the others came out, Ada punched Sybil in the arm. "There they are," she whispered superfluously.

Sybil returned the punch. "Knock it off."

The other car pulled out onto the road. Sybil started the engine and began to follow, from the main road to smaller and smaller roads, twistier and twistier. She was able to track the car only because the night was a bit foggy and its lights made a soft floating island of light that could be seen from some distance. When the car finally turned into a driveway, Sybil drove past.

"What are you doing?" squeaked Ada.

"Making sure we don't look precisely like we were following them. We'll drive on for a while, then drive back, so maybe they'll think we're a different car. Then we'll park a little way down the road and walk in."

"How are we going to make a quick getaway when we find him? What if he's drugged and we have to fucking carry him through the fucking bush?"

"One problem at a time. Right now it's more important that we actually sneak in, instead of driving up and beeping the horn."

"Yeah, but there's nothing wrong with planning ahead, is there? Isn't that what you're always on about? And I'm finally giving it a go, and you're telling me not to. Jesus, Sybil! Make up your fucking mind." Her voice cracked in distress.

"Ada! If you are in this state when we go up to that house, you—will—get—us—killed. Now take a deep breath. I didn't hear it, try again. That's better. Now another. All right? All right. Now keep doing that."

"For how long?"

"Until we have Oliver back again. Or you pass out. Whichever comes first."

Chapter 22

In Which Nestor Encounters
Many Difficulties

Nestor paced—it felt good to work out his tension in a physical way again. They'd got the boy for him, that was a relief. He desperately needed the boy's power, as his distance from the staff was making him far more vulnerable to fatigue and pain than he'd expected. There was a complication, though: Nestor had thought that the boy had no idea of his own strength, and that Nestor would have to expend little of his own in the process of establishing the conduit. Somehow, in just the past few days, the boy had discovered his own wellspring of power. Perhaps he'd begun having relations with the girl; that could conceivably have triggered this sudden burst of confidence.

Nestor cursed. Again, a woman foiling his plans. Natalie, back in England, with all her mocking. Violet, in Sydney—he'd been ready to do anything for her, anything. Ruby, falling in love with Nicholas. That mannish thing, Sybil. And now the girl. Women would suffer worst of all when he finally got to Sydney and set his plans in motion.

* * *

Sybil and Ada sat in the darkness, watching and listening. Sybil was impressed; Ada sat entirely still, entirely quiet, her eyes glittering in the light from the windows. People walked back and forth, but nobody did anything definitive, or spoke loudly enough for them to hear anything except the vaguest murmurs.

Without any warning, Sybil felt the air go tense, even taut, hard to draw into her lungs. And cold.

Ada clutched at her arm. Sybil glanced over; Ada's eyes were wide and frightened. "Something's happening," she whispered.

"Sh."

The tension grew and grew. "I have as much time as you do," came Nestor's voice. "I know—oh, I know—how much pain this is causing you. Just give in. Then it will all stop. You'll have peace. Quiet."

Sybil's skin crawled. *Oh, Oliver. Apparently he can't kill you, or he would have by now, but he will make you long for death, I'm sure of it.*

"Stop it," said Oliver. "Please." He sounded completely drained.

"I need you, boy. I need your power, and your youth, and your extreme, extreme sensitivity. You are my source, my fountain. Together, we will make the world anew."

Oliver's voice rang out. "No. Fuck you! 'You cannot buy the revolution. You cannot make the revolution. You can only be the revolution. It is in your spirit, or it is nowhere.' Ursula K. fucking LeGuin!"

Nestor screamed, "That has nothing whatever to do with this, stupid, stupid boy! I have had enough!"

"'In this possibly terminal phase of human existence, Democracy and Freedom are more than values to be treasured, they may well be essential to survival.' Noam Chomsky, fuckers. Suck on that!"

Nestor gave an inarticulate, animal howl of frustration and rage.

"Uh-oh," said Ada. "Let's go. Storm the place. Before he kills Oliver." She leaped up, dragging Sybil with her. "Now or never. Come with me or I'm going alone."

Sybil dug her heels in, and they poised there. Then Ada flung

Sybil's arm away and cried, "What is wrong with you?" She ran onto the verandah and flung the door open. "Oliver," she bellowed. "Oliver!"

"Shit," cried Sybil. "Ada!" She followed Ada into the house.

The house was small. Ada had already looked in the front room and the kitchen. Someone came out from one of the bedrooms and grabbed her; she fought, a chaotic, snarling whirl of elbows and nails and teeth. In a moment, Sybil was up to them, and although it was difficult to get a clear shot, she managed to get behind the attacker and snap a kick up between his legs. Not as effective as a knee to the groin from the front, but definitely enough to distract him. Ada took advantage of the situation to turn and deliver the strike properly, followed by the knee to the head.

"You learn quickly," said Sybil.

There was only one door left off the narrow hallway. Ada flung herself at the doorknob and rattled it frantically. "Oliver!"

"Ada!" yelled Oliver. "Get out. Get out now! I'll be fine."

"You won't fucking be fine. How do I get in there?"

Sybil whispered, "Keep the talking going," and went back outside. She grabbed a broom that was lying on the veranda, then found the window of the room where Oliver was.

"Who's in there with you?" Ada yelled.

"That weedy little shit Nestor."

Nestor howled.

"No one else?"

"He's plenty, believe me."

"Are you all right?"

Silence.

"Oliver! Jesus Christ, are you all right?"

"Yes," said Oliver.

Sybil punched the broom handle into the glass, over and over, knocking out the panes. Hopefully, she'd be able to reach some sort of latch.

Nestor loomed abruptly in the window, a silhouette. Sybil rammed the broomstick into his stomach. She heard him grunt, but there was no other effect.

"No, you can't have him," said Nestor. "But I'm so glad you're here. He's not cooperating, and your presence will be a much more effective persuasion. Now come inside. The girl is already captive."

"No she isn't," yelled Oliver.

Nestor clapped a hand to his forehead. Then something seemed to snap. He yanked a knife from his belt and whipped around to attack Oliver. "You can't be the only one—I'll find another. I'm done with you."

Sybil pushed up on the window frame, which didn't budge. She frantically fumbled for a window latch—nothing. Finally she wedged the broomstick horizontally between the now-glassless panes and swung it around to splinter the wood. She clawed at the twisted frame until there was a gap big enough to get through. She could feel splinters tearing at her, but ignored them.

Oliver was on the floor, his hands tied behind him. He was kicking out frantically at Nestor, who circled him, knife in hand. Nestor was wild with anger, but Oliver was just as wild, spinning and striking.

Sybil thought, *I'm getting a little tired of fighting.* She dragged the broom in after her; Nestor was too frenzied to even notice. She didn't know whether it would do any good—after all, he'd taken a full-on jab in the stomach with no more than a grunt. Would a crack on the head make any difference? She had to do something, as it was only a matter of time before Nestor made it past Oliver's feet to stab him. She positioned the broomstick on one side of her body, then swung it around with a vicious flick to strike at his head. She connected, but as she feared, he kept on darting around Oliver and feinting with the knife.

"Oliver!" screamed Ada from the hallway. She started pounding on the door.

Sybil had no other plan than to keep hitting Nestor and hoping the blows would add up and he would finally collapse. It was a nightmare that kept on going: the noise, the confusion, her aching arms and hands, the blood from the cuts on Oliver's feet and legs—and Nestor, mad, unstoppable, terrifying. Sybil struck and struck and struck, until at last, oh God, at last he dropped to his knees, and then forward onto his face.

Sybil dropped the broomstick and opened the door. Ada tumbled into the room, then ran over to Oliver. "Oh, Oliver, look what he—are you—Sybil, is Oliver going to be okay?"

"Come on," Sybil said simply. She took Nestor's knife and cut Oliver's bonds, then she and Ada helped him to his feet.

"Should we, you know …" said Oliver shakily and nodded at the knife in Sybil's hand, and then at Nestor's inert form.

"I don't want to kill anyone," said Sybil. "Let's go before he wakes up."

In less than a minute they were in the car and back on the road.

"If it weren't for Hoyle, we could just go back to Sydney," said Ada. "But since we're stuck here, is there a hospital? Oliver's hurt."

"There's one in Katoomba," said Oliver weakly. "But I don't want to go to the hospital."

"I know, honey," said Sybil gently. "But some of those cuts will need stitching."

"Scars are cool, though," said Ada.

"Infection and muscle damage aren't," said Sybil with finality. She drove them back to the lights of Katoomba and asked for directions to the hospital. It was a busy night: plenty of fights, a drug overdose, two car crashes, and a kid who'd fallen off a skateboard. It was a while before anyone saw to Oliver.

A nurse came over to where Ada and Sybil were waiting, sipping at cups of instant coffee. "Are you Oliver's friends?"

"Yes," said Ada eagerly. "He all right?"

"The cuts aren't so bad, but we're a little worried about his heart rate and temperature. He's showing signs of extreme exhaustion—what's he been doing lately?"

Spending hours resisting torture and brainwashing from the slave of a weird magical stick, thought Sybil. "Studying for an exam," she said. "Then he sort of went wild and got, um, on the piss with a mate, and they got into some trouble."

"Well, we're going to keep an eye on him overnight. Why don't the two of you go home and sleep, and come back in the morning? You don't look too much more chipper than he does."

"No, thanks, we'll wait here," said Sybil.

"You got any money?" said Ada when the nurse left. "I'm starving."

"You have got to be kidding me."

"No, why would I kid? I always get hungry at times like these. It's a stress response."

"Ada Drake, when have you ever been in times like these?"

"Okay, I haven't. But I'm still hungry. Can I have some money, please?"

"Here you go. It's not going to last forever, though, you know. Then Hoyle and I will have to go home."

"So why shouldn't you stay in Australia?"

"They don't let you just stay. If we overstay our tourist visas, that gets us into quite a bit of trouble, and they kick us out into the bargain—and we'll never be able to come to Australia again."

"Oh," said Ada, and she looked genuinely troubled. "That wouldn't be good at all. Hey! Can Oliver and I come to America with you?"

"Maybe."

"Cool! Where do you live in America?"

"Washington, DC."

"Wait—real people actually live there? I thought only the president lived there. Is it a cool place?"

"Pretty cool."

"Would Oliver like it?"

"He'd be in heaven, all the politics. So much to protest against."

"Looks like he's found plenty to protest against here. That was so creepy, especially right before we ran into the house. What *was* that?"

"Maybe it was a little foretaste of what the whole world will be like once the staff takes over."

"Ew. We're not going to let that happen, are we?"

"I guess not."

"Good, then," said Ada. "That would suck."

* * *

Nicholas said, "We're getting closer."

Hoyle said, "Yeah." The sick, greasy feeling in his mind was definitely stronger. He longed to talk about it—actually, he longed to complain about it—but he was trying to provide an example to Nicholas on staying positive. But what chance did workplace platitudes stand against a century of bitter hatred and betrayal?

How in the world was he supposed to convince Nestor to join with them in defeating the staff? Nestor loved the staff. He loved the ageless power, the freedom from the incessant demands of the body, the exhilarating feeling of being caught up in something bigger, stronger, *weirder* than dull, plodding, normal life. He loved sticking it to weaker people.

What could Hoyle hold out in exchange for that? Inescapable, ineluctable pain, followed by a life of mediocrity—if they survived at all. Hoyle himself would be sorry to say goodbye to Sybil and Ada, but aside from that, he really didn't feel all that emotional about the prospect of sacrificing his aimless life. In a way, it was even a step up: his life was finally about to mean something, in its very last moments.

He was willing to go with the flow, see what happened. The voices had seemed as clueless as he, but they weren't particularly frantic. So maybe he could relax. Except for needing to depend on the Ivory brothers. And, oh, yeah, the little question of unstoppable human suffering if they failed. And the fact that while he now knew he wasn't as useless as he'd thought, he still didn't feel particularly prepared for the demands of saving the world.

Okay, he told himself as they trudged along the streets of Katoomba, homing in on the nastiness that was Nestor. *If you can't solve the whole thing right now, what can you do? You can get you, the staff, and those two clowns all in the same place. Then maybe the next step will reveal itself. Or not. But your friends, the voices, gave you this one lead, and it's all you've got.*

Nicholas raised his head. "Something's …"

"Yes?" said Hoyle.

"Not right. Something's wrong with Nestor."

"Many, many things are wrong with Nestor. Can you be more specific?"

Nicholas shot him an annoyed look and picked up the pace. They got to an intersection; a smaller road wound away from the main highway into the darkness. "This way."

Hoyle, too, felt the directional discomfort that told him they were headed the right way, but except that he couldn't feel anything about Nestor one way or the other. After another turn or two, they found a small huddle of wooden houses, each more cluttered and neglected than the last. Even in the moonlight, Hoyle could see that the last one in the row had a badly broken window frame around the side: the wood was twisted outward in splinters, and broken glass lay everywhere. Hoyle wondered how anyone living in a house this shabby could have anything worth breaking in for.

"This is it," said Nicholas. "He's in there."

Hoyle could feel it, too. "You're not rushing up the steps."

"No."

"You're not chickening out, are you?"

Nicholas smiled wryly. "I'm well past worrying about that sort of thing. " He walked up the steps and into the house.

Hoyle followed. The inside was even more disordered than the outside, with things knocked to the floor and broken wherever he looked. There was a dark smear on the linoleum at his feet.

"Look, Nicholas," he said. "I think it's blood."

Nicholas glanced down, then moved on. Hoyle was puzzled—wasn't a blood smear something they should be paying attention to? If only to warn them to be careful, if not to help them sort out what had happened. As soon as they'd entered the house, Nicholas had stopped interacting with him at all; he'd always been grim, but now he was hostile and remote. Hoyle was surprised at how much this bothered him.

Nicholas glanced into each room. At the last doorway on the left, he stopped and stood quite still. Hoyle peered in around him.

Nestor lay on the floor. His face was battered into near-shapelessness. As they watched, his arm twitched.

"Jesus," said Hoyle. Nicholas made no move. Hoyle pushed past him, saying, "If you're not going to help him, I will."

He put the staff down and knelt next to Nestor, wishing desperately for Sybil and her fathomless expertise. Nestor was breathing. That was a relief; Hoyle hadn't been looking forward to having to try his own made-up version of CPR. *Note to self: learn CPR when you get back home. If you get back home.*

"Hey," said Hoyle, touching Nestor's shoulder. "Nestor? You okay?" The arm twitched again.

"Just pick up the staff and use it to finish the job," said Nicholas.

"No," said Hoyle. "We need him."

"We need him not to be connected to the staff. If he's dead, the problem is solved."

"I don't think it works like that. We need him to say no. He's the willing slave. His 'no' is going to mean a lot more than yours or mine."

Hoyle unwrapped one end of the staff and shoved it against Nestor's hand. There was a soundless shout of energy, and Nestor stirred. He gripped the staff reflexively, but Hoyle yanked it away and wrapped it up again.

Nestor's face was healing as they watched. In less than a minute, he sat up painfully. "Oh," he said, squinting at Hoyle. "Hello, old boy. And you, Nicholas. Pleasant of you to come and visit me."

"What happened?" said Nicholas blandly.

"A thug broke in looking for money, no doubt to support some loathsome drug habit or other. He had a large and effective metal pipe with him—even the vigor of the staff couldn't keep up with it, not without its being in my hand." He made a show of noticing the re-swaddled staff in Hoyle's hand. "My! Is that it? What a happy coincidence." He reached for it; again, Hoyle snatched it out of his reach.

"We need to talk," said Hoyle.

Chapter 23

In Which Yet More Decisions

Must Be Made

Ada sat in the back seat with Oliver, who lay limply against her shoulder. They drove in silence through the tiny, mostly tree-obscured towns along the Great Western Highway until Sybil saw a McDonald's. None of them were at all hungry, not even Ada, but it was a busy, well-lit place to park.

"How are you doing, Oliver?" said Sybil. "Need another—what are these—codeine? They let you walk out of there with a packet of codeine pills? What the hell is this?"

"What?" said Ada. "They do that all the time. You can get them at the chemist, anyone can."

"Prescription only in the States."

"Wow, what a nervous country. Codeine never hurt anyone."

"No, I'm fine, thanks," said Oliver. The circles under his eyes were deep and dark against his pallid face.

"Can you talk about it?" said Sybil.

"Not sure," said Oliver. Ada hugged him more tightly. "I just kept thinking of you guys. Of you, Ada. He wanted me to … he kept trying to make me …"

They waited.

After a while, Oliver spoke again. "He said I was special. He said I was crucial to … to something, I never quite got that. But he wanted me to, I don't know, some kind of telepathy thing. 'Let me use your power,' he kept saying. 'I need your help.' 'Help to do what?' I kept asking him. But all he did was … laugh. It was really scary. And then, when he saw I was scared, he tried to convince me we were friends. He … kept touching my hair. The creep. He pressured me and pressured me. I don't know how, but I actually felt it inside my head. Hey, did you know it was Hoyle who made me want hot dogs? Why did you let him do that? You shouldn't fuck with me like that, it isn't nice."

"It was an accident," said Sybil.

"Oh. Nestor told me. He said it meant I was special. Sensitive. I bet he thought that meant I was weak. That I wouldn't be able to stop him using me. But I did. I fought and fought, and I stopped him. It really hurt, everything hurt, because I sort of wanted to … I wanted to help him. Isn't that creepy? But it wasn't like wanting to help you. It was a kind of crawling feeling. With you, though, I feel like I'm better. What did you do to him? I was kind of out of it. I'd been shouting for hours, trying to keep him out of my head."

"Sybil bashed him unconscious. It took some doing, too, let me tell you."

"Wow," said Oliver drowsily. "You did that for me?" And he was asleep.

"Sybil?" said Ada.

"Mm?"

"Is he going to be okay?"

"I don't know."

Sybil suddenly felt like her eyes were being crowbarred from her head. "We've got to find a safe place to sleep," she said. "I'm going to start hallucinating from sleep deprivation in a minute."

"No shortage of hotels in the Blue Mountains," said Ada. "Let's go."

They stopped at the first place they found. Unsurprisingly, based on the look of it, there was a vacancy. Sybil paid, and they trudged to the room. Ada and Oliver fell onto one bed, Sybil onto the other. All three were asleep instantly.

Sybil woke suddenly to the sound of hoarse screaming. Ada was shaking Oliver, shouting, "Wake up, Oliver! Wake up. I'm here. It's all right. Stop it. Stop it!"

Sybil turned a light on. "Ada! Quiet. Yelling isn't going to help. You've got to make him feel safe, for God's sake." She hoped Ada would be able to hear over the sounds of Oliver's terror.

"Oh." Ada controlled herself with visible effort, then held Oliver close and rocked him. "Shh, baby, shh. Shhhh." Gradually the screams subsided.

"What time is it?" said Ada.

Sybil looked at the clock radio. "Three-thirty."

"So we've been asleep for …"

"About an hour."

Ada sighed. "Let's try this again." Sybil turned the light off.

Oliver woke them at five-fifteen, six o'clock, six-thirty, and eight o'clock. Each time, the screams got quieter and quieter as Oliver lost his voice. *Just as well*, thought Sybil, *or else they'd chuck us out of here.*

At nine a.m., housekeeping knocked.

"When's checkout?" muttered Ada sleepily.

"Ten," said Sybil.

"Checkout's at fucking ten," yelled Ada. "Fuck off until then!"

A few minutes later came another knock. "Manager."

Ada groaned in annoyance. She took a deep breath to do more yelling, but Sybil said, "No, Ada, wait."

She got up, every joint aching, and shuffled to the door. "Yes, what is it?"

"I'm sorry to disturb you, but I need to ask you to check out now."

"Why?"

"The other guests are complaining."

"Which other guests?" called Ada. "The junkie, the hooker, her pimp, the drunk, or the guy whose wife kicked him out last night?"

"Ada, you're not helping," said Sybil. "It's all right, we'll get our things together and go."

"Thank you," said the manager.

Ada squawked.

"I don't want to argue about it," said Sybil. "I really don't. And I have no idea at all what we should do now: go to Sydney, or see if we can't find Hoyle and try together to handle Nestor."

"You sound like Hoyle would be able to help us get rid of Nestor," said Ada.

"Maybe he would."

"He didn't do so good before," said Ada dubiously.

"I think Hoyle's connection to the staff is a vulnerability that Nestor's forgotten about. Hoyle's got a way in. I'm betting he can guess what Nestor's going to do next, he can sense when Nestor is afraid and why. He may even be able to turn the tables on Nestor and do a little of the ordering around himself. He's our secret weapon. So. How are we going to find Hoyle?" said Sybil.

"You're asking me?"

"Just driving aimlessly around is not going to do it. Besides, I'm sick of doing that. I feel so … useless."

"Yeah, useless. You. Okay," said Ada, and rolled her eyes.

"Is Oliver awake?"

"Let me see. Hey, baby," she said tenderly. "Come on. Time to wake up."

Oliver rubbed his eyes with the backs of his hands, like a small child. "Okay," he mumbled.

"How handy that we're already dressed," said Ada. "Jesus, they can't even give us time to take a shower?"

"We'd just be putting the same filthy clothes back on," said Sybil. "Everything in my pack is this dirty."

They emerged into the glaring sunlight to see the manager, her arms crossed and her face wary, watching to make sure they left.

"All right, all right, we're going," said Ada.

"Sorry about the noise," said Sybil, and trudged over to the car.

How can I take care of Ada and Oliver, find Hoyle, and stop Nestor? She had never felt so alone, and so responsible.

A tear dribbled down her cheek, then another. She wiped them off quickly, before Ada could notice.

* * *

Nestor laughed, a long, screeching cackle.

"I'll take that as a no, then," said Hoyle.

Nicholas shook his head. "I told you he would—"

Hoyle turned on him. "Look," he snapped. "I have about had it with your negativity, all right?"

"He's immune to reason—listen to him," Nicholas shouted back. "He's mad, and you're a fool."

"Then we have to leave reason alone and find another way," said Hoyle. He let the words roll around in his head: *We have to leave reason alone.*

What was reason? Logic, cause-and-effect, things you could think through step by step. Hoyle had always thought it was the only way to understand things. But reason had been less and less reliable of late. Was there another way to think? Another sort of logic? Hoyle didn't know. There was intuition, but that meant knowing what to do by things feeling right. Nothing had felt right for—well, if he was going to be honest, the only thing that had felt right for years now was the moment he'd told Sybil he'd come with her on this adventure. And even that had turned out to be a disaster.

Hoyle closed his eyes and sighed.

"Look out," shouted Nicholas at the same moment.

Just in time, Hoyle opened his eyes and jumped back, taking the staff with him as Nestor clawed at it.

"I did not sense that coming," said Hoyle. He looked at Nestor, who was unabashed at his failed attempt to grab the staff. "It looks like the staff is on your side, Nestor. That's not such a good thing."

"I think it's a jolly good thing," said Nestor. "Particularly as it seems that nobody in the world is on your side. You think Nicholas is your ally? Look more deeply into his heart, as I know you can. You will see that it's as black as mine."

"Look all you want, Marchand," said Nicholas. "I don't care what you see. I'm not doing this for you."

"Doing what?" said Nestor mockingly. "Trying to spoil my fun yet again? How many years before you finally grow up and get tired of that game?"

"Yes, exactly," said Nicholas. "I'm trying to spoil your fun. You are a foul little tick, and your fun means the misery of countless others."

"You were just as horrid as I. Why this sudden rush of virtue?"

"The way we used to do things has got to stop. Ruby is dead. How I hate you for that—"

"I didn't kill her," said Nestor jovially. "It was that madwoman—"

"*Shut up!* She was trying to stop you. If it weren't for you, Ruby would still be alive. If you hadn't loved the power of the staff, if you hadn't craved that sick, sick feeling … I'll make you pay!"

"Oh, Christ," moaned Hoyle. "Nicholas, *you* shut up. You're both poisoned. Years of hatred, years of just … giving up, refusing to think things could ever be better, ever be fixed. No wonder the staff was able to suck your life right out of you until you were worse than ghosts."

"I have no time for this," said Nestor. "The boy proved useless, but there will be others who can serve me. I must be off to find them."

Hoyle tried to block his way to the door, but as he moved, he was wracked with waves of pain. He dropped the staff, but the pain went on, until he crumpled to the floor. He was vaguely aware of the two brothers struggling, but could do nothing to help. By the time the pain eased and he could make sense of things, Nestor was gone again. Nicholas had the staff.

"It was more important to keep him from it than to stop him," said Nicholas. "As bad as he is now, he'd be unstoppable if he had his hands on it."

"Nicholas, what are we going to do?" said Hoyle. "Look what he did to me. And he can do that anytime he wants."

"He didn't do it, the staff did," said Nicholas. "It's got … instincts. It wants to be with Nestor."

On an impulse, Hoyle said, "Tell me about Ruby."

"Good God, why? Focus, man!"

"It's important."

"I can't think why."

"There's something we're missing. Something that will tell us how to break the staff's hold. And we can't think what it is. So there must be some other piece of information."

"Why won't the voices in your head tell you, if it's so important to them to stop the staff?"

"Don't scoff at my voices. Until recently, you were just one of the voices in my head too."

I still am, came Nicholas's thought. *But you certainly don't do what I tell you.*

"That was kind of funny," said Hoyle. "I didn't know you could be funny."

"I'm out of practice, it's true. But at one time I was the toast of the junior common room for my wit."

"Don't distract me. Tell me about Ruby."

"All right," said Nicholas. "Nestor and I had been knocking about the bush for far, far longer than we cared to think, all the while picking at each other. I'll admit I was no better than he. The misery, the boredom, the sheer, petty *spite* of it all were unbearable—and yet bear it we must, year after year after year.

"Then one day, a handful of wanderers appeared. By that time, the staff had nearly spent whatever I could give it, and I was, if you will, a shadow of my former self. I could only just have an effect on the world around me: it took all my strength to make a leaf flutter. I was visible, audible, but nearly powerless. Nestor was in far better shape; he'd had a talent all along for manipulating the staff, and that made me a far easier source of food for its ravening hunger. He was winning, and he knew it. He must also have known that once the staff was done with me, it would turn and consume even him—but look! Here was new food for the staff, here were his bulwarks against the staff's gluttony.

"At first, I was as relieved as he. But I soon began to regard them as people, not prey. I was desperate for company, you see—imagine having only Nestor around for a hundred years. Right away, I was taken with Ruby. She was not particularly beautiful, not as I had been used to judge these things, but my God! Her intelligence, her fire, her strength. She was a queen among them, just and wise, and all of them obeyed her in everything."

Unbidden, the image of Sybil arose in Hoyle's mind, and he felt a sweet and exciting spasm of longing, followed instantly by grief and fear and a loathing of the staff that had messed up everything, everything!

"Or nearly all of them," Nicholas continued. "There was one who always hesitated just that instant, asked that one pointed question, let slip just that one exasperated sigh. I should have seen, and watched Dianne much more carefully. But I only had eyes for the glorious Ruby. I waited for what seemed an eternity before making myself known to her, during one of the rare moments when she was by herself. When she got over her surprise, we spent many hours together. At first she could only just feel my touch, and we soon yearned for more substantial contact. And in that yearning, what joy we found: her love seemed to pull me away from the staff and give me form again. We talked of running away together. I was certain that with her help, and the power of her love, I could break free of those constraints that bound me to the staff and to the place. But Dianne had grown suspicious of Ruby's time away from the others and had begun spying on her. Eventually she overheard Ruby and me planning to run away. And, as you heard, she became convinced that no one connected to the staff could be let loose—and we were all now connected to the staff, as far as she saw it. She knew she could do nothing to harm either Nestor or me, as the staff looked after its servants. But there was one thing she could do to keep me there: she could destroy my salvation. And now Ruby's dead," he finished simply.

"What … what would you have done, if you'd gotten away?" said Hoyle. "Where would you have gone?"

"Did it matter? We would have been together, and away from the staff. Away from Nestor."

"Dianne had a point, though—wasn't it dangerous to just let the staff keep doing what it does? Wasn't Nestor proof enough that people will be the worst kind of shits, given the chance? Wasn't it … *selfish* to just run away?"

"Yes, damn you, of course it was! Why do you think I'm here now? To atone for my folly. If I hadn't distracted her with my idiotic daydreams, she would have seen the danger and put a stop to it, before it had had a chance to taint her life and destroy her."

Hoyle doubted Ruby had been entirely the flawless creature Nicholas described, but he wasn't about to say so. Instead, he said, "I guess we'd better go." As he reached for the staff, however, something Nestor had said struck him. "What boy?"

"What?"

"Nestor said the boy was useless. What boy?"

"I have no idea."

"Oliver. And Oliver was with Sybil and Ada. They'd never let him just go with Nestor. Which means they might be in trouble, too. I need to find them."

"Now who's being selfish?" said Nicholas. "Whatever he did to them, it's done. We need to stop him. That's the only thing either of us can afford to think about now."

Hoyle owed Sybil everything, and he loved her. What kind of friend would leave her to suffer, maybe die? And Ada—so innocent, despite all she'd seen. She hadn't signed on for any of this.

And what if Oliver were still alive? How could Hoyle just walk away from them to pursue some fool's errand, when they needed him? And yet—wouldn't they tell him that they'd be all right, just go and save the fucking world, already? He could hear Ada saying it, could see Oliver's earnest nod and Sybil's steely gaze as she waited to see what he was made of.

Nicholas was at the door. "Let's go," he said. "We have work to do."

Hoyle stood up. "All right."

Chapter 24

In Which the Search Begins in Earnest

Ada was getting worried. There was something wrong with Oliver, something that wasn't getting better no matter how much he dozed or what he ate. He wasn't complaining—he was just … different. He wouldn't talk much. He didn't reach for her hand. He didn't make even his usual lame jokes. She would have been more than happy to laugh at them, even the really wordy ones that she didn't get.

And that was another thing: Oliver was always so smart, but he was only saying a few dopey-sounding things. Ada kind of liked being the practical one, but this was ridiculous. If it kept up, pretty soon he'd be no better than a baby at taking care of himself.

She looked at him across the picnic table. His eyes were half-closed, and his head lolled over to one side.

"Hey," she said softly. "Hey, Oliver."

His eyes opened just a bit.

"You okay?"

"Sure," he said. "I had a hard day. A hard couple of days. I'm not … up to …"

"You're sure not. Here, have some more Coke." She handed him her cup. He obligingly drank a sip.

Ada and Sybil exchanged concerned glances.

"You want to talk about it?" Ada said to Oliver.

Oliver shuddered once, enough to make the Coke slosh in the cup. "I can't. I can't tell you what it was like. I don't …"

"I think it would help," said Ada. She came around to sit next to him and put her arms around his waist. He didn't push her away, but he didn't hug her back, either. Sometimes people got like this; she'd seen it. But that didn't mean she had to just let it happen. If she could help him, she would.

"I'm really tired," he said unexpectedly. "But I'm afraid of what's going to happen when I fall asleep."

"Why?" said Sybil.

"Last night. I had these dreams, right? And then this morning they kicked us out of the motel. So … did I make something bad happen? In my sleep?"

"I didn't hear a thing," said Ada.

"Yeah, but you were asleep, too," he said. "I never made anything happen in my life. But then Nestor kept talking about how important I was, how I was special. What did he mean? That I could make scary things happen to people? I don't want that. I want everyone to have a good life. That's why I became an anarchist." He snorted. "Although we see how well that turned out. Looks like anarchism is just the same as everything else: people trying to trick each other into giving up their power. Ironic, isn't it? Because, like, anarchism is all about people *having* power."

"What are the dreams like, Oliver?" said Sybil.

Oliver blinked and looked distressed. "They're … they've got lots of people in them. And the people are all scared and screaming. And … I'm the one who's scaring them."

"What are you doing that's so scary?"

"That's just it. I'm just standing there watching them be scared. And in the dream … I'm … I'm liking it. It's horrible. Am I really like that? Deep down inside? And every time I try to tell myself no, and to stop the dreams, everything gets all vague and I can't think straight. And the dreams start up again. What's wrong with me?"

"Nothing," said Ada indignantly.

"Then how could I have those dreams, if I wasn't that person, deep down inside?"

"Maybe," said Sybil slowly, "they're not coming from deep down inside. Maybe they're coming from Nestor."

"Ugh," shrieked Oliver, animated at last. "Ugh, no!"

"Maybe he formed some kind of connection with you during that ordeal, and even though you were too strong to become his slave, that connection is still there."

"No! Maybe … maybe it was Hoyle. He tried to get me to do things, too, you know. He made me want to eat hot dogs. That was criminal. He's bad, too. It was Hoyle."

"Maybe," said Sybil.

"You don't think so. You think Nestor got me. Well, I fought him. I fought him and he couldn't beat me. He thought I was weak, but I'm not."

"I know," said Sybil.

"I know," said Ada. "It's okay."

"It's not okay. You think—you think—"

"I do not," snapped Ada. "Shut up and believe me when I tell you things, damn it!"

Oliver wilted. "Sorry. It's just—"

"Oliver?" said Sybil. "Do me a favor, would you?"

"Depends," said Oliver warily.

"Can you see if you can find Hoyle? If there is some kind of connection, maybe we can make it work for us."

"And then what?" said Oliver miserably. "The whole thing starts again?"

"No. It'll be different this time."

"How?"

"All right, I don't know. I just have a feeling."

"Wow," said Ada. "That's not like you. You're Ms. Plan."

"Tell you the truth, I don't even have a feeling. I'm just shooting in the dark," said Sybil. "But try anyway."

"It's going to hurt," whimpered Oliver. "And feel horrible. Everything having to do with that fucking staff feels horrible."

"Please try," said Sybil. "I'm all out of ideas, aside from that."

"So I'm important, you're saying? I'm special? You know, I used to dream that someone would say that to me. 'Oliver, it's up to you!' 'Oliver, you have to seize the airplane controls and save the day!' I don't want that anymore."

"Nobody wants you to suffer, Oliver," said Sybil. "But we need to keep that staff, and Nestor, from doing any more damage. Who else is he trying to control? How long before he gets to enough people to start causing real problems for Australia? For the whole world? Come on, Oliver, cut the crap and do what needs to be done."

Oliver looked back and forth between them until Ada wanted to scream and shake him. Finally—*finally*—he said, "What do I do?"

"Jeez, I don't know," said Ada. "Maybe you just sort of … think towards him?"

"I don't know where 'towards him' is."

"Did you ever get the feeling someone was looking at you from across the room?" said Sybil.

"Oh, man, I feel like that all the time," said Oliver.

"Me too," said Ada.

Sybil scowled at her, then said, "Just see if you can sense anything that—that reminds you of Hoyle. Ready, go."

An anxious thirty seconds ticked by as Oliver closed his eyes and breathed in … and out … and in … and out …

"Nope," he said.

"Try again," said Sybil. "Maybe you're just afraid, and it keeps you from finding him. Try again."

"Of course I'm afraid, Sybil, for God's sake!"

"We're right here. We'll be with you. Try again. Please."

Oliver nodded wearily and closed his eyes again.

"Oh," he yelped.

* * *

"Oh," squawked Hoyle.

"What?" said Nicholas.

"I—I could swear someone—I—*Oliver*?"

"That useless whelp." Nicholas cocked his head. "Ah, yes, there he is, brought into the corrupt fold, no doubt by my even more corrupt brother."

"At least he's alive. And he needs me. Nicholas!" Nicholas looked uninterested, and Hoyle was suddenly frantic to find Oliver. And Sybil. "Can't we—can't we use Oliver as a signal to lead us to Nestor? Won't Nestor be following him to try again to control him?"

Nicholas considered this. "How strong is your contact? Mine's almost imperceptible."

"Getting stronger. A lot stronger. He recognizes me! This way," said Hoyle, and started walking.

It only took a half hour to reach Leura. It was quaint, a much, much smaller, idealized version of Katoomba, packed with well-dressed people sauntering from shop to shop. There was a bookstore that in other circumstances would have drawn Hoyle in like a magnet; today he only glanced in to see if Oliver were there. Every few minutes he would check with his inner sense to correct their course, although that was starting to get tiring.

"Oh, Jesus," he heard. "Hoyle! *HOYLE*!" Suddenly Ada slammed into him and wrapped her wiry arms around him. In quick anxiety, he checked to see that Nicholas and the staff were nowhere near her, then hugged her back.

"Sybil," Ada yelled. "Over here, over here! Oliver, you did it! I knew you could do it!"

And there was Sybil, drawn, filthy, exhausted, and utterly beautiful. Hoyle peeled Ada's arms from his waist and rushed to her. They held each other close for an endless moment. Then, somehow, he was kissing her.

"Marchand?" said Nicholas. "If you please, old boy."

"What?" said Hoyle irritably. "Christ, Nicholas, can't you give a man some peace? And quit calling me Marchand. We're adults here, and this is not a cranked-out school story in a cheap annual anthology."

"Woo-hoo!" said Ada. "You go, Hoyle."

Now that the mood was broken, Hoyle thought to look for Oliver in the flesh. "Holy crap, Oliver, you look awful."

"Thanks, mate. So encouraging."

"Sorry. But—what happened?"

"Denny, that guy, you know?"

"No."

"Anyway, they shoved me in his car and then he drove off, and I tried to get away but there were three of them and only one of me, and then we got to the petrol station, and Denny had a needle, and then I woke up in a house over that way," he waved vaguely, "and Nestor was there and … and … he tried to make me do things, and then—"

"What things?" said Hoyle.

"Maybe not now," murmured Sybil. "He's had it tough."

"Sorry."

Oliver continued: "And so I fought him, but I was almost done, and just then Ada and Sybil found me, and they hit Nestor until he was knocked out, and then, and now, here we are."

"What about you?" said Sybil.

"It looks like we were pretty close to you all along," said Hoyle. "We found Nestor unconscious."

"Did you finish the job?" said Ada.

"No," Hoyle said in a shocked voice. "I used the staff to heal him up."

"Wait, what?" said Ada.

Hoyle was about to attempt an explanation when Nicholas broke in. "Hoyle's got an idea that Nestor is required for some sort of plan to break the power of the staff. He does not know in what way Nestor will be required, nor of what the plan actually consists. Therefore, unfortunately, he is loath to rid the world of Nestor."

"Besides," said Hoyle, with a dark glance at Nicholas, "Nestor is still protected by the staff. Obviously not as protected as he thought—you guys beat him up pretty good—but enough that he'd probably take a lot more killing than we think."

"Does anybody know where he is now, or what he's doing?" said Sybil.

Nicholas said, "He's getting further away. Heading … east."

Sybil said, "Ever been in a car, Nicholas?"

* * *

Nestor had given up on getting anything done in the Blue Mountains. He would stand a much better chance of finding susceptible people in Sydney—if he could get there with his body intact. This was in no way certain, as every step was taking him further from the staff. Still, it couldn't be helped. He was already learning how to tap into its power from a distance; it was quite a bit easier than he'd thought. Clearly, the staff wanted to help him. At last he, and not Nicholas, was the golden child, the darling. He'd bounce back stronger than ever, and once he had the staff actually in his hands, there'd be nothing to stop him.

He was troubled by the fact that Nicholas and that booby Marchand wouldn't just give him the staff and be done with it. Marchand's idiotic plan to destroy the staff, if you could call something so rudimentary and disjointed a "plan", was nothing more than a small boy's daydream of nursery heroism. He couldn't destroy the ancient and beautiful power of the staff!

Nestor neither knew nor cared where it came from; he only cared what he could do with it. Soon he'd be among the poor, desperate people of Sydney, who would be eager for guidance.

The lights of Sydney spread out before him—good Lord, the city had grown in a century! London itself was scarcely greater. With a wild grin on his face, he started down the mountain road.

Chapter 25

In Which Nestor is Pursued

"Hey, wait," said Ada. "I thought you guys were trapped up there in the mountains. How did you get loose?"

"Funny thing," said Hoyle. "Seems there were two forces fighting it out. The staff wants to control people. But there are these, um, mysterious beings who wanted to make sure nobody left, so that the staff's influence couldn't spread. Quarantine. But when the anarchists ended up wanting to scatter, there were too many people pulling in too many directions for the beings to control, and in the chaos, Nestor took his moment and slipped away. So the beings said, 'Uh-oh.' And they sent Nicholas and me after him."

"Oh, yeah?" said Ada, crossing her arms. "And why should you do what *they* say? Sounds like just another mob getting their kicks out of ordering people around."

"They seemed okay," said Hoyle lamely.

Ada smacked her forehead.

How could he communicate the bizarre certainty of their benevolence, so different from the twisted nausea he felt whenever he thought of the staff? "They don't have a lot of answers," he began. "But they want to do the right thing. They want to stop Nestor."

Ada said, "Well, they can be my guest."

"They can't. They're all sort of … used up. That's why they need us."

"Are they, like, space aliens?"

"Not as far as I know. Maybe they evolved here. Like us."

"Where are the fossils, then?"

"I don't know," said Hoyle irritably. "Maybe nobody has dug that far down yet. Or something."

Sybil was frowning. "I won't say it makes sense. But can they at least give us information as we go? Suggestions?"

"They're, um, relying on us a lot. But yeah, they've helped a little so far."

"The watchers," said Oliver suddenly. Everyone looked at him. "Nestor said. He said the watchers were always trying to stop him. He said, 'The bloody watchers needn't have worried—you're stopping me just as effectively as they would, stupid boy.' I was proud, but I wondered who the watchers were."

Sybil murmured, "The enemy of my enemy …"

"For God's sake," said Ada. "Why don't we just build a bonfire and be done with it?"

"I don't know how Marchand would fare," said Nicholas, "but chances are good it would finally send me to my long-postponed grave."

"And Nestor, too, right?" said Ada.

"And Hoyle," Sybil reminded her.

"Maybe … maybe it would be worth it," said Hoyle. But he found he didn't mean it. As of a few minutes ago, everything had changed, and now it mattered whether he lived or died.

"Don't be ridiculous," said Sybil.

Hoyle fought the urge to grin. It was still sinking in: Sybil loved him. *Sybil loved him!*

"If nobody else dies, then that's a win," said Sybil to the group. "No more death, all right? Loss of life is never an acceptable risk."

"Yeah, but that really cuts out a lot of options," said Ada. Sybil gave her an irritated look.

"We have to find Nestor," said Hoyle. "That's what the … the watchers said. If even one of us is still connected with the staff, it can keep doing what it does."

"And you're absolutely, positively sure that it's only the three of you?" said Sybil. "Just check, would you? In whatever way you have to check."

Nicholas nodded curtly, then closed his eyes. After a moment, he said, "I—oh, no."

"What?" cried everyone else in alarm.

Nicholas opened his eyes. "I don't know how he did it without the staff actually in his hand, but this is very bad news. Hoyle," he said, stumbling over his first use of the name, "you check."

Hoyle also closed his eyes. There was Nicholas, loud and clear. And Nestor, a writhing, slimy presence. But—there. So faint, but not far. Close. Very close. As close as—

"Oliver," said Hoyle. "I hate to say it, but somehow Nestor's managed to patch you into the staff. It's probably why you feel so miserable, but also probably why what he did to you didn't outright kill you. And if he can do it to you—"

"He can keep on doing it to other people," said Sybil.

"So there's no time at all to waste," said Nicholas.

* * *

"We can all fit in your car," said Ada to Sybil, who was frowning.

"We can keep the staff in the trunk," said Hoyle. "I'll sit in the back with Ada and Oliver." That would mean nobody had to snuggle up against Nicholas in the back seat.

Nicholas shot Hoyle a look that said very clearly that Nicholas knew why Hoyle had volunteered for the back seat. Hoyle felt a flicker of guilt—was the guy going to have to keep being an outcast, now that he finally had someone to talk to after a hundred years who wasn't Nestor? Nicholas would just have to put up with it. He knew what he was, after all. As freaky as a ghost, already proven to be manipulative and self-serving—what was there to love? Maybe he'd been different with Ruby. He would have had to be.

Nicholas was a puzzle, that was for sure. He could have refused to help, doomed Hoyle's efforts to free himself from—and, hopefully, destroy—the staff. He could even have joined forces with Nestor: surely two of them together would be more than enough to use the staff for whatever they wanted. *Or whatever they could agree on*, Hoyle thought wryly. Instead, here he was, jammed into Sybil's tiny car with the rest of them, off on an impossible task, impossibly incompetent.

Hoyle stowed the staff in the trunk, making sure every square inch of it was thoroughly wrapped in the sheet. It was a child's bed sheet, with hundreds of grinning Harry Potters flying past on broomsticks. Magic. Ha ha. So much fun.

"It can't take us long to catch him," said Oliver. "He's on foot, right?"

"No guarantees," said Sybil. "He's good at getting people to do what he wants—like maybe giving him a lift into Sydney. Guys?" she said, glancing at Nicholas. "Any clues as to where I should point the car?"

Hoyle reached out, and felt Oliver and Nicholas doing the same. "Sydney," all three said in unison.

"Okay, that's settled. When we get to Sydney, we start homing in, or look for clues," said Sybil briskly. Hoyle's heart swelled with admiration. Even now, she was so capable. The days when that made him feel frightened and useless were long past. And besides, hadn't she kissed him? Hadn't she? A slow grin kept trying to seep across his face, but that seemed so inappropriate while they were trying to save the world.

Ada missed nothing, though. She nudged him, glanced at Sybil, and raised her eyebrows. *See? I told you!*

Hoyle blushed.

"What's that?" said Oliver. "Over there, up by that house."

A group of about five or six people were huddled around something on the ground. They looked anxious. One of them kept looking up and down the road. Sybil pulled the car off the road near them and got out.

"Everyone okay?" she called.

"We're waiting for the ambos," a woman called back.

"What happened?"

"We don't know. He's having a … a fit or something."

A minute later an ambulance pulled up. Sybil eased herself out the group and walked matter-of-factly to the car. Only after she'd gotten in, gotten back on the road, and driven for a mile or so did she speak.

"It's a pretty brutal trail he's leaving us," she said. "That poor bastard was twitching like a fish and drooling bloody foam. What *is* Nestor?"

Nicholas said, "Even I don't know. Not anymore."

Ada said, "So … what made Nestor such a creep?"

"We can't blame the staff," said Oliver. "*You're* not like that. It's not like the Ring."

"What ring?" said Nicholas, an unfamiliar note of rising panic in his voice. "There's something more we have to worry about?"

"Sorry. Just something in a book," said Oliver hurriedly. "It's not real. Anyway, my point is that it doesn't turn you evil. I mean, look at you, helping us. And look at Hoyle. If anything, he's an even better person than he was."

"I am?"

Oliver nodded.

"Does it matter?" said Nicholas wearily. "It only matters that we reach him, keep him from doing more damage, and convince him to—" He stopped abruptly.

"To what?" said Hoyle.

"Sh! Can't a man think, for God's sake?"

They waited tensely until Nicholas said, "Nestor will want to believe the staff is compelling us to bring it to him, to join him in his blood- and power-lust, with him as leader. He'll be more than happy if it will mean he finally, indisputably gets to be the Ivory in charge. That will be our chance. He will have voluntarily let himself link up with us through the staff. That's when we get him to renounce it, and it will wither and die—possibly within minutes."

"Anyone besides me seeing the tiny flaw in that plan?" said Ada. "It happens … oh, right about the 'get him to renounce it' point. Or is that just me?"

"Beats anything else we've got," said Hoyle. "I'm willing to give it a try."

Oliver laughed shakily. "I'd rather chew open a vein than face him again. But if we gotta, we gotta. Are—are you sure you can't just drop me off in, like, Penrith or something? I mean, I've already shown how little use I am."

Sybil said, "You're connected to the staff now, somehow. So, unfortunately, we can't risk not having you there. If there's any way that power can keep a foothold in humanity, it will. And if we end up where you're its only foothold …"

"All right, all right. Oh, God."

"Why did he wreck that person?" said Ada. "He doesn't need to eat or drink or … or anything. He's not like a vampire. And so—why?"

"Maybe it's a false trail," said Oliver. "It's so … self-consciously gruesome."

"It's the only trail we've got," said Sybil. "So we follow it as quickly as we can, to minimize the number of breadcrumbs he feels he has to leave for us."

"A point doesn't determine a direction," said Hoyle. "Where do we go?"

"There is only Sydney from here," said Ada.

Only a moment later, they were looking down at the lights of Sydney, spreading out from the base of the mountains until they vanished in the haze. Nicholas, for all his world-weary attitude, gasped audibly.

Ada leaned forward and said to him, "Does that mean, 'Oh, by Jove, look at that enormous city, how are we ever, ever going to find my nuisancy brother amidst that throng'? Because it bloody should. There are a lot of people he can mess up down there."

"I will point out one thing," said Sybil. "He has no idea what he's getting himself into. Before, he had surprise and our own ignorance to help him. Now, though—is there any one of us here who is the same person they were before all this started?"

Nobody spoke.

"All right, then," said Sybil. "All right, then."

Chapter 26

In Which Nestor Sets a Trap

Hoyle and Nicholas progressively directed Sybil through western Sydney and into a neighborhood Ada said was Marrickville, and finally to the parking lot of a warehouse. "Spitshine Theatre" was painted, graffiti-like, on the side of the building as part of a huge, exuberant mural.

"Know anything about this?" Sybil asked Ada.

Ada snorted. "Theaters? Me? I don't even go to the movies very much."

"Oliver?"

"One of my roommates was an actor; maybe she said something. Let me think … something about … no. No, that was some other theater. Oh! This was the one where there kept being all those worker's comp issues from actors getting sliced open on pieces of metal sticking out and toilets overflowing and stuff. And oh, yeah, the dressing rooms had rats in them."

"That's it. I'm not going in," said Ada.

"We're all going in," said Sybil. "How could we make it work without you?"

"Make what work?"

"Defeating Nestor. I don't know which one of us is going to save the day, as you put it, and it's as likely to be you as anyone. Do you want to miss your chance at your destiny?"

"Jesus, you sound like Oliver. All right, all right. But I swear to God, if a rat runs over my foot I'm going to pick it up and shove it right down someone's throat, and I'm not going to care whose."

"Do we leave the staff here or take it with us?" said Hoyle.

Sybil and Nicholas said, "Take it with us." At the same moment, Ada and Oliver said, "Leave it here."

"We don't want him just breaking into the car and taking it while we're distracted," said Sybil.

"We don't want him just getting the drop on us and taking it while we're dead," said Ada.

"Five of us are going to be awfully hard to surprise."

"If all five of us are on the same side."

Sybil, Oliver, and Hoyle cried, "What!"

Nicholas merely said, "No, I can't blame her. Why should she believe that I want to stop Nestor at least as much as any of you? Why should any of you?"

"Well … you …" Hoyle tried to express in a word all the impressions that together made him think that, after all, Nicholas was not such a bad guy. Nicholas's stereotypical Victorian childhood, almost as familiar to Hoyle from countless adventure heroes' fictional biographies as Hoyle's own; his love for Ruby—maybe it was only because of those few moments here and there when it seemed like Nicholas thought that he, Hoyle, was not such a bad guy.

Nicholas clapped him on the shoulder. "Don't worry about it, Hoyle. Ada can keep an eye on me while the rest of us are keeping an eye out for Nestor. Right, shall we go in?"

Sybil merely opened the trunk and motioned for Hoyle to pick up the staff.

They tried the first door they found: locked. But around the back, behind enough rusty, twisted junk to make Oliver's actor friend seem like an optimist, was another door. Without hesitation, Sybil reached out and opened it. The room inside was crammed with costumes and props. A huge clown head was festooned with feather boas and greasy orange overalls. Filing cabinets lined one wall; every drawer had been jammed shut over protruding sheets of yellowing paper. Wires and pipes drooped and dangled from the ceiling, and every one that could bear the weight held hangers from which hung dresses, tights, doublets. An untidy teepee of swords took up one corner. Another corner contained a rickety desk piled with ancient makeup and topped with a cracked and greying mirror. There was a rustling sound, and one of the piles of sequined fabric on the floor twitched.

"Rats, oh my God, that was a rat, that was a rat," quavered Ada.

"Didn't you ever see them at the Happy Guest House?" said Hoyle.

"Of course! Was cleaning their shit out of the kitchen supposed to make me love them? The little bastards used to eat the packets of rat poison and come back every night for more."

Hoyle was glad they hadn't gotten room service.

"Quiet," said Sybil.

Hoyle listened hard, listened with his ears and with the odd awareness that the staff gave him. He could clearly sense Nicholas doing the same, and could just barely catch the feeling of Oliver's effort. Poor, brave Oliver—he was having the worst time of any of them. Only he had been outright tortured by Nestor, only he would have to confront the one who had caused him indescribable torment and humiliation. Hoyle hoped Oliver could keep it together.

"He could be anywhere in here," said Ada. "He could be hiding with the rats."

"Or he could be in another room," said Sybil. "Let's assume he didn't draw us here to hide from us. Come on."

The door across the room led into the wings. The same dim light that had shone in the storage room lit the stage as well, and again, Hoyle had no trouble scanning the house from where he stood. Empty. He looked up at the … the place where the techies sat, it probably had a name. Booth? Did he see a shadow moving there? He nudged Nicholas. "Up there."

Nicholas peered into the gloom, and grunted.

"Nestor," Hoyle called.

"Is he here?" said Sybil. "You sense him?"

"Better. I actually see him. Nestor! What the hell is this?"

The sheet collapsed and dangled from his fist. The staff was gone.

* * *

Hoyle braced himself for the pain he knew was coming. Like that moment between knowing you stubbed your toe and feeling the agony. Only worse. Much worse.

The seconds ticked by, but the pain didn't show up. Oliver was staring at him, sweating and shaking. "What—"

Oliver spoke through clenched teeth. "I'm trying to protect you."

"Protect me from what?"

"From the staff, stupid," said Oliver. "As soon as you think you can keep it together, let me know, because doing this for both you and Nicholas is damn near killing me."

Hoyle felt a rush of shame. He said, "It's okay now, Oliver, I'm ready to try."

Oliver nodded. Hoyle felt every muscle in his body grow tense as a stretched wire as he braced himself. Slowly, slowly, the loss rose within him again, but his concern for Oliver and his own damaged pride gave him the strength to contain it. "Now what?"

"Ada is still jumpy about rats, so we may as well go back outside."

"Yay," said Ada. She jogged to the back of the room and tried a door. "Uh-oh," she said. She ran back up to the stage and into the storage room. "Uh-oh." She darted around the building, trying every door and window. "Uh … oooooohhhhhhhh. Hey, guys, guess what? We're locked in."

"Why?" said Hoyle. "Nestor's got the staff. What more does he want?"

"Us, apparently," said Ada.

"He's … not still in the building, is he? Ada, did you notice anything?"

"Jesus, I didn't think of that. He could have been anywhere."

"Never mind what he could have been," said Sybil. "Did you actually see or hear anything?"

"I thought I heard rats. Maybe it was Nestor."

"Everyone hush. See if we hear anything."

There was silence as they listened. But nothing broke it, not even the rustling of a rat through the piles of props.

"Why doesn't he just kill us?" said Hoyle impatiently.

"The staff still protects us," said Nicholas. "You, me, Oliver. And he knows we'll protect Ada and Sybil."

"So … he wants to keep us out of action, but the only way he can do that is by locking us up," said Ada. "Terrific. All that trouble I've gone to all these years to avoid going to prison, and now look."

"It's not prison," said a voice from the booth—Nestor. "It's more like a zoo. You're kept here because you can do damage, but I'm not at liberty to either send you back where you came from or kill you."

"I should have strangled you in the nursery," Nicholas said conversationally.

"But this way I get to live out the fantasies of power and self-indulgence you were too weak to pursue," said Nestor. "I have not been idle since I left you in the mountains. You may wonder how it was that I could bear to walk away from the staff. The answer is that I am the one deemed fit to bring the staff's purpose to fruition. I have, as it were, a direct conduit into the vast energies of its creators; and this I have learned to exploit. The petty enhancements I knew in the mountains, and which are all you will ever know, are the vague, weak movements of a baby's limbs compared to the bounding purpose and strength I enjoy now. And oh, I do enjoy them. I do indeed."

"Ada, Sybil," said Hoyle. "He can't stop you from going. You have no link to the staff."

"Uh, the doors are still locked," said Ada.

"Moreover," said Nestor, "you're quite mistaken. You are operating on old information, old boy. I can do whatever I wish to whomever I like."

Sybil cried out.

Hoyle rushed to her, but she held up a hand. "I'm all right," she said shakily.

"What did he do to you?"

"Hoyle! Focus, for God's sake." She pushed him toward the stairs.

Hoyle started to run up to the booth, but Nicholas grabbed his arm as he passed. "Don't waste your energy. He's bound to slip up sometime—he always was a careless idiot."

Nestor's only response was to laugh.

Nicholas said, "Everyone. A moment, if you would." He gestured to bring them closer.

"Won't he just be able to overhear everything anyway?" said Hoyle.

"It's not for him I need us close. It's for … for us. All right, the watchers' plan was idiocy. All it's done is bring the staff into Nestor's reach. This is all my fault, I know it. I could have stopped this a hundred years ago. Instead, I wasted both our lives, and now I've ruined yours. And Ruby's dead. It's well past time I faced up to my own actions. I'm going to go up there, and I don't expect to come back out. Maybe the staff will survive us. If it does, Hoyle, you'll need to do what I wasn't strong enough to do: destroy it. Do you understand?"

Nobody said anything.

He screamed, "DO YOU UNDERSTAND?"

As the echoes died away, Ada said, "Sure, mate. Yeah."

Nicholas whirled away from them and dashed up to the booth. Hoyle tried to follow—*Nobody should have to face Nestor alone*, he thought—but Nicholas was far quicker.

There was no doubt about the start of the battle: a flash, a grinding screech like metal on metal, then a low wub-wub-wub that grew louder until it was beating on Hoyle's ears like a club. He knew it: the pulse of the staff. He felt his muscles pulling against each other, so that they ached with exertion, but did not allow his body to move at all. The smell of his own sweat filled the air around him. His breath came in gulps.

He was aware of Sybil, Ada, and Oliver; they, too, were motionless, trapped in the tension that filled the theater. It was unbearable—one of the brothers would have to snap.

The flashing began again, each flash accompanied by a boom that shook Hoyle where he stood, and through it all the horrible pulsing. Why weren't the police storming this place? Could he possibly be the only one who could sense the battle raging? He yearned to cover his ears, crouch under the seats, run—anywhere—away from the assault, but still his body was caught in the strain of the fight.

Then, in an instant, it was done. Hoyle took a huge breath; he heard the others gasp, too, followed by the sound of one of them crashing to the floor. He turned; it was Oliver, but Ada and Sybil were already next to him. Hoyle took advantage of their inattention to do what they surely would have prevented: he ran up to the booth and burst inside.

Black terror settled in his stomach as he saw Nestor, gleeful and triumphant, eyes wide and chest heaving. He held the staff upright in front of him.

Of Nicholas there was no sign, and there was only emptiness where he'd been in Hoyle's mind.

Nestor pointed the leaf-blade end of the staff at Hoyle. A ball of force shot toward him and knocked him backward; he lost his balance and landed heavily on the floor.

"One conquered, two to go. Your turn, old chap. Then the spotty boy, and the staff will be mine alone!"

"No," cried Sybil. Damn—she'd followed Hoyle after all. She pushed past him. Hoyle cried out in horror as she reached out and grabbed hold of the staff. Her presence rushed into his awareness, hot and bright and beloved, yet he shook with fear and regret.

"Ada!" she yelled. "Get up here."

Ada thundered up the steps.

Nestor was struggling with Sybil, trying to dislodge her grip, but even with all his knowledge of the staff and its powers, he couldn't break free. Somehow she was stronger than—

Hoyle knew how. He could feel his own strength joining to hers.

Ada ran into the booth. Sybil said sharply, "Grab the staff, Ada. Grab it and don't let go."

Ada's eyes met Sybil's, and she reached out and took hold.

The three of them—four, because Hoyle could feel Oliver, very faintly—gathered themselves. At Sybil's urging, they flung themselves at the wall Nestor had put up. The feeling of belonging was exhilarating: they were working together in a way Hoyle had never known before. He felt like he could do anything, defeat anyone, change the world. Again and again they attacked, again and again they were thrown back. But each attack was a little weaker, a little less coordinated. Each time they fell back, it took them a little longer to recover. And Nestor's face gradually changed from fear to exultation as he realized that, even together, they didn't have enough power.

Finally they weakened enough that he could wrench the staff away. They could feel him gathering power for a final strike. They huddled together, eyes closed, waiting for the blow to fall.

The seconds went by.

A growing unease, rapidly escalating into all-too-familiar panic, told Hoyle what had happened: Nestor had escaped, taking the staff with him.

"Hoyle?" said Ada, and Hoyle could hear the same panic in her voice. "What the fuck? What the fuck is this?"

"He's taken the staff," said Hoyle, trying to at least sound calm. "It's not going to kill you, it just feels like it will. Don't be afraid."

"Jesus, Hoyle—how long does it stay like this?"

"Um, all the time."

Sybil was doing her best to keep her composure. "Well, if—if it's all the time, we'll get used to it. That's all. We'll just have to get used to it. Until we can—can—"

Hoyle still had his arms around both of them; he hugged them close. He tipped his head back and yelled, "Oliver! Are you all right? Can you come up here?"

"Okay," Oliver said in a weak, frightened voice. "Are—is everyone okay?"

"Yeah," lied Hoyle.

Oliver came up to the booth. "Where are they?"

"Nicholas is dead, we think. And Nestor is ... gone. He took the staff."

"And I hate that, I hate that," Ada said frantically. "I hate that. We have to go get it. We have to go get it. Why are we just standing here?"

Hoyle took his arm off Sybil's shoulders and grabbed hold of Ada with both hands. "Look," he said. "I know it hurts. I feel it too, and so does Sybil. But remember what I said: it's not going to kill you. It isn't. If you're not scared of being scared, it's a lot easier to deal with. Try it. Try thinking, 'I'm just scared. That's not fatal.'"

Oliver came close and hugged her. Tears were streaming down his face. "Why did you touch the staff?" he said. "Now you're never going to be free. Bad enough for me, and I never even laid a finger on it. Why did you—"

"Because I told her to," said Sybil. "And it almost worked. With all of us together, including you, it almost worked."

"But remember what those watchers told me," said Hoyle. "It's not just a question of getting the staff away from him. Someone has to break the connection, break the chain. And now it's more complicated than ever. Maybe ..." He turned to Sybil. "Maybe you shouldn't have done that."

"Well, I did. So, now what?"

"We chase him?"

Oliver groaned. "I'm sick of chasing Nestor."

"It doesn't seem to get us the results we want," agreed Sybil. The words were casual, but Hoyle could hear the strain in her voice, and see the sweat that had started to form on her forehead. The demands of managing the panic were starting to tell. "So we have to make him come to us."

"How?" cried Ada. "That crazy fucker wants to take over all of Sydney. 'Oh, come back and be defeated, Nestor, yeah?' 'Rightio, chaps, be with you in a swivet.' I say let's go after him anyway. At least we'd feel better being closer to the staff."

"No," said Hoyle. "I've got an idea."

Chapter 27

In Which Hoyle Has an Idea

"You know how he got the staff from me?" said Hoyle. "Just … whisked it away? If he can learn how to do stuff, even while someone else has the staff, so can we. And we can do it faster. First, we already know it can be done. Second, we're smarter. Third, we've got the moral high ground. Fourth, there are four of us and only one of him."

"Maybe," whispered Ada in a horrified voice, "maybe he sort of ate Nicholas alive, and so there are two of them."

"That's all the better," said Hoyle. "It means he'll have internal conflict to deal with as well. Nicholas is on our side."

"If there's any Nicholas left," said Ada. "Let's just go find the staff, okay?"

Sybil said, "Ada, we can't have any internal conflict. You have to trust us. I know you're hating how you feel right now. So am I. So are all of us. But remember how things were for you when you were growing up? Lurching from crisis to crisis, always acting on the spur of the moment? Now you know differently, don't you? You know how to plan, how to think about more important things than just right now. You know you're strong enough to put up with some unpleasantness to achieve something amazing and good."

"I do?"

"Ada, don't try to be funny. This is for real," said Sybil sternly.

"No, I was really asking. I don't feel like I'm any of those things. I've just been tagging along with you guys—first, because my best alternative was spending the next few weeks running away from Johnno until he got arrested for some dumb trick or other, and second, because, um, you're my friends. And then I met Oliver, and I'm not leaving him anytime soon."

"What?" said Oliver excitedly. "You mean it?"

"But just sticking around doesn't make me some kind of adventure hero. That's you guys. You're the heroes. I just tricked you into letting me come with you because I was scared. Okay, when I reached for that staff, I thought for a second that maybe I *was* special. But no. We lost, and he's gone, and *I want to go get that fucking staff and I don't care why.*"

"Ada, please, trust me and stay here."

"You think I can't find it by myself? I can, you know. It's that way." She pointed, and the ache in Hoyle's mind confirmed it: she knew, all right. They all did, even Oliver.

"If we want different results, we have to do different things," said Sybil urgently.

"So let's make ourselves comfortable," said Hoyle, "and we can get started."

This was very different from Hoyle's tentative explorations of the staff back at the campsite. This time, he had a purpose: to get so connected to the staff that he could physically wrench not just the staff—what good would that do?—but Nestor himself back to them. Plus, he had his friends. And he had, for the first time in his life, the liberating feeling of not worrying in the slightest what anyone thought of him. The only people who mattered were right here with him, and the days of agonizing over whether they liked him or what they were saying behind his back were long gone. He had never felt such trust in anyone, never felt so unconcerned about himself. The beauty and power of this moment did a lot to counteract the fear and panic the staff was triggering. A whole lot.

They sat in a circle, for no particular reason. "Is this, like, a séance or something?" said Ada. "Should I close my eyes?"

"I guess," said Hoyle. "If it helps you concentrate."

"Concentrate on what?"

"We'll figure that out as we go along," said Sybil.

Hoyle closed his eyes and became very conscious of the sound of everyone's breathing. Slowly, he gathered his awareness of them all in his mind. He heard Oliver whispering, "Did you really mean it? You're not going to leave me?"

"Will you shush?" she whispered back impatiently. "I'm trying to do a séance here."

"Everyone shush," said Hoyle. "I'm going to try a few things. Just back me up, okay?"

"I don't even know how to do that much," said Ada.

"You will," said Hoyle.

"How do you know?"

"Shh," said Sybil. "Go ahead, Hoyle."

Think about the staff—no, that's too easy. If it were just a question of wanting the staff, Ada would have had it back ten minutes ago. The trick has to be something Nestor's capable of, so it can't be anything noble. It has to be a greedy, selfish thing. But I can't be like that, that would just make me his … accomplice. I can't use his way. I have to find our way. And our way is trust. I can't trust the staff, it's just a thing, and not a nice thing at that. But I can trust the watchers. At least, I think I can. At least, I guess I have to. Hey! He called out to them. *Talk to me!*

His mental voice fell flat and limp, like a wadded-up tissue thrown hard at a trashcan.

"Guys?" he said out loud. "Think about wanting to help me. Send all that wanting to me—you can feel the way to send it, can't you? You can feel where I am. It doesn't matter if you don't know what to do. Just the wanting is enough. Go!"

Again he called: *Talk to me, you bastards!*

The reply came, bemused and worried. *Nobody's ever tried this before.* The voice was much clearer than it had been, much richer, more real inside his head. In fact, everything seemed easier and clearer, now that the others were with him.

I need more help, thought Hoyle, aiming his intent at the vague sense he had of the watchers' presence. *I need to know how to bring Nestor and the staff back here and keep them here. And I need just a little more information on how to get a power-hungry madman to voluntarily break his connection with the staff. I also wouldn't mind knowing a little more about you guys.*

Yeah, Ada echoed.

You're not helping, Hoyle told her.

We sense what you're thinking, and you've guessed correctly, said the voice. *The staff is our fault. We made it, and we had no idea what we were doing. We still don't.*

What? thought Hoyle.

Did you assume that because we're many and ancient, we're also automatically wise? That's very unfortunate. We were hoping you'd come up with something.

Who are you, really? Come on, now.

Exiles. Willing sacrifices to contain a great evil.

Exiles from where?

Do you really think you people are the first ones to emerge on this world? You're only the least foolish so far. We saw you arrive, or evolve, or whatever it was you did, all those centuries ago, and we were relieved: at last, someone to sort things out. And, indeed, you've done a better job than we did. Only a few of your inventions have turned in your hand, whereas we have a very dismal history indeed.

Hoyle felt a coldness settle over him. There would be no sudden rescue from unseen powers, then: that, like so much else, had been something that would only happen in books. There would be no rescue, no dash to safety, no breathtaking climax. Hoyle would spend the rest of his life chasing after Nestor, doing his weary, dreary best year after year to limit the amount of damage Nestor could do. The staff would keep them all alive, to play this horrible game forever.

What were you thinking? he snapped. *How could that staff possibly have seemed like a good idea?*

We … were trying to create an amplifier, to heighten perception. It would have been a useful tool for a ruler who wished to be both canny and just. Only …

Hoyle filled in the blanks. *Only the staff didn't just boost your perception. It was an amplifier: it revealed, and then exaggerated, who you really were, just like it does us. You were shallow, vain, and fearful, desperate for something to make you feel brave. Do I have it right?* He should have been angry, but all he felt was cold and scornful.

Essentially.

At least it's not going to turn me evil if I'm not already. That's something. But it's going to be a very long eternity trying to keep Nestor out of trouble.

It's all right, Sybil said. *We're with you.*

As she spoke, Hoyle knew in the deepest part of his soul that, in fact, the most important part of all those stories he used to read—maybe the only important part—had come true after all: he had companions with whom he had faced a hundred crises, a hundred times where someone had needed pulling back from cliffs or out of dungeons, a hundred moments of warm, rushing relief to see each other still alive. There was no silliness about who liked whom anymore; there was only the utter certainty of approval and love. Without knowing it, he'd figured it out in that moment when he'd turned to Nicholas and offered him the only thing he had of value: his trust. And he knew it again now, a wave of joy that he, Sybil, Ada, and Oliver—the most unlikely people in the world—were bound by something far stronger than the tendrils the staff had wound around them all.

But would it be strong enough to capture Nestor and the staff? Strong enough to protect them from his vicious, devastating rage? Nicholas was gone—the staff was no longer a refuge for its servants. Anything could happen. What few rules Hoyle had managed to puzzle out were already irrelevant in the face of Nestor's increasing power and madness.

And there was so much more to lose now: his companions were infinitely precious to him. Even the loss of Nicholas had hurt—what would it be like if something happened to Sybil? And how badly would it hurt her if something happened to him?

"Don't worry about that," said Sybil aloud. "For God's sake, here we are, as close as two people have ever gotten, and you still think I give a damn about keeping myself pristine and pain-free? If I'd wanted that, I'd have stayed back in DC, reading old books. Instead, I have you, and if that isn't way, way more than I had any right to expect, I don't know what would be. So cut the bullshit and let's figure out what we do now."

"Yeah," said Ada. "Let's cut the bullshit."

"Yeah," said Oliver, although he sounded like he didn't quite get what was going on.

"All right," said Hoyle. "Here's what I want to try. It's no good trying to reason with Nestor, and no good trying to catch him, let alone overpower him. That means we're going to have to trick him. And the only bait we have is Oliver."

"What?" screeched Ada. "That's the creepiest fucking thing I've ever heard. If you think for one minute—"

"Wait, wait," said Hoyle. "Holy hell, could you please be a little more gentle with your objections, now that we're all on an open channel? It's like you've just scraped the inside of my skull with a screwdriver. Nestor needs something Oliver's got. He went to an awful lot of trouble to try to get Oliver on his side. I'm betting Nestor still wants whatever it is, but has decided to cut his losses, because fighting all of us to get it is too much trouble. What we have to do is convince him that Oliver's had some sort of big fight with us and sees things Nestor's way. Or something. Then Nestor comes back, and we … we make him think that Oliver can't properly connect with the staff while Nestor is in control of it. When he lets go of it, even if it's just for a second, we can let go of it, too, and keep him from touching it again. Then the staff will, I don't know, starve or something."

"And how long is that supposed to take?" said Ada. "That's the lamest plan I've ever heard in my entire life. You want to risk Oliver's life doing something that stupid? I can tell you, there's no way it's going to happen—"

"Yes, there is," said Oliver. "I want to do it. I want to stop Nestor, so he never does to anyone else what he did to me. Okay, yeah, the plan is lame. But we have at least a little while to work on it. Even Nestor has limits to how much damage he can do in a half hour."

"All right," said Hoyle. "We're going to do our best to keep radio silence."

"What's that?" said Ada.

"We're going to try to keep our thoughts to ourselves."

"Oh. That may be a problem."

"It needs to not be, or Oliver's a dead man before we even start," said Hoyle.

Ada looked chastened, so Hoyle continued. "Oliver, you remember the kinds of things Nestor was saying to try to get you to go along with him?"

"Way, way too clearly."

"Tell him as loudly as you can that you've changed your mind. Make up whatever lies you think might work, maybe that you and Ada had a fight or something, but try to be convincing. When he gets here, give us a signal, and we'll do our best to trap him. Somehow." Hoyle rubbed his forehead.

"What signal? Yelling out loud, or something, like, telepathic?"

"Yelling is probably safest. If you yell 'Nicholas,' maybe it will weird him out for a second—and a second may make all the difference."

"Okay," said Oliver. "I'll try to remember."

"You think you can reach him without our help? If he thinks we're boosting you—"

"I'll do it," interrupted Oliver. "I'll be fine. Can we get this over with?"

"All right. Come on, guys, let's go wait in the storeroom."

Ada hung back. "I'll be with you in a minute, okay?"

Hoyle nodded. He and Sybil went down through the theater and onto the stage. Hoyle turned and looked out at the empty house. He spread his arms. "To be," he boomed, "or ... NOT to be. THAT is the QUESTION."

"You're a great loss to the profession," said Sybil blandly.

"Yeah, I always thought so," said Hoyle. "On the other hand, being me is so challenging, I have no idea how I would have handled being other people on top of that."

Sybil smiled. "You do all right at being you, you know."

He smiled back. "Thanks."

"Ada," called Sybil. "Come on."

"All right, all right!" Ada emerged from the booth, looking both distressed and irritable. "I sure hope you know what you're doing, Hoyle."

"Not me. Best guess only. But it's all we've got."

We're disappointed, frankly, said the watchers. *We could have done that much ourselves.*

But you didn't, said Hoyle. *So get fucked.*

He'd never said that to anyone in his life, let alone a throng of unseen, ancient non-humans. Was he acting a role now after all, or had his real self—decisive, determined, maybe even a bit cocky—been waiting all along for this moment? For him to finish acting the part of a timid, pasty weakling?

The three of them went back into the storeroom. Sybil arranged some of the flats so they could hide well enough from a quick glance, but still have room to rush back into the theater when the time came. They stood uneasily, not sure what they were waiting for or what they would do when it happened. Sybil took Hoyle's hand.

Hoyle resisted the temptation again and again to reach out and try to sense what was happening. From the twitchy, staticky feeling from the others, he assumed they had the same problem.

Suddenly the atmosphere became sharp and dangerous, and Hoyle could sense a buzz like cicadas that rattled him to his bones and deeper. And under it all, the familiar and horrible pulsing of the staff.

Oliver had done it. Nestor was on his way.

Chapter 28

In Which Nestor Gains the Upper Hand

Hoyle exchanged glances with Sybil and Ada. There was no doubt; they felt it, too.

"Join up," said Hoyle quietly. "We have to be ready."

Even in this moment of dread, he relished the warm rush of affection and trust that poured into him and back through him to the others. Nestor had nothing like this—only his own cold, lonely self.

A scream from Oliver stopped his musings.

Without a word, they ran back out and up to the booth. They burst in to see Oliver clinging to Nestor with arms, legs, nails, and teeth. Nestor still had the staff, but using it as a bludgeon was impossible with Oliver pinioning his arms. Oliver kept screaming through his clenched teeth, which were sunk into Nestor's shoulder. Nestor, too, was screaming. Hoyle wondered irrelevantly if he was so happy to have his body back now.

He threw himself at Nestor and Oliver, dragging them to the floor. At the same time, he flung a mental net over all three of them, hoping that his intent would be clear enough to get a result. He felt Sybil and Ada making the net more solid and more firmly anchored to this place. Holy hell, they were doing a good job; even Hoyle himself could hardly move. He could hardly think, either, with all the noise.

"What have you done, Marchand?" snarled Nestor.

"I know you're too pitiful and nasty to let go of the staff, the only thing that's ever made you feel like a big man. But maybe you'll let go of it if you know what it's doing to you."

Nestor laughed. "It could turn me inside out and dance on my entrails, for all I care," he said. "I just came back to get the boy. It's his choice. Let us go."

"It's not that simple," said Hoyle. "Now that we've got you here, we need to talk."

Nestor gave a tense, breathless laugh. "Oh, do we?"

The attack took Hoyle completely by surprise. Even as the shrieks and the stabbing pain began, he berated himself. How stupid of him not to see that Nestor was playing possum.

Of course I was, you bloody idiot, snapped Nestor silently.

The pain redoubled.

"No," screamed Oliver. "Hoyle, he's making me! He's making me help him, he's making me hurt you. No, I don't want to. *That's not who I am. I hate you, I hate you!*"

That's enough, boy, said Nestor, and Oliver was silent. *Next, the girl—pity it's come to this. She was the only one of you who was worth a damn.*

Hoyle could hear what Nestor was saying to Ada—he knew this was part of the torment, that Hoyle could not shut him out.

You wanted so badly for them to rely on you, didn't you, idiot girl? sneered Nestor. *And here you are, just as helpless and incompetent as ever. Moreso, because so much more was at stake. And you failed. As you always fail.*

Hoyle could actually feel Ada's spirit collapse, taking his along with it. *Why are you letting him do this to you, Ada?* he wailed. *Why is it so easy for him to win?*

The staff. It amplified everything. Power, perception, hopes, ambitions, fears. It made everything larger than life. It was like they were all characters in a book, where everything was so much more intense than dull, slogging, everyday life, and the fate of the world always seemed to hang in the balance. Well, they'd gotten their wish, then, hadn't they? Pity it was nowhere near as exhilarating as the characters always seemed to find it. They never felt this kind of humiliation and pain. It was all, "Buck up, lads, let's show these villains what we're made of." What facile, shallow writing! All those writers who had churned out book after book, breathless adventure after breathless adventure, jungles, deserts, idols, treasures, long-lost relatives—they'd been cheats and frauds and cowards, unable or simply afraid to imagine what it would actually be like to live through something like this.

He realized who would be next, and began to tremble.

And now, and at last, said Nestor, *that horrible woman. Freak!* he barked. *Mannish, ugly, unwanted freak! You're no good as a woman, and not good enough to be a man. And now they're all going to die, and it's because of you and your revolting urges to dominate them. You're unnatural and disgusting, ugly and useless.*

Sybil didn't scream, like Oliver, or collapse, like Ada. Instead, she grew cold, and dreadfully quiet, until her presence just snuffed out, like a pinched candle wick. The emptiness within him howled, and with everything he had left, he reached for her. *Sybil!*

There was no answering presence, no warmth, nothing at all. Sybil was gone in every way that mattered. Nestor's revenge was heartless and complete.

Nestor leaped up, laughing, as the pressure vanished. Hoyle started to struggle to his feet as well, but Nestor slammed the net back down with a savagery that nearly broke Hoyle's back.

You still don't understand, he boomed in Hoyle's mind. *Every moment that passes, I learn more, can do more. Every challenge you've thrown at me has only taught me more about what the staff can do. And now that I've destroyed you and your friends, Sydney is mine. And once I'm done here, I'll embark for London. And can you imagine the fun I'll have there?*

Nestor turned to go, then paused. *You'll die here, of course. The staff won't even bother to protect you anymore, not against me. And really, there's nothing it can do, because I won't actually be doing anything to you. I'll just leave you here as I take the staff farther and farther away, until the connection just … snaps. And with it, you. It won't be pleasant, but I can't help that. Well, now, I'll be completely honest: I want you to suffer. And so you will.*

Hoyle felt like his mind was a moth, fluttering weakly and chaotically against the roaring wind that was Nestor's exultation. From Ada and Oliver, Hoyle could feel only the faintest thread of pain.

He cast back frantically to remember all the ways he'd ever read about to defeat a villain. If he was inside a book—by now he was fairly certain that nothing this weird and horrible could happen outside of one—then the techniques in books ought to be just the ticket. Villain's change of heart? Not likely. Deus-ex-machina revelation from the watchers? They'd already proven themselves essentially worthless. Sudden realization of hidden magical powers within himself? Oh, he'd searched and searched, and found himself again and again to be nothing special—no better than the watchers. Would the anarchists track Oliver by his cell phone and burst in to save them all, in contrition for what they'd done and in the strength of their rejuvenated convictions?

No, came a familiar voice, grim and determined, but very, very quiet. *None of those.*

Hoyle started to cry out: "Nicholas!" But it was as if a hand had clapped over his mouth.

Radio silence, old boy, said Nicholas, and this time "old boy" sounded warm, not mocking. *This is a private channel, but you ooze thoughts through every orifice in your head. So please shut up in all the ways you know how, all right?*

Hoyle held very still. With luck, Nestor would think he was immobilized with fear and guilt. But—wasn't Nicholas dead?

Obviously not, Nicholas snapped. *Now shut up. The watchers were idiots. They were right in that we all need to be here—all the thronging hordes now attached to the staff,* he added sourly. *Bloody hell, Hoyle, why did you let Sybil and Ada connect themselves? That increases the complexity exponentially. Don't answer that, just keep quiet. But we're never going to starve the staff, not while it can still* reach out and grab someone new, as it did Nestor and me. We're going to have to overload it. At least your bringing them in on this gives us more firepower for that. We have to get them back from whatever hell Nestor drove each of them to. Good work keeping your self-control—he was counting on your being weak and suggestible. But you've changed, old boy—the warmth returned for a moment—you've changed a great deal.

How were they supposed to overwhelm the staff? Hoyle permitted himself to feel a tiny moment of questioning.

Nicholas replied, That's much better control. We're going to flood it with the strongest, wildest emotions we've got. It amplifies, no? Then let it amplify itself to oblivion.

Won't the backwash kill us?

Are we much better than dead anyway? But we have to get the other three back with us. That is, you do. You're the one they trust. You're the one they love. But one thing I can do is keep Nestor busy until you can get them back. He didn't kill me last time, so he might not this time either.

What did happen? Hoyle asked gingerly.

I know his weaknesses. He can't resist a gloat. I feigned defeat, then as he was doing his little victory strut I slipped away to wait for you. Bloody stupid of me to go in there without you in the first place—apparently I have my own weaknesses. Right, then. You gather the troops. I'll draw his fire.

And Nicholas was gone.

A moment later, the pulsing of the staff resumed, and grew louder and more chaotic until it deafened Hoyle both inside and outside his head. How was he going to reach the others in all this noise? By habit he raised his hands to run them nervously through his hair, then stopped with the hair poking out from between every finger. He could move. He could move!

Knowing every second was precious, he flung himself over to where Sybil sat on the floor, hunched over with her arms over her head.

"Sybil," he cried, even though he was pretty sure that between the noise and her own isolation she couldn't hear him. He put his arms around her and held tight. He found he was rocking back and forth, and Sybil, impassive, was letting him rock her. He could get no response from her at all, and he was afraid. The fear began to grow as well, like feedback from the speakers at a rock concert.

What do you want to have amplified? he asked himself angrily. *Fear, or love?* He took a deep breath. "Sybil, listen—come back. I need you. And oh, God, I want you. I want you with me forever and ever. I want your strength and your intelligence and your amazing beauty. You're the most wonderful woman I've ever met." He fed all that into the staff and felt the feelings surge. The intensity was almost more than he could stand, but stand it he would. For Sybil. Riding on the power of it, he reached out with his thoughts, searching, searching. He no longer bothered with the struggle between Nicholas and Nestor, no longer noticed the pulsing of the staff.

When he caught the awareness of Sybil, he flew toward it. But it was such a chilly, fragile thing. His arms tightened again around Sybil, and his mind carefully eased closer and began to flow around what there was of her, as if coaxing flame from an ember.

"I love you, Sybil." He said it over and over, backing it up with all the awe he felt for her, all the trust. Slowly, she raised her head and looked into his eyes; slowly, her presence gathered and grew, and slowly turned toward him.

"Hoyle …"

He kissed her once, very gently. She reached for him and drew him closer yet, and answered his kiss with one of her own—yearning, desperate, anything but gentle. Hoyle didn't mind. He let the moment increase, on and on, up and up.

"Wait," said Sybil, but Hoyle rejoiced even in that, because he'd feared he'd never hear her again. "Ada. Oliver."

"Okay, let's give it a try. We'll try to talk to Ada first."

Ada had slumped down in a corner, head resting against the wall, eyes staring desolately at nothing as the tears continued to spill out and drip down her face. She made no sound.

"Hey, buddy," said Hoyle. He shook her shoulder. "Hey. Mate. Hey."

"Let's both try," said Sybil.

Hoyle felt Sybil link her intent with his, and they went in search of Ada. She was easier to find than Sybil—perhaps, more accustomed to despair, she was less damaged by it.

"It's okay, Ada," said Hoyle. "It's all okay. You've been amazing, this whole time. Finding things out, figuring things out, and making sure nobody gets too—what are you always saying?—too up themselves. And Oliver—Ada, buddy, you can't leave him alone. He needs you!" He felt Sybil backing him up, and it occurred to him that he'd been feeling her support for weeks now and hadn't recognized it until now. He always wanted that feeling, for the rest of his life.

With Sybil's force of personality added in, he let the amplification happen. He felt Ada's shame and fear start to dissolve, and knew when the first, hesitant hope took shape. Was it possible that she really did have friends who weren't just waiting to hurt her the moment she dropped her guard? Could they really care about her? And she about them?

Yes, said Hoyle urgently. *Yes to all that. Come back, Ada. Nestor lied. Show him that he couldn't fool you after all. Show him that he's the fool.*

It was this last that finished the job of revitalizing Ada's impish spirit: the chance to laugh at Nestor.

"Right," she said. "Where's Oliver?"

But when they got to Oliver, he was faint, like a half-exposed film image. He lay on the floor, limbs flung haphazardly, and they could see the floorboards through him.

Ada touched his face. "Oh, Jesus, so cold," she said. "Oliver!

Get up. What the fuck is wrong with you?" She started to cry again.

The power for all this amplification had to come from somewhere. And poor, sensitive Oliver, incapable of defending himself against the demands of the staff, was as used up as Nicholas and Nestor had been: disembodied, weak, and passive. If they stuck to Nicholas's plan of overloading the staff, Oliver could—probably would—die.

Chapter 29

In Which Hoyle Fears All Hope Is Lost

"You have to," said Oliver, his voice already frighteningly quiet. "Who knows how long Nicholas can distract him? Maybe it will all be okay."

Ada was frantic. "You don't know that. You could die!"

"It's okay," he said, patting her on the arm.

"Jesus, I could hardly feel that—what's happening to you? How can you say go ahead? There's already almost nothing left of you. Hoyle, we can't. Sybil!"

The glass at the front of the booth shattered, and a body landed loudly among the seats, its arms and legs draped at grotesque angles. It was Nicholas, his chest a crushed and bloody ruin.

Nestor leaned through the window. "Ha!" he shouted. "Ha! The staff has many talents, including burying itself point-first into my brother's body. Well, maybe I helped a little, what? Ha!" He disappeared, and they could hear him thundering out of the booth. In a moment, he would be in the theater and upon them. Hoyle knew none of them could either outrun him or defeat him in a physical fight, not now.

"It's too late," said Sybil. "We've got to stop him now."

"No," wailed Ada.

Oliver gave her a pleading look, then turned solemnly to Sybil. He said, "Do it."

Nestor burst into the house and ran toward them.

Now, cried Sybil silently. *Everything we've got! Everything we are!*

Hoyle desperately sought for each of them, gathering their connections together like a fistful of kite strings. He knew he'd have to be the one to focus them all into the staff; apart from Nestor, none of them was as fully linked with it as Hoyle. As he concentrated on his awareness of the staff, Sybil and Oliver began to pour energy into him. He felt his muscles tense and sweat begin to trickle down his face as he channeled everything they gave him into the staff. This stream was Sybil: strong, determined, heroic—just feeling her this close, knowing that she was willingly braving terrible peril, simply because it was *right*, made him want to weep from love and admiration. And here was Oliver: so bright with zeal, so guileless and eager. Hoyle was alarmed at how thin and weak Oliver felt, but there was nothing he could do—everything had to go into the staff.

But the staff merely absorbed it all—they were feeding it, making it stronger. Despair inundated Hoyle. They'd never win, they'd only end up helping Nestor instead of stopping him. Nestor would be able to do whatever he wanted, and it was all because of Hoyle's stupid idea, all Hoyle's fault. The pulse of the staff swelled yet again and beat on Hoyle's ears and mind and even body. It felt as if Nestor were actually thrashing him with it, although he could see that Nestor was merely standing there, holding the staff and exulting in the rush of energy they were so thoughtfully providing. Hoyle fell to his knees.

Sybil cried, "Ada! God damn it, we need you."

Oh, thought Hoyle. *That's right. Ada's missing. Not that it can make any difference. Maybe if we still had Nicholas, we could have made this work.* And grief for the odd and awful death of a man who'd—astonishingly—become his friend added to Hoyle's pain and despair.

"But it's killing him," came Ada's voice.

"Ada," snapped Oliver in a voice that, while faint, was suddenly crisp with anger. "Remember we talked about standing by when there is evil to fight? This is the fight. This is finally it, Ada, it's finally real! All those months wasting time in the bush, I dreamed of the chance to actually do something. You're taking that away from me—and even worse, you're letting Nestor win. And with him, all the bastards you've ever known. He's going to find plenty of people who will do whatever he wants, and he's going to find plenty more who won't do a damn thing because of what it might cost them. Ada, you're not one of those people. You're so wonderful, and I love you so much, I can't stand the thought of you helping Nestor, even if you don't mean it. It doesn't matter what it costs. It really doesn't. Now! Everything we've got, everything we are!"

Hoyle could hear Ada snuffling wetly. Without warning, her energy slammed into Hoyle, solid, irresistible. He scrambled to manage it and guide it into the staff, himself taking strength from it as he channeled it. Sybil and Oliver, too, found renewed vigor, and the four of them suddenly remembered how to reinforce each other. Their power built and built, and the beating of their own hearts began to drown out the pulse of the staff. Nestor frowned, puzzled, as his reverie was disturbed; a moment later his face was contorted in rage, then fear, as the staff began to tremble in his hand.

Even though Hoyle was several yards away from Nestor, he could feel the heat building up in the staff and coming off it in waves.

"Yah!" he yelled in wild exultation—it was working! "Yaaaah!" Even as he poured their power into the staff, he found he could still urge the others on, bolstering them where they were weakening, leaning on them where they were strong. Through it all he felt a manic joy, and he remembered Oliver's words: *This is it, it's finally real!* He was the hero he'd always wished he could be, and it was a thousand times better than he'd imagined. And what made it so good, so fantastically, astonishingly good, was having Ada, Oliver, and—most of all—Sybil with him in the fight.

Without a word exchanged, they simultaneously knew it was

the moment to end this. Each had been straining with all their strength, but each found they'd been holding onto just that small fear, that one self-doubting thought—and these were luxuries they could not afford. At the same reckless moment, they abandoned themselves completely, thinking nothing at all about what would happen next.

The staff began to let out a shrill squeal that Hoyle could only hear for a few seconds before it deafened him. He looked at Nestor, whose mouth was open in a shriek of terror and denial. Nestor clung mindlessly to the staff, although it was hot enough to burn him, and the more it shook, the closer he clutched it to himself, until he was staggering as it pulled him from side to side. Smoke began to curl up from where he gripped it, and he screamed again and again as he stared at his hands with horror, but he could not, would not let it go. The struggle filled the room—the room? The whole world!

The staff shattered in a dreadful crash that shook Hoyle to his bones. Splinters flew past, lacerating his face and arms and embedding themselves into the walls and floor. Hoyle had covered his eyes by instinct, but the chaos subsided in a moment, and he gingerly lowered his arms and looked at where Nestor had been standing. The staff was no more; only the splinters were left. As for Nestor, Hoyle could only assume the weathered and crumbled old bones on the floor were his.

Hoyle quickly scanned the room to see where the others were. A very solid and corporeal Oliver was staring, hollow-eyed, where Nestor had been. Ada clung to him, gasping, but otherwise motionless. Sybil was looking at Hoyle, her expression a mixture of concern and wariness.

Hoyle moved toward her, then stopped. His body felt thick and slow, clumsy and weak. He was suddenly and acutely aware of his cells burning sugar, his lungs breathing waste products into the air, peristalsis working along his bowels, his bladder slowly filling.

In the next moment, he also realized how alone he was—the others, whose presence he had rapidly come to love and lean on, were gone from his awareness. It was as if he stood in the middle of a winter steppe, with unbridgeable space all around him, and only coldness wherever he reached. *Sybil?* There was not even an echo, just his thought falling limply into silence.

Hoyle was the man he'd been at the start: powerless, incompetent, alone. Why had he been so stupid as to want to destroy the staff? It had made him a hero—made him into a man Sybil could love. And now she would go back to DC, perhaps think fondly of him from time to time, and sigh with gentle regret that on his own he hadn't been half the man the staff had made him.

Whatever the staff had wrought was undone.

Everything.

Hoyle stood in the dim light of the theater and sobbed as though his heart were breaking.

* * *

He had no idea how long he'd been crying before he finally opened his red, swollen, waterlogged eyes and wiped his nose on his sleeve. The others would no doubt have left; what need was there for them to stay around? He'd make his way back to the Happy Guest House, and then to the consulate to sort out a flight back to the States. He no longer cared about his devastated library or worried about getting a new job. He was of no importance, and what happened to him from now on was also of no importance.

"Ew," said Ada from behind him. He whirled to see her sprawled across a couple of theater seats, grinning. "Ever hear of tissues? Gross, mate."

Oliver came in from the storage room. "Hi, Hoyle," he said shyly. "Look, I'm all here now." He held up his hands and showed them to Hoyle, back and front.

Hoyle dared to look around the theater. Sybil had gone, of course she'd gone. She—

She was running up the aisle, straight toward him. More out of instinct than decision, he caught her in his arms. He had no time to worry about what would happen next: she was holding him so tight it hurt, and kissing him not with the urgency of someone unsure, nor with the soft regret of someone who was about to walk away. These kisses were the strong, confident kisses of someone who knew what she wanted and was already certain it was right and good—and what she wanted was to be with Hoyle.

When they paused for breath, Hoyle said, "I thought you—now that I'm not special anymore—"

Sybil actually shook him by the shoulders. "Do I have to explain *everything*? The staff didn't make you special. It amplifies, remember? It doesn't create. It only made it easier to see how special you are. Everything you were with the staff, you are now. Better, in fact. Really, now, who do you think I see when I look at you?"

After an awkward moment, Hoyle just shrugged.

"Well, I'll tell you. No, wait, I won't. I'll show you." And she kissed him again. Hoyle's knees almost buckled as a rush of desire flashed through him.

"Whoa," said Ada. "Hey, Oliver, come on. Let's go take a walk."

"What?" said Oliver vaguely.

"I said," she enunciated, "let's … go … take … a … walk."

"Oh." Oliver giggled with sudden enlightenment. "Okay."

"And, guys?" said Ada. "I think there's a pile of carpets or something in the storage room. Just sayin', is all."

"Thanks," said Sybil. When they heard the door close behind Ada and Oliver, Sybil said, "Okay. There's a lot we have to relearn, now that we don't have the staff."

Hoyle didn't know exactly what she meant, but he was ready to find out.

Chapter 30

In Which Hoyle Can Finally Relax—

For Now

The four of them stood in front of the Happy Guest House.

"'Nice wisdom and kindness for you,'" read Oliver. "That's really sweet," he added sincerely.

"Joke's on you," said Ada sourly. She peered into the darkness of the hallway. "Uh-oh. Melati's in there. Maybe I'd better go."

Sybil said, "After all you've been through, you're going to let Melati scare you?"

"You got a point," said Ada. "What are we doing here, anyway?"

"Hoyle and I need a place to stay until we figure out what we're going to do next. In all the running around, I don't have a passport or a credit card anymore, and I don't think Hoyle does either."

"Nope," said Hoyle. A month ago, the mere thought of being in a foreign country without a passport—let alone without money— would have thrown him into a diagnosable panic.

"Plus, we're filthy. There's a lot to do, and at least this is a famil- iar place we can stay in while we do it."

"How are we going to pay, though?" said Hoyle. "They won't let us stay here unless we pay in advance, will they?"

"Melati sure won't," said Ada. "Ask me how I know."

"Um," said Oliver. "I didn't realize it was that bad—I thought maybe you'd rented a safe-deposit box or something for your documents. So, um, my mum runs a coal-mining company. And my dad is in the state parliament. So maybe I can get one of them

to let you stay at their place. And get some help getting new pass-
ports. And stuff."

"Wait," said Ada sternly. "You're rich?"

"No," he cried. "No, no, I'm not rich, my parents are rich!"

"Oliver, you have not told me the whole story. Have you?"

He looked down.

"*Have you?*"

"I'm not rich," he repeated doggedly. "I'm not going to take a
cent from them." Then he added hastily, looking from Hoyle to
Sybil, "But that shouldn't keep you from—"

Melati came out onto the verandah. She stared at them, astonished, then said, "Get out. Go away! Ada, you go too. I sack you
already, now go. Bad things follow you around. Johnno, he never
stop looking for you. I chase him away—"

"Oi!" said a man walking toward them along the sidewalk. "Oi,
Ada!" He was tall, and he had a peculiar, slouching swagger to
his walk. A tight blue t-shirt stretched over his muscles, but did
nothing to obscure the tattoos that completely covered his arms.
He came up to them and frowned, slack-jawed and malevolent,
at Ada. Some of his teeth were missing, and his close-cropped
hair was parted by several large and angry scars across the top of
his scalp.

"Oh, God," said Melati, exasperated. "Here he come again."

"Oh," said Ada casually. "Hi, Johnno."

Johnno frowned. Clearly this wasn't going the way he'd
expected. "Where you been?"

"Went bush for a while. You miss me?" She made a mocking
kissy-face and grinned. Oliver looked back and forth between
them, puzzled and resentful.

"What about me money?"

"*Your* money? Get stuffed."

"I been waiting long enough."

"No, wait a little longer, would you? Hey, Johnno, look: I'm not
scared of you. First, Melati can call the cops any time now. Second,

it's not your money, and I don't owe you anything. Third—" She grabbed his shoulders, hugged him close, and drove her knee into his groin. "That."

"Jesus," he grunted, as he curled up and sank to the sidewalk. "I'll fucking kill you."

"Um, no, I don't think so. You won't kill me, and you won't … do any of those other things you were doing to me, either. That's done. Now piss off before I kick your tiny, limp dick into your guts and out through your arsehole."

From where he lay, he looked up at her, panting and incredulous.

"*Now*, thanks," she said in a bored, irritable voice. When he still didn't move, she hauled off to kick him. He scrabbled out of range, got painfully to his feet, and hobbled away.

"Ada," said Hoyle uneasily. "Don't get into the habit of liking this. It's easy to hurt people. Look how Nicholas got sucked into it."

"And are you going to try to tell me Nestor was just a victim, too?" she said.

"I'm just trying to tell you—" A million words rushed into his head to say. He knew a lot more about hurting people than he'd ever wanted. He'd felt the pulsing of the staff, felt Nestor's bitter rage and the terror that had underlain it all, felt how tempting it had been to grab hold of the staff's power as the ultimate guarantee against anyone being able to hurt or humiliate him. How could he tell Ada what it had been like to fight his way out of the storm of fear, confusion, and self-absorption that had been his first days of connection with the staff? How could he convince her how important it had been to make that choice?

He looked at Ada, her eyes flashing and posture upright and proud as she enjoyed her victory. He understood. It was good to feel powerful for once in your life. To his own sick shame, he found he missed the power and confidence the staff had given him. But that was exactly what he dreaded for Ada.

He waited for another moment to see if the right words would come to him. When they didn't, he reached out and pulled Ada into a quick hug. He said to Oliver, "You stick with her, okay?"

"What do you mean?" said Ada. "I thought we were all going to stick together. Aren't we?"

"Of course," said Sybil briskly. "We'll figure out what to do next, make a start on it, see it all go horribly off course, and sort it out. Then we'll do it again. And maybe again after that. I'd rather that than go back to DC and read books and wish I were somebody else. I'm getting to like being the person I always wanted to be."

"Cool!" said Oliver. " So much better than planning political turmoil. And, um …" He looked at Ada and blushed.

"I get it," said Ada. "You don't have to say anything more."

"Hoyle?" said Sybil, and her voice faltered. "What do you say?"

Could Hoyle let them all depend on him again? He was so weak without the staff, so isolated and clumsy—how could he risk it?

Very faintly, inside his head, he heard one of the watchers say, *The staff only amplifies what's there, remember?*

Oh, he thought. *You again. Didn't we do enough for you before?*

You did plenty, said the watcher. *Now go do some more.*

You'll make a bloody good hero, said another voice, warm and familiar.

Nicholas!

The watchers scraped me off whatever cosmic surface I'd been plastered to, I gather as a sort of thank you. It's not so easy to die when you've been a hundred years with the staff. I'm sort of … an honorary watcher now. But I've got to tell you, they're an unusual bunch. Don't know how it'll be, spending eternity with them. Still, it beats oblivion. Oh, and I found out what happened to that tick Ingraham. As it turns out, he really did put clues in the book so that someone would eventually find their way here and sort all this out. He'd been horrified and disgusted to see Nestor's true self, amplified through the staff, but he knew he wasn't strong enough to fight him. So he did what he could. Obviously, he couldn't be overt about it—the situation in Europe was already moving toward war, and he couldn't risk revealing the staff's true nature to a world of Nestors. He must have died despairing that anyone would ever figure it out—apparently he once even wrote Rider Haggard, coming clean and asking for advice, but Haggard was immensely famous by then, and just wrote him off as a madman. But all that's by the way now. Off you go, my friend, have your adventures. You're a better man than you know, even now. I'm mistaking you for a hero. Make me be right.

"Hoyle? Are you all right?" said Sybil.

"Sure. Sorry. Just thinking." Maybe it could work. He could stay with Sybil. They could have adventures, and figure out how to keep getting visas and buying food as they went. It couldn't be any harder than what they'd just done, could it? "Yeah, let's do it. Hey, Oliver, where are we going to sleep tonight?"

"I'll call my parents. I'm pretty sure they're still speaking to me. Me, I'll go find some of the others and ask if I can sleep on a couch somewhere—"

"Don't be an idiot," said Ada. "You can come to Punchbowl and sleep on our couch. It'll be fun. It opens out, we can both fit. Mum won't mind and neither will her boyfriend. Or the dog."

"Okay," said Oliver dubiously.

"Ada, I don't think that's a good idea," said Sybil. "Just sort things out with your parents, Oliver. Just for one night. Then be as principled as you like."

Hoyle was fairly certain that none of this would go as smoothly as it sounded when Sybil talked about it. But right now he needed food and sleep, and while he was enjoying needing them again, before too long it would stop being fun. Meanwhile, he was also enjoying being with Sybil, and caring about Ada and Oliver, and not having to save the world. Just for a little while.

Acknowledgements

I would like to gratefully acknowledge the unfailing support and perspicacious guidance that Dr. Van Ikin has given me throughout the writing of this novel and beyond. I further thank those people who helped me with their expertise: Dave Bere and Greg Nash of the NSW State Emergency Service, Wollongong City Unit; and Steve at anteater.com.au (don't ask).

Thanks also go to Cathyann Sweeney, who has been utterly stalwart not only in her friendship, but in her enthusiasm for my writing, without which I would almost certainly have abandoned the whole writing enterprise at several despairing points. Moreover, although it would be indelicate to relate them here, our many adventures at various WorldCons, bookshops, and pubs on several continents (not to mention one particularly epic Skype session) have provided me with much-needed jollity in the darkest, as well as the brightest, of times.

I have, over the years, experienced the great good fortune to find communities of writers and writing enthusiasts who have encouraged and enlightened me, and I thank them all: my NaNoWriMo Coffee Shop buddies (and other NaNoWriMo and Script Frenzy mates—you know who you are), my writing students, my Egoboo buddies, my Wollongong writing colleagues, my fellow SWISHErs, the Writebulb Moment mob, Gillian Polack, Margo Lanagan, Cat Sparks, Rob Hood, Anne-Louise Rentell, Joe Dolce, Craig Allen, Rod Bartlett, Chard Nelson, Helena Fox Dunan, Susan Kennedy, Steve Hockensmith, Tansy Rayner Roberts, Rebecca Carstens Collis (criminal mastermind of the Great

Notebook Caper), Dirk Flinthart, Ion Newcombe, the fabulous people of Moonburn Productions, and—most of all—my fellow Clarionites (students, tutors, and organizers). They have all bestowed on me friendship and insight without stint or measure, and made me deeply glad that whenever I write, I do not write alone.

I want to thank the wonderful team at Odyssey Books, who are daring in their vision and unshakable in their support. Thank you for seeing my idiosyncrasies as strengths, and my weaknesses as manageable.

Finally, I wish to express my deepest love and appreciation to my husband, Dr. Houston Dunleavy; our daughter, Margaret; and my mom, Dr. Elspeth Goodin. Your love, example, encouragement, and support mean absolutely everything to me. Absolutely everything.

About the Author

American-born writer Laura E. Goodin has been writing professionally for over thirty years. Her stories have appeared in numerous publications, including *Michael Moorcock's New Worlds, Andromeda Spaceways Inflight Magazine, Review of Australian Fiction, Adbusters, Wet Ink, The Lifted Brow,* and *Daily Science Fiction,* among others, and in several anthologies. Her plays and libretti have been performed on three continents, and her poetry has been performed internationally, both as spoken word and as texts for new musical compositions. She attended the 2007 Clarion South workshop, and has a PhD in creative writing from the University of Western Australia.